"It's no...

Sam jerk...

"What ar...

"The gray," Kevin replied. "It's not painted on, so you can't rub it off. No matter how hard you try."

"Talk like that makes you sound like an old poop."

"Maybe I am."

"Oh, for heaven's sake. You weren't old the other night. You were a man. Not an old man. Just a plain, wonderful man...."

Dear Reader,

What better cure for a hectic holiday season than settling in with romantic stories from Special Edition? And this month, we've got just what you've been searching for.

THE JONES GANG is back, with bestselling author Christine Rimmer's latest title, *Honeymoon Hotline*. Nevada Jones is November's THAT SPECIAL WOMAN!, and this adviser to the lovelorn is about to discover love firsthand!

Andrea Edwards's latest miniseries, GREAT EXPECTATIONS, continues this month with *One Big Happy Family*. If Big Sky Country is your kind of place, you won't want to miss *Montana Lovers*, the next book in Jackie Merritt's newest series, MADE IN MONTANA.

And the passion doesn't end there—for her first title in Special Edition, Helen R. Myers has a tantalizing tale of reunited lovers in *After That Night…*. Rounding out the month are a spellbinding amnesia story from Ann Howard White, *Making Memories*, and a second chance for two lovers in Kayla Daniels's heartwarming *Marriage Minded*.

I hope you enjoy all that we have in store for you this November. Happy Thanksgiving Day—all of us at Silhouette would like to wish you a happy holiday season!

Sincerely,

Tara Gavin
Senior Editor

Please address questions and book requests to:
Silhouette Reader Service
U.S.: 3010 Walden Ave., P.O. Box 1325, Buffalo, NY 14269
Canadian: P.O. Box 609, Fort Erie, Ont. L2A 5X3

ANDREA EDWARDS
ONE BIG HAPPY FAMILY

SPECIAL EDITION®

Published by Silhouette Books
America's Publisher of Contemporary Romance

For Zeke, the most recent addition to our happy family.
Isn't it awful what we youngest siblings
have to put up with?

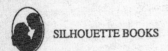 SILHOUETTE BOOKS

ISBN 0-373-24064-3

ONE BIG HAPPY FAMILY

Books by Andrea Edwards

ANDREA EDWARDS

is the pseudonym of Anne and Ed Kolaczyk, a husband-and-wife writing team who have been telling their stories for more than fifteen years. Anne is a former elementary school teacher while Ed is a refugee from corporate America. After many years in the Chicago area, they now live in a small town in northern Indiana where they are avid students of local history, family legends and ethnic myths. Recently they have both been bitten by the gardening bug, but only time will tell how serious the affliction is. Their four children are grown; the youngest attends college while the eldest is a college professor. Remaining at home with Anne and Ed are two dogs, four cats and one bird—not the same ones that first walked through their stories, but carrying on the same tradition of chaotic rule of the household nonetheless.

Once upon a time, a mother duck hatched her eggs. All her babies were small and golden, except for one. He was big and gray. The other mothers said he was too big; he was too ugly. The other ducklings liked playing with him, but they all heard the comments about his size and his ugliness.

Little by little, the ugly duckling began to swim by himself and keep away from even the little ducklings who still wanted to be his friend. Then one day, new birds came to the pond—big beautiful birds that called themselves swans. They said the ugly duckling was one of them and that he should come live with them. The big duckling went with the swans, happy to find a place where he belonged....

Prologue

July, twenty years ago

"**S**amantha!" the counselor called out. "Aren't you supposed to be swimming?"

Samantha got to her feet, looking at the teenager striding down the path toward her. It was Jenny Rizzo, the bossiest counselor in the whole camp. Jenny didn't listen to anybody. She would never let Sam stay here and wait for the big kids to go to lunch.

"Come on," Jenny said as she got closer. "I'll walk you over to the beach."

"I can't go," Sam said and pointed to her knee. "I gotta show Fiona I scraped my knee."

"You don't have to show your sister now," Jenny replied. "She's busy having fun with her friends."

Sam pulled her backpack into her arms. She wished she was a squirrel. Then she could climb really high and run around to the other side of the tree trunk where Jenny couldn't catch her. Or she could run all over camp and make sure Fiona and Cassie were still here and that the social worker hadn't come to take them to a new home and forgotten all about her.

But Sam wasn't a squirrel. She wasn't even a frog. She was just a little six-year-old kid. The littlest kid in her family. And, except for Billy Sherman, the littlest kid in her kindergarten class. If it wasn't for Billy, she would be the littlest kid in the whole world. That was why people were always bossing her around.

"Fiona said I gotta tell her if I hurt myself," Samantha said.

Jenny stopped right in front of her, smiling down with a mean kind of smile that meant she was going to make Sam do something she didn't want. "You can tell her when you get home," Jenny said, reaching out for Sam's backpack. "Come on. I'll take care of your—"

"No. You can't have my backpack." The words came out so tough-sounding that Samantha almost fell over in surprise. Jenny looked like she was surprised, too. "I'm gonna go find Fiona," Samantha said and, pushing past Jenny, quickly ran down the path.

"Samantha, stop being silly!" Jenny called after her. "No one wants to steal your backpack."

But Samantha didn't slow down. Not even the teeniest-tiniest bit. You never knew what other people might take. And everything important that she had was in her bag. Stuff like her fuzzy puppy slippers, a monster eraser, a little doll with blue eyes that closed and brown hair that you could comb, and the picture book Mommy had given to her before she and Daddy went away.

Samantha dodged among the bushes and branches, running until she was sure that Jenny wasn't following her. Then she stopped, put the bag on her back, and continued walking down the trail.

She just wanted to talk to Fiona, that was all. It was mean of Jenny to try to stop her. Sam and her sisters had been living with a bunch of different people for a long time now. Ever since Mommy and Daddy went away and got dead. Fiona and Cassie were all the family Samantha had, and sometimes Sam just had to talk to Fiona.

Though not so much anymore. Sam swallowed the lump in her throat. Now she and her sisters were living with the Scotts and they were the nicest people in the whole world. Except for her real mommy and daddy, that is.

The social worker had brought Sam and Cassie and Fiona to the house and then left, just like she always had before. Samantha had been carrying her old brown paper bag with all her stuff in it.

When Mrs. Scott had asked her what she had in the bag, Samantha had told her it was stuff that was hers and no one else's. And how she always carried the bag with her so when they had to move, she wouldn't leave anything behind.

A blue jay perched on a branch above Sam and hollered down. Samantha looked up at it. "You're just like Cassie," she told him. "Always yelling about something." She watched the bird fly off. Then, once it was out of sight, she started walking faster again.

Mrs. Scott didn't do anything about Samantha's bag. She didn't try to take it away like some people did. She just helped Cassie and Fiona put their stuff away. Then she took all of them to this big store and bought Samantha her very own backpack. After they paid for everything, Mrs. Scott took her into the ladies' room and they put her stuff into her backpack. Sam put the brown paper bag in it, too, in case she needed it again later.

A rabbit dashed across Sam's path and into the bushes. "Hi, bunny, bunny," Samantha called after him. He didn't answer back but she wasn't bothered. Rabbits didn't like to stand and let other people see them; they might get hurt.

Sometimes she wished she could be a bunny and run away where no one could see her.

Suddenly Sam heard voices. Down by the big trees where the path bended a whole lot. Mad voices. Familiar voices. Fiona was there. Sam hurried ahead.

As she rounded the bend her feet slowed and she sighed. Both her sisters were up ahead, walking along and arguing. Cassie and Fiona were always arguing. They hollered at each other more than they hollered at anyone else in the whole world.

"Where are you guys going?" Samantha shouted, hoping her yelling would make them quit arguing.

It did make them stop. But instead of being glad to see her, they looked all frowny and mad.

"Go back to camp," Cassie told her.

Fiona would have said it nicer, but Samantha could see that her oldest sister didn't want her around, either. Well, tough. Sam stood and glared at them. They didn't even notice her skinned knee, but went stomping off toward the lake. For a moment Sam was so surprised, she just stood there. When she realized they were going to ignore her, she ran after them.

"There she is." Cassie was running toward the lake. "There's Juliet."

Samantha looked to where her sister was pointing and her hands flew to her mouth. Oh, no. Something was wrong with the mommy swan. Juliet was in some branches in the water and her wings were all droopy. Samantha held her breath and watched Cassie wade into the lake.

"Cassie, you can't go in the water!" Fiona cried. "There's no lifeguard around."

Fiona was right, but Juliet was in trouble. Samantha wondered whether she should run and get help. Why couldn't her sisters stop arguing and tell her what to do? She could run really fast if she had to. Not as fast as Cassie, but faster than Fiona.

Now clutching her hands together, Samantha watched Cassie splash out toward Juliet. Suddenly, the bird flapped its huge wings and Samantha gasped. Cassie could get dead, too, just like Mommy and Daddy. The counselors had told them how really, really strong the swans' wings were.

"She's trapped!" Cassie shouted.

Samantha's stomach jumped. She hoped Cassie would be able to rescue Juliet. She had to. But she didn't want Cassie to get hurt, either.

"Her foot's caught in one of those plastic-ring things from pop cans!" Cassie was shouting.

"We need to tell Mrs. Warner!" Fiona shouted back.

"She won't do anything. You know how she went on and on that first day about swans being mean." Cassie was flapping her arms like they were wings as she splashed back to shore. "She won't let anybody near them. She'll just call somebody and Juliet will die before they get here."

"She might not," Fiona said.

Samantha wanted to punch them both. Juliet needed their help and those two were fighting like they did over who was going to get the last piece of cake. Big kids always thought they were so smart.

"Come on." Cassie yanked on Fiona's arm. "We can help her. We just need something to cut the plastic."

But Fiona didn't budge. Cassie jerked harder and Fiona had to move. Breathing a sigh of relief, Samantha followed after her sisters. They would help Juliet. But then Cassie turned to frown at Sam.

"You stay here," Cassie told her. "Keep Juliet company."

"Me?" Samantha stopped, her feet suddenly glued to the ground. "What am I supposed to do?"

"I don't know, Sam." Fiona sounded just as mad as Cassie. Why was the whole world mad at her? She didn't do anything. "Sing to her. Read her a story. Show her all that junk in your bag. Just stay out of the water."

Why did she have to stay? Why not one of them? Samantha wanted to shout. Fiona should stay; she was the slowest. Samantha and Cassie could be back before Fiona was halfway there.

But her sisters were already gone, disappearing through the bushes before Samantha could get the words out of her mouth. She felt tears sliding down her cheeks.

That was the way it always was. She would have some really good stuff to say and nobody would listen. Nobody ever listened to a little kid. Nobody.

Suddenly a squawky sound came from the lake. Samantha quickly turned. Romeo was swimming around Juliet, telling her everything was going to be all right. But Juliet looked like she was really tired.

"Juliet!" Samantha called. "Hold your head up. You gotta. If you don't, you'll—"

As she was talking, Samantha was walking toward the birds. Suddenly she found herself in the mud at the edge of the lake. And her shoes were dirty. Now she really felt like crying. The Scotts would never adopt them now. Mommies and daddies didn't like kids who got their shoes dirty.

Maybe if she wiped them off, everything would be okay. She could always hide behind Cassie and Fiona. Or she could go barefoot. And when it snowed, she would always wear boots. With six kids—the Scotts already had three boys—they couldn't notice everything anyway.

Romeo called out again, making Samantha forget about her dirty shoes. "I'm sorry," she said. "What do you want me to do?"

The daddy bird didn't answer. He just swam around Juliet. Samantha clenched her fists. Romeo was acting just like a big kid. He wanted her to do something but he wasn't saying what.

"You want me to sing you a song?"

Her ankles felt wet and Samantha noticed that she'd gone farther into the lake. Fiona had said not to go in the water, but Sam couldn't just stand here and holler at the swans.

"I don't sing very good. That's what Fiona and Cassie say."

She moved closer to the birds. Juliet was still hanging her head but Romeo was looking at Samantha.

"Fiona and Cassie are my big sisters. They're the two big mouths that just left." She noticed that Romeo looked really scared. "But don't worry. They'll be back. They just went to get something to cut with."

Neither of the swans seemed impressed. Samantha went farther into the water. It was up to her knees now.

"You want me to read you a story?"

Juliet lifted her head to look at her. Samantha smiled. She'd finally found something the big bird was interested in.

"I read pretty good. I mean, for a kindergarten kid."

Both birds squawked. And Romeo put his wings out.

"You don't want me any closer?" Samantha asked. "But you won't be able to see the pictures. Pictures are what really make a book good."

They squawked again. It sounded like a definite no.

"Okay. Maybe you got good eyes." Samantha reached around into her backpack and pulled out her book. Then she squatted down because she never liked to stand and read. The cold water washed over the seat of her pants.

"Oh, swell. Now my butt's all wet. I bet I have to stand on the bus all the way home."

The swans didn't say anything. Boy, even birds didn't care what happened to a little kid.

"Okay," Samantha said. "This is a story about a baby swan who lives with a duck family. It's really, really good."

The birds sat there and stared at her.

"You really could see the pictures better if I got closer." They didn't even blink. "Oh, all right."

"'Once upon a time...'"

Samantha shifted the book to one hand. She didn't need the book to tell the story. She'd heard it so many times, she knew it by heart, but she was trying to match the words in her head with the ones on the page, so she followed the string of words with her finger. Fiona said that first graders weren't allowed to do that. But Sam wasn't in first grade yet—not until September.

"'... there was a mommy duck with a whole nest full of eggs.'"

"Samantha! I told you to stay out of the water."

Sam had been concentrating so hard on her words that she didn't hear her sisters come back. In fact, she didn't even know they were there until Fiona hollered. Then Sam just about jumped out of her wet pants.

"I had to show her the pictures." Samantha began splashing out of the lake. "You always show me the pictures when you read to me."

No one said anything to Sam as Cassie went into the water. Samantha vowed that when she was a big kid she was going to be nice to everybody. No matter how big or small they were.

She ran the last few steps out of the water. Then she turned and watched Cassie.

"Stop it, you dumb old bird. We're just trying to help you."

Cassie was splashing around in the water around Juliet. The birds were getting excited and waving their wings around. Samantha held her breath.

"Fiona!" Cassie cried out. "I can't cut the plastic away unless she holds still. You've got to come over here and help."

"In there?"

Fiona didn't want to do it. Samantha clenched her hands. She could help. She knew she could. But if she tried, her sisters would just tell her to get out of the water.

Without another word, Fiona inched into the water and Samantha let all the air out of her lungs. Her oldest sister was moving slow, but she was moving. She circled out around to the other side of the swans.

"When she's looking at me, you cut her free," Fiona told Cassie.

Cassie nodded as Juliet kept watching Fiona.

"Hi, Juliet," Fiona said. "You remember me? I'm Fiona."

Of course, Juliet remembered her, Sam thought. What did Fiona think, that the bird was dumb?

Cassie was whispering something to the bird and Samantha couldn't hear what it was. But the bird was only looking at Fiona, and Cassie was getting closer and closer. Samantha held her breath and squeezed her fists and her eyes shut.

Then, suddenly, she heard Juliet flapping her wings. Sam's eyes flew open just in time to see Cassie kind of lying in the water. For a minute Samantha couldn't breathe or anything. She thought one of the birds had hit Cassie, but then Cassie stood with a whoosh.

"Look at this stupid junk." She was waving a piece of plastic over her head as Juliet and Romeo were swimming away. "People who throw this stuff in the lake ought to be hung by their necks with it."

Cassie didn't talk nice when she was mad, but that was okay. Everyone was safe now.

Fiona followed Cassie out of the water. "Come on." She took Samantha's hand but was talking to Cassie. "We'll go back to camp by the nurse's office. We can say we went there with you."

"Whatever."

Nurse's office? Samantha stared at Cassie. Her sister was never sick. Why were they talking about going to see the nurse? Sam wanted to ask, but when she opened her mouth, no words came out. An old woman was coming toward them, looking kind of scary.

"I saw what you did," the woman said.

"So?" Cassie replied.

Samantha bit her lip. She hoped they weren't going to get in trouble.

"It was my fault." Fiona was always trying to make things okay after Cassie got mad. "I'm the oldest and I should have known better."

The old woman laughed. "The gods will smile on you," she said. "You fought so love might live. Someday, the spirits will return to fight for your love." She disappeared into the trees.

Spirits? Weren't they the same as ghosts? Sam wondered. What kind of ghosts was the woman talking about? Swan ghosts?

Samantha didn't think she wanted any kind of ghosts coming around, and she edged over, closer to Fiona, clutching her backpack again. Did ghosts take backpacks?

Chapter One

"You're history, you leaky old pipe," Samantha Scott muttered as she spread her tools out around her on the tiled bathroom floor.

The small white hexagonal floor tiles were charming—a quaint reminder of the solidity and strength of houses built around the turn of the century. Just like the heavy paneled-oak doors, the wide cove molding around the ceilings and the brass light fixtures. These ancient water pipes were another story, though.

Sam picked up a wrench and pulled the ever-present plastic bucket out from under the pipe, tossing it onto the bathroom floor behind her. Then she crawled into the cabinet, faceup, so that she was staring at the bottom of the sink. One of the advantages of being small was you could squeeze into almost any space. A fat, cold drop of water fell onto her nose. But it felt almost good compared to the hot, sticky August air.

"Welcome to you, too," she muttered and fitted her wrench around the nut at the top of the corroded supply pipe. "I may not be able to do anything about the pipes in the wall, but I can sure take care of you." She gave a mighty push against the nut. It didn't budge. Not a smidgen.

"Sam?" Light footsteps came closer, followed by her sister Fiona's face peering through the cabinet door—complete with frown. "What in the world are you doing? You can't fix the plumbing in this old place along with everything else."

"I'm not fixing the plumbing," Sam corrected her, continuing to try to budge the stubborn nut. "I'm replacing a leaky supply pipe. Minor surgery."

"I don't care that Cassie said this place was in good shape. There's no such thing as minor surgery when you're dealing with old plumbing."

Fiona sat on the edge of the claw-footed bathtub so Sam could only see her feet and legs. Her sandals were speckled with drops of water. It must still be raining outside.

"This place is ready to fall apart. I don't know what you and Dad were thinking of."

Sam knew exactly what she'd been thinking of—that light of excitement that came back into Dad's eyes each time he talked about his dream of having a bed-and-breakfast. A dream that Sam feared had died with Mom six years ago.

"Our bed-and-breakfast is going to open by the end of September. We have to. We've got reservations for the first football weekend in October."

"Sam, you know it's not that we don't want you to succeed."

Fiona's voice was high—a telltale sign that she was about to make a pronouncement for someone's own good, a pronouncement based on the collective wisdom of Sam's two sisters and three brothers.

"Lord knows, we all think this inn would be the best thing in the world for you and Dad, but you can't fix everything yourself. It's just too much. You don't know what you're doing."

"Sure, I do." Sam squirmed to avoid the residue flaking off the nut, *not* her conscience, and hoped Fiona wouldn't notice the *Reader's Digest Complete Do-It-Yourself Manual* on the top of the toilet tank. But the sound of pages being flipped told her that was a useless hope.

"This book is two weeks overdue." Sam heard the dull thump of the book being placed on the floor. "Your library card is going to be revoked."

"I'm a librarian," Sam reminded. "They won't revoke my card."

"They might," Fiona said. "You have to obey the rules, too, you know."

Fiona had had this thing about rules ever since she, Sam and Cassie had been kids. Their parents had died when Sam was four and she could barely remember them, but she did remember Fiona always worrying that one or another of them was breaking some rule. Even after the Scotts had adopted them, Fiona had followed Sam and Cassie around, filling their ears with deep sighs as she tried to keep them in line.

"Sam," Fiona was saying, "the father of one of my students does plumbing repairs on the side—"

"I don't need his help." And can't afford it. Even if the savings and loan did approve their request for a larger mortgage.

"He can get parts at cost and—"

"I don't need any help," Sam repeated.

"I wish I could believe that." Fiona stood. Her sandals were out of sight and the hem of her skirt just peeked under the edge of the cabinet opening. "I'd better get going. Alex and I are shopping for new kitchen wallpaper tonight." Fiona and Alex had bought Dad's old house and were redoing it. "I left a casserole in the fridge for your dinner."

"What for? I had dinner planned."

"I know. I saw the pizza coupons on the counter. See you later, hon."

Her footsteps disappeared softly down the hallway and Sam let her shoulders slump. Her adoptive brothers were no better than her sisters; all her siblings seemed to think she needed watching over. If they hadn't meant well, she would have run away from home long ago. She'd been well loved and well supervised, but didn't they realize she was grownup? Yeah, she was the baby of the family, so they wanted to keep the bandages handy. But they should see she needed to ride without training wheels.

A bundle of tabby fur climbed into the cabinet and settled on Sam's chest.

"You know this place is going to be a success, don't you, Toby?" The cat blinked his agreement and purred as she resumed her attack on the recalcitrant nut.

"Hello? Miss Scott?"

Toby started at the sound of the male voice and so did Sam, but probably not for the same reasons. The man's voice was as smooth and thick as maple syrup, with a husky depth that was almost enough to set Sam to purring. She took a deep breath and steadied her nerves. Toby tensed as a pair of tan slacks came into view.

"Miss Scott? Are you up here?"

"In here," she mumbled, as Toby backed into her face.

She shoved the cat off to the side as the stranger stooped down and looked into the cabinet. Her breath caught as she stared at him. His dark brown hair had just faint streaks of gray at the temples, his eyes were deep dark pools of mystery and passion. And his shoulders—encased in a rain-dampened, navy sports coat over a pale blue shirt—were broad enough to carry the weight of not only plumbing problems, but electrical, as well.

The man smiled. "Is this your office?" he asked, waving at the inside of the cabinet. "Or am I intruding on your private quarters?"

Sam let her breath out slowly. Her insanity was due, no doubt, to the close confines of the cabinet. She was not about to get hyper over a handsome face. "Why don't I come on out?" she said.

He stood, giving her room to move, to breathe, to think. She squirmed out of the cabinet, well aware of the fact that her dignity, as well as her equilibrium, had long since disappeared. Who was this guy, anyway, to come in here and discombobulate her?

She made it out of the cabinet, then carefully got to her feet. Unfortunately, his presence was just as unsettling when she was vertical. Not a good sign. Maybe a frown would keep those magic male rays from affecting her. She was not some weak, simpering female, ready to go faint at the sight of a handsome man.

"Now, what can I do for you?" she asked.

"Kevin Delaney," he said, holding out a business card and his hand.

She took the card and, without looking at it, placed it on the edge of the sink. Then she slowly shook his hand.

"I met your sister on her way out and she told me you were up here. I hope I didn't come at a bad time, but this was the only time I could squeeze you into my schedule."

Aha. Fiona had sent him up. Fiona, who just happened to know someone who did plumbing repairs on the side. Fiona, who just happened to have shown up a few minutes before Mr. Delaney. Except that her sister never "happened" to do anything in her life.

This had to be Fiona's plumber. Sam's temper lurched into high gear, ready to take off, and she had to hold it back with both hands.

"This isn't a bad time," Sam repeated carefully. "Though I'm afraid you've made the trip for nothing."

He had been opening up the notebook he was carrying and stopped to stare at her. "I beg your pardon," he said slowly.

Toby came out of the cabinet and jumped up on the edge of the sink to butt his head into Sam's hand. She petted him slowly, trying to match the even rhythm of his breathing to her own. It wasn't this stranger's fault that Fiona was organizing Sam's life again. She should at least be polite to him.

"I don't need your help, after all," she said simply. "I have everything under control here."

He frowned and glanced around him, his gaze taking in the tools scattered over the floor, the do-it-yourself repair book and her skinned knuckles. "You have plumbing problems?"

No, she was having a picnic here in the north suite's bathroom. "Only minor ones," she replied. "I'm not so foolish as to touch the wall pipes. They're probably being held together by rust and mineral deposits, so I'm steering clear of them."

"If they're that bad, they could cause you big problems in the future."

"Then that's when I'll worry about it—in the future." She stepped over the repair manual and, with a regal wave of her hand, got him to move slightly closer to the door.

He frowned, reminding Sam of her father, her brothers, her brother-in-law Alex and her brother-in-law-to-be Jack. "That's not a very sound business attitude," he said. "You should at least—"

That did it. First of all, his good looks assaulted her heart and now he was rivaling Fiona as chief advice-giver. "Look, Mr. Delaney, I'll thank you to butt out. I've done just fine up to this point without your or my siblings' interference. Just because you've got business cards and a leather notebook, doesn't make you an expert on running an inn, you know."

The deep brown eyes suddenly turned hard. "It hardly takes an expert to see that this place needs more than just a few cosmetic repairs," he observed. "And any reasonable businessman knows that preventive maintenance is always cheaper than wholesale replacement."

"And you just happen to be offering a special bargain rate on your services now, right?"

"What I'm trying to offer is some advice, but you seem to be too stubborn to listen."

"And you're too stubborn to admit that somebody might do quite well without your advice."

His nostrils flared as the heat of anger flashed though his eyes. He closed his notebook with a snap. "I've never yet forced anyone to do business with me. You have my card if you change your mind, but don't count on my cooperation."

"And don't count on my call," she snapped.

With that, he turned on his heel and left. His footsteps echoed on the bare wooden steps and across the marble-tiled foyer. The front door opened and shut hard, the angry sound reverberating through the house. Then everything was silent and still.

Sam took a deep breath and let it out slowly. She shouldn't have been so rude to him. After all, it hadn't been his fault that Fiona had told him to come. But Sam was glad he'd gone, glad that it was over. Toby mewed softly and pushed at her hand for attention.

He was so certain she would call, too. If that wasn't just like a man. She might have his card, but not for long. The house could be awash in leaky pipes, with furniture being swept down the stairs and out into the yard by rushing waters. And she still wouldn't call Mr. Kevin Delaney to ask the time of day. She reached around Toby and picked up the business card.

"I'll just file this under *N* for never." Suddenly her heart stopped. "Oh, no!"

"Michiana Savings and Loan. Kevin Delaney. Vice President. Loan Department." She hadn't chased away a pushy plumber. She'd bounced the moneyman!

Kevin stared out his office window. It was pouring outside and he thought he could hear thunder in the distance. He hoped they wouldn't get too much rain. His basement tended to flood when there were downpours, and he didn't look forward to bailing it out around midnight. Of course, he would have been home a lot earlier if he hadn't agreed to that stupid poker game. It was just that he was tired of Stacy bugging him to go out every time she called. You would think she was the parent and he was the kid.

Of course, he hadn't acted very adultlike in getting so angry at that Scott woman. He shook his head, trying to dispel the image of soft womanliness from his mind.

He never got angry. It was the standard joke here at the savings and loan. Cool-tempered Kevin. Nothing ever made him blow up. The savings and loan could be robbed, his car could be destroyed in a hijack attempt, and wild dogs could break into his kitchen and work their way through the frozen dinners. None of it would faze him in the slightest. He would call the police, then find a corner to read the newspaper.

A knock at his office door woke him from his thoughts.

"Hey, Kevin." Dick Hayes poked his head in the door. "We've got to cancel the poker game. The power's out at Tom's house."

"No problem," Kevin said and hoped that his relief wasn't too evident in his voice. He could just go home and—

"We're going out for a drink instead," Dick added. "Maybe get something to eat."

"I think I'll pass," Kevin said. "I should get on home and make sure my basement hasn't turned into a swimming pool." Dick left with a wave and silence shrouded Kevin's office once more.

He wasn't a social being—not anymore. Maybe he'd never been one. Debbie had loved socializing and parties and just being with people. She'd started dragging him along in high school, and by the time they married in college, he'd left his hermit status far behind.

That is, until she'd died two years ago. Then he hadn't even been able to talk to his kids. It was no wonder they preferred their grandparents' company to his. Or that Stacy chose to stay at Purdue over the summer and that Jon moved in with her to get a head start on his freshman year.

"Mr. Delaney." Cindy Baumgartner, his secretary, was at the door, her umbrella and purse in hand. "There's a Miss Scott here to see you. I told her it was closing time, but she's very insistent."

Miss Scott? "Samantha Scott?"

"Yes," Cindy replied. "She said she's a client of ours."

Kevin rubbed his face with his hands. Why did that woman have to come here? He'd just about wiped her out of his mind.

"Shall I tell her you're indisposed?"

A vision of shorts and a soft T-shirt filled his mind; shapely legs that could lead a man to the ends of the earth and full breasts that would push him over the edge. He could not believe how attracted he was to this woman. Maybe the storm had something to do with it. He'd heard that low-pressure weather systems had strange effects on people and animals.

"No." Kevin leaned on his desk and sighed. "Show her in, Cindy."

For the first time in his career with Michiana Savings, Kevin wished it were a bigger institution. Then he would just give her application to someone else. He didn't need that woman in his life. Maybe he would be lucky, though, and learn she'd come to cancel it in person.

Cindy held the door open and Samantha Scott came through, her blue eyes tentative and wary. She'd changed her clothes—a prim-and-proper white blouse covered her top half, and the worn shorts that had clung so sweetly were gone. In their place was a soft blue skirt that swirled enticingly around those legs, clinging for a moment, then falling free as she stepped farther into the room.

Kevin was slowly getting the feeling that it didn't matter what Miss Scott wore. She would still have the same unsettling effect on him. There was something wrong, here. Maybe he'd taken too many antihistamines for his mosquito bites. He put a businesslike frown on his face.

He would be okay. All he had to do was keep her on the other side of the desk and beyond arm's reach. "I got the impression earlier that you wanted to cancel your loan application," he said.

"I made a mistake," she replied.

Her hands were clutching her purse. The look in her eyes was pure bravado, and about as thick as the sheer hose that gave a slight sheen to her legs. One more bark from him and it would be gone. But he could never resist helping a poor little kitten.

"Sit down." He sighed, waving to the chair in front of his desk.

She took it quickly. "It was all a mistake," she said. "I thought you were someone else."

"Someone you disliked?"

Her eyes flashed as a grin split her lips. "Someone I was prepared to dislike," she admitted in a low, confiding murmur.

"I see." He clenched his teeth, wishing that he'd never let her into his office. Her application said that she had just turned twenty-seven. He was almost forty. That meant he'd been in junior high when she'd been born. He was too old to be attracted to her.

"I thought you were someone my sister had sent," Sam went on. Her eyes, framed in sheepishness and glittering with laughter, drew a reluctant smile from his heart.

"So it's your sister you dislike." He tried looking at a spot beyond her left shoulder but his treacherous eyes wouldn't obey.

"Oh, no." She looked genuinely shocked. "I love her. I love both of my sisters and my brothers, too. And they love me. That's why they're always trying to help."

He began to see more than just those legs. She looked young but she was handling a difficult situation with more maturity than your average twentysomething. "You love them, but you don't always want their help."

Sam ran her fingers through her short brown hair, tempting him to... Tempting him to listen very carefully to her words.

"Fiona had just left when you came upstairs."

"Fiona?"

"She's my oldest sister."

Her hands fluttered in a most delightful way. Like two hummingbirds dancing. Kevin squinted and forced himself to look into her eyes. Not that it helped all that much.

"She'd been telling me about some part-time plumber and wouldn't listen when I told her that I had everything under control. Then the next thing I knew, you turned up. It fit her pattern perfectly."

She leaned forward then, without really coming all that close. Not nearly close enough. But, just to be safe, Kevin pushed his chair back from his desk.

"I'm so sorry for everything I said," Sam assured him. "If I had known you weren't Fiona's plumber, I would never have treated you that way."

"I have to admit most people don't treat their bankers like that."

Worry came back to shadow those eyes, turning the calm blue into stormy gray. "I don't, either," she said quickly. "That's why I came to explain. I didn't want you to be mad at me and turn down the loan."

Kevin got to his feet—he had to do something before the adrenaline ate out his insides—and went to the window to study the dark August storm washing the parking lot. What he saw was Sam's reflection in the window.

She shifted her position and recrossed her legs. Not that that showed him anything. Her skirt had demurely covered those shapely legs. But his collar felt tight and he had to swallow hard before he could speak. He needed to get this thing over with.

"We're a bit more businesslike than that, here." He cleared his throat once more to rid himself of his unbusinesslike desires, then turned to face her, irritation with himself riding high. "We have to base our decisions on fact, nothing else. While your outburst surprised me, it'll be the building's condition and your potential for making money with it that will determine our ultimate decision."

She was on her feet now. "I can't tell you how glad I am to hear that," she said. "Because the place is great—well, it's going to be great. And soon."

He forced a frown onto his face. "Even with pipes held together with rust and mineral deposits?"

"I just said that to get rid of you," she replied, waving away her negative comments. Her eyes had lost their worry and replaced it with an infectious gleam. "You really need to see the place for yourself."

"I tried to."

A beautiful rose color filled her cheeks but his rough tone seemed to have no effect on her enthusiasm.

"When can you come again? I'll take you on the grand tour and show you what a terrific investment our bed-and-breakfast is."

He returned to his desk and sat down, flipping through the calendar. He should avoid this, a little voice whispered. But the words were coming out of his mouth before he had a chance to think through a more businesslike course of action.

"How about tomorrow morning?" he was saying. Best to get this wrapped up and over with fast. The attraction was probably just a fluke and would be gone by tomorrow, anyway.

Sam sat down in her chair. "Tomorrow's Saturday," she said.

"So?"

She shrugged. "I just thought you'd be busy. You know, doing stuff with your family."

"I usually schedule work on Saturday mornings," he told her. "It's more convenient for a lot of our customers."

"Okay, then," she said with a grin. "Tomorrow's fine. I'll be waiting."

"Around ten?"

"Super."

She stood. Instead of leaving, though, she came around the desk and extended her hand. He stood his ground.

"Thanks for being so understanding about all this."

"No problem," Kevin said. He shook her hand firmly, Just like he would shake the hand of any business client. Sure, her touch was smooth as silk, warm and soft as a kitten's breath, but he was totally unaffected. There was no need to reassign this application. He could handle it. No sweat. "See you tomorrow, then."

She flashed him a smile as she left. It was only after the door had closed and Kevin had flopped back into his chair, that he realized he'd been holding his breath. He let it out slowly, feeling like a balloon deflating.

He'd been attracted to other women since Debbie's death. Hell, he wasn't dead. But this thing was different. It had come on before he'd had a chance to blink. Like one of those snow squalls that blew in off the lake.

Then, for the first time, he relaxed and smiled. Those squalls came in quick but they disappeared just as fast. By tomorrow he would have everything under control. Samantha Scott would be just another loan applicant.

Kevin stared at the papers on his desk. The pile of loan applications seemed to mock him and he pushed them impatiently away. It was almost six. Maybe he would just grab a movie at the video rental and a pizza at Ruelli's. A cold shower wouldn't hurt, either.

Sam was thrilled that she'd gotten everything straightened out with Mr. Delaney. She felt such a surge of confidence; she knew she could be a success at anything. He wasn't convinced the inn would be a good investment; she knew that. But he was willing to listen with an open mind, and that was enough to make her want to celebrate.

But with whom? Her dad had a dinner meeting at his senior citizens' club tonight, leaving only Toby. And the cat's idea of a great evening was a can of tuna, followed by a snooze on top of the refrigerator.

Sam started back toward the parking lot. Rain was great in April; it put everyone in a spring mood. It was nice in May when you were planting your garden. But by August, a downpour was torture, adding to the humidity, making the area feel like a rain forest. She stopped in front of a video store and looked at the posters in the window. A movie might be fun, or at least a way to not feel so alone.

The store was packed. Everyone in town seemed to have the same idea. But most of the crowd was around the new-release rack, so Sam moved over to the classics section. Only one other person was there . . . a tall, dark-haired man in a blue—

Sam considered running. Turning around and tiptoeing out the door. But the Scott girls never snuck away from anything.

"So, Mr. Delaney. We meet again."

Kevin turned toward her. "Miss Scott." Surprise raced across his face, then an indefinable mixture of emotions—something that sent answering shock waves along her spine.

She'd forgotten the effect he had on her when they were close. "Sam," she corrected him, then dragged her eyes from his with difficulty. "Looks like we both have the same plans for our evening."

"Rescuing fair damsels from distress?" he asked as he picked up the tag for *Red River*.

"Fighting for what's ours," she said decisively, and took the tag for *Gone with the Wind*.

"I never could see the appeal of that movie," Kevin remarked.

He seemed ready to start an argument, which was fine with her. It was probably the best way to keep her silly heart in line. The last thing she wanted at this stage in her life was to feel weak-kneed over some man. Especially one her brothers' age who acted as know-it-all as they did!

"I never could see the appeal of John Wayne," she said as she started toward the counter.

"You don't like the Duke?" Kevin walked with her. "You've got to be kidding. Everybody loves the Duke."

"Not me. He's a male chauvinist of the highest degree."

"He can't help that. His movies reflected the attitudes of the times."

"And I can't help it that he sets my teeth on edge. You ever see *The Quiet Man?* He literally drags Maureen O'Hara over the hillside because he 'knows what's best' for her." Sam was getting riled now—with herself, mostly—but the subject was convenient.

"Maybe that was a woman's idea of romance back when it was made."

"I find that hard to believe." She handed her tag to the clerk and dug into her purse for her membership card.

"Isn't there a scene in *Gone with the Wind* where Rhett carries Scarlett up to their bedroom, against her will?"

"So it has a flaw or two. I never said it was perfect."

"I think it's the most romantic movie I've ever seen," a new voice said. Sam looked up to find the clerk was back with the movie and a dreamy expression on her face.

Sam shoved her money at the girl, then signed the rental paper. "Well, I think a man should respect a woman's intelligence, not play caveman."

"You've never dreamed of being carried off by a knight in shining armor?" Kevin asked.

Sam felt her cheeks turn fiery. "Never," she replied. "I think that caveman act is something a man thought up."

"Maybe," Kevin said, reaching in with his membership card as Sam reached in for her movie.

Their hands brushed and warmth flooded over Sam. Warning bells went off in her mind, but her eyes flew to his. The flame was back, but this time more potent, more dangerous. The room became stifling and breath hard to come by. Sam would be glad to see August and its damn humidity go. She grabbed her movie.

"I'll see you tomorrow, Mr. Delaney," she said, and turned to flee.

But before she was out the door, he had gotten his movie and was next to her. "I'll walk you to your car," he said roughly. "It's dark out and even a little burg like South Bend can be dangerous at night."

But where did the danger lie? "It's really not necessary," she told him. "I'm just parked in the city lot in the next block."

"It's on my way," he said and stepped out into the rain with her. "I was stopping at Ruelli's to get a pizza."

The idea of a pizza was tempting, but Fiona's casserole was waiting. And although Sam didn't really want it, she couldn't ignore the fact that Fiona had gone to a lot of trouble for her. It would be like rejecting a Christmas present.

Sam jumped instead on Kevin's words. "Ruelli's is on Division."

He shrugged. "So I circle the block. I'm not like you, with someone at home waiting for me."

"Actually, I'm on my own this evening," she admitted, shaking the damp hair from her forehead. "The only one at home now is Toby, our cat."

His laugh was reluctant. "That would be your plumbing assistant. I believe I met him this afternoon."

Sam refused to blanch at the reminder of the afternoon's encounter. "Yes, and you should feel quite honored. He rarely hangs around when strangers appear."

"Maybe he could sense my cats, Duke and Duchess."

Sam groaned. "Don't tell me. John Wayne's influence again?"

But rather than laugh with her, Kevin's voice grew distant. "No, my wife named them. She thought they seemed so snooty when they were kittens, like royalty."

"I didn't realize you were married," Sam said.

He looked at her with a smile that glittered almost too brightly in his eyes, like raindrops catching the neon lights— all reflected light and none from inside. "I'm not anymore." He paused to clear his throat. "Debbie died two years ago."

"I'm sorry. She must have been so young."

He shrugged, but it seemed too practiced to be anything but a facade. "Life isn't fair sometimes."

Sam stared down at the wet sidewalk. Suddenly the space between them was filled with pit traps and bramble bushes so that she didn't know which way to turn without causing him more pain.

He took a deep breath and let it out. "So what about you? I know you're single, but do you have a man on the hook—one you're just waiting to reel in?" A careful detachment coated his voice.

"Hardly," she said. "I'm not into caveman stuff on either side."

"I forgot. You're too independent for all that nonsense."

"Well, there are things I have to do before I settle down," she agreed. "I need to try my wings for a while before I get tied down to a man."

"Marriage doesn't have to tie you down."

"Any relationship will, if it's worth anything," she said. They stopped at the corner, waiting for the light to change. "When you love someone, you want to consider their feelings. You can't just rush headlong into things. At least, if the relationship is meaningful, you shouldn't."

"So making the inn a roaring success is your number-one priority."

Sam wasn't so sure that was true, or that she wanted to open that Pandora's box to a man she barely knew. "Is that so strange?"

"No. As your banker, I find it admirable."

The light changed and they started across the intersection. "The inn's been a dream of my dad's for years. He and Mom always talked about starting one once all us kids were grown up. But then Mom died and he didn't seem to have an interest in anything anymore."

"Until you brought it up again."

She sensed something in his voice to take exception with. "And what's the matter with that?"

"Nothing," he said quickly.

Too quickly. "Why'd you say it like that, then?"

He shoved his hands into his pockets. "It's just that you said you want to try your wings before settling down, but here you are chasing someone else's dream for them."

"I am not!" she cried.

"Are you following your own dream?" he asked.

What was this? Someone else telling her how to lead her life? "Maybe I think my father's happiness is more important right now," she snapped. "My own plans can wait a bit."

"Maybe it's safer to complain about not having your own life than it is to fight for it."

"I was not complaining!" she insisted. "I was merely making small talk. But maybe you've spent too much time counting money and don't understand these little nuances in conversation."

Luckily they'd reached the parking lot and Sam was almost free. "I don't want to complain," she mocked. "But I'd better get my car before I have to put another quarter in the meter."

Without another word, she hurried between the parked cars, darting down the middle aisle to her car. What an idiot she was! She shouldn't have been sucked in by her crazy heart. He wasn't something special just because her breath caught when he was near. She fumbled with the lock of her car door as the steady drizzle formed little rivers on her cheeks.

"Sam." Kevin was there behind her, breathing hard.

She stiffened her resolve enough so that she could turn and face him. In the dim streetlight, his eyes looked almost worried. But then she was probably reading that wrong.

"Sam, I'm sorry. All that came out badly."

"All what?" she said breathlessly, then thought she might be carrying it a bit too far. "Oh, you mean about living someone else's dream? Heavens, I'd already forgotten about it."

She'd thought she'd said that well, that her tone had been just right, but Kevin continued to frown.

"You were right." His voice was quiet. "I spend too much time with numbers and not enough with people. I didn't mean to sound critical."

Sam shrugged. "It's okay."

"No, it isn't. You're a thoughtful, unselfish woman in a selfish world."

"Oh." The world was suddenly very still. Just her and Kevin and her foolishly racing heart. "Thank you."

He put his hands on either side of her, trapping her against her car door. Gentle rain was falling like silent kisses on her face. She couldn't have moved if she had wanted to, but she certainly didn't want to.

"Your father is lucky to have you helping him," he said.

Suddenly there was just the two of them, staring into each other's eyes. Sam's gaze moved slightly, down to his lips. What would they feel like, pressed against hers? What joyful heaven would they bring? His sudden intake of breath told her he might be having the same thoughts. Then he pulled away, freeing her—although, for all the world, she still felt like a prisoner.

"You'd better get on home," he said, his voice sounding raw.

She nodded, her mouth too dry to form words just yet. He waited while she unlocked the door. Or tried to. Her hand was shaking so, it took three tries to get the key in the lock. By the time she'd gotten inside, she'd found a topic she could cling to.

"Looks like the rain is stopping," she said.

"Lock your door."

He stood there watching while she closed and locked her door, then backed out of the parking spot. By the time she was on the road, her nerves were almost steady enough to drive. That is, until she realized she would see him again tomorrow.

Chapter Two

Sam didn't dress any differently the next morning just because Kevin was coming over. She put on the same old shorts she normally wore when working on the house, and the same faded Indiana University T-shirt. Kevin was coming to see the inn, not her. It was the shape of her business that would influence him, not the shape of her body.

Sam was on her hands and knees scrubbing the soot-encrusted stone around the fireplace in the front room-cum-lobby when her father came in, carrying cans of paint for the kitchen.

"You look like Cinderella over there," he teased. "Prince Charming coming down the chimney soon?"

"Dad, Santa comes down the chimney. Prince Charming comes through the front door."

"Speaking of which, I got your tickets last night. I put them on your dresser."

"Great." Her father's senior-citizen club was sponsoring a Las Vegas Night next Saturday to raise funds for the children's literacy program.

"So who's going to be Prince Charming next week?" he asked.

Sam stopped her scrubbing to stare at him. "Next week?"

"You know, for the Las Vegas Night. Who you gonna let sweep you off your feet?"

She just shook her head and went back to her scrubbing. "I wasn't actually planning on using those tickets," she admitted. "It's for a good cause, so I bought them."

"Be a shame to waste them, though." He stopped at the door to the kitchen, a thoughtful frown on his face. "Maybe Larry can find someone for you to take."

"Dad!" But it was too late. He was already in the kitchen, the door swinging shut behind him. Damn. If she wanted to go to the Las Vegas Night, she could find herself a date. She certainly didn't need her brother to help her. Sam attacked the dirty stonework with renewed vigor.

Nancy, Larry's wife, dropped in a few minutes later. "I'm taking some stuff to the cleaners," she said. "You need anything while I'm out?"

Sam sat back on her heels and gave her sister-in-law a wry look. "No, thank you." She shook her head. "Rosemary stopped by first thing this morning with some milk and bread. I told her we're capable of buying a gallon of milk ourselves, but she said she was already out and what did it matter."

"I hope she bought two-percent, not whole. And was it wheat bread?"

"Yes and yes," Sam replied. "But we can still buy our own stuff. And we can take our own clothes to the cleaners."

"Dad in the kitchen?" Nancy asked, ignoring Sam's words. "I'll go say hello." As she turned, her sister-in-law stopped and peered out the front window. "Oh, wow. Hunk alert.'' Her eyes took on a new gleam as she turned back to Sam. ''You expecting somebody? Somebody tall, dark and handsome?''

''He's from the savings and loan,'' Sam said and perversely went back to scrubbing.

''So? Hunks have to work, too.'' Nancy opened the door. ''Come on in. Cinderella's on the hearth, as usual. *Ciao, sis.*''

The door closed behind Kevin and Sam heard Nancy's footsteps cross the room and fade into the kitchen.

''Is that your other sister?''

''No.'' She put down her brush and got slowly to her feet, brushing back some of the unruly curls from her forehead as Kevin came closer, his all-too-familiar frown in place. ''She's my brother Larry's wife. But she's just as bossy as my regular sisters.''

The frown disappeared, was replaced by a crinkly-eyed smile. Sam snatched an old towel off the floor and dried her hands with it. Then, as she was about to drop the towel on the floor, Kevin took it from her and wiped at her forehead.

He was close to her—too close, for she had to fight back the urge to move even closer, into his arms, into his embrace. He seemed taller, his shoulders broader than she remembered. Nice, but not Prince Charming. At least, not *her* Prince Charming.

''Traces of Cinderella,'' he explained, showing her the sooty smudge now on the towel.

''I see.'' She stepped away from him but his soft, spicy scent followed her, wrapping her spirit in the promise of his embrace. She breathed it in, letting her heart dance for a moment, then called her common sense back in control. She had too much to accomplish before she could allow romance into her life. ''So how do we do this? Want to look the place over first or see my business plan?''

"Let's check out your facilities," he suggested. "I've got the notes from Dick's inspection when you applied for your first loan, but I should see everything for myself."

She nodded. He didn't really seem like he was spoiling for a fight. Maybe his initial frown was just part of his business attire. It wouldn't hurt for her to put one on herself, just to keep her silly heart in line.

"This is the former living room that we'll use as a lobby," she said, waving her hand at the spaciousness surrounding them as she led him across the floor to the next room. "And this is the dining room. It's not especially large, but since we're only going to be serving breakfast, it should easily take care of all our guests in two sittings."

"The woodwork original?" he asked.

She nodded. "The place is in great condition. The wood needs some refinishing, but at least it's never been painted over."

"When was the house built?"

"In the 1890s." Sam slid a massive oak door with thick glass panels out of the doorframe and ran her hand slowly over the surface. "I think I fell in love with these doors. They're all over the place, between all the rooms down here and between the hallways upstairs."

Following her example, Kevin ran his hand appreciatively over the wood. "They don't make houses like this anymore. No one wants to take the time." His voice sounded less clipped, less brusque.

"Or has the money," she suggested.

He walked over to one of the tall windows that looked out over a rolling lawn and opened a cabinet that was part of the window frame.

"Shutters." She joined him, pulling out wooden shutters from the opposite cabinet so that the bottom half of the window was covered. "All the windows have them."

He seemed preoccupied and Sam wondered if something was bothering him. Did he think the building was too old, not maintained well enough?

"It's not the money that's lacking." He put the shutters back into their little closets. "There are houses up in Shamrock Hills that cost three times as much as this place that aren't nearly as well made. Good things take time. What can be made fast, can spoil fast."

"I guess," she said uncertainly. "Come on into the kitchen and meet my dad before I show you the suites upstairs."

He followed her through the swing door at the far end of the dining room and into the kitchen. Nancy was gone and her father was spreading drop cloths over the kitchen cabinets. He stopped to let Sam introduce them and shake hands with Kevin.

"So, Mr. Delaney, you going to give us the extra money we need?" he asked.

"Dad, we've hardly started discussing it," Sam said.

But Kevin ignored her. "It seems like a sound investment, Mr. Scott. And we take pride in helping the small businessman get started."

Dan Scott winked at his daughter. "Well, Sam, here, is small, but she's not any kind of man," he joked. "Maybe you need to take a closer look at her?"

"Dad!" This was too much, especially after last night. Sam could feel Kevin's gaze on her and knew without looking that, although his lips might be sharing her father's joke, his eyes were not.

"Why don't I show you our guest suites?" she suggested.

"Good idea."

She led him to the back stairs, conscious all the while of his eyes on her. She imagined that he could feel his breath tickling the back of her neck and that his gaze was as aware of the snug fit of her shorts as she suddenly was.

"We have four suites that can each sleep up to four people, and two that could sleep eight with rollaway beds," she said briskly. "Not that we'll always have that many guests here. We—"

"Samantha," her father called from the sink.

She stopped, even though a little voice inside her was urging her to run. "Yes?" she asked without turning around.

"Bankers usually know a lot of people in the community."

"So?"

"Maybe your banker friend would know of a Prince Charming who's at loose ends at the moment," her father suggested.

Sam turned just enough to flash her father a tight smile, but not enough to catch more than a glimpse of Kevin. "It's all right, Dad. I can handle it." She went up the stairs as quickly as she could and still maintain her dignity.

"Do most people call you Samantha?" Kevin asked from behind her. "Or do we get our choice?"

She mixed a smile with a shrug as she waited at the top of the stairs. "My sisters decided it was too much of a mouthful when I was younger. Fiona would find someone had been in the cookie jar right before dinner, but before she could get my whole name out, the evidence was gone."

"Sounds like you should have refused a nickname. It took away your edge."

"I guess. I answer to either, though, so take your pick."

"No contest. I'll stick to Sam."

His tone was as odd as his words had been but before she could question them, he moved to an open doorway. She followed.

"This is one of our smaller suites," she told him. "A small sitting room, with a bedroom and bath."

"Nice." He stepped inside and flicked the switch to light up the brass ceiling fixture, then walked into the bedroom.

"The wallpaper and drapes are still on order, so it's hard to get an idea of what it'll look like when it's finished."

"I've got a good imagination." He stepped into the bathroom and tried the faucets. "Is this one of the bathrooms held together by mineral deposits? Or are you just using rust in here?"

If he was trying to intimidate her, it wouldn't work. Not his reminder of yesterday's fiasco or the chill creeping back into his voice. "There's a plumbing report in your file, I'm sure," she said. "We had the place inspected before we bought it. I'm just trying to correct the minor drips on my own."

"I see."

She was about to explain just how minor the minor drips were, when she heard footsteps on the stairs.

"Sam?" Fiona called.

What great timing. "In the corner suite," Sam called back, then grimaced at Kevin. "It's my sister Fiona."

Fiona bustled into the room. "Ah, there you are, Sam. Oh, I'm sorry. You have a guest."

"No problem," Sam said and introduced Fiona to Kevin. "I think you met briefly yesterday."

"You sent me upstairs to interview Sam in her office," Kevin noted.

Fiona's eyes reflected her confusion. "Her office?"

"The sink cabinet in the north suite's bathroom," Sam said, wryly. "What can I do for you?"

"I just happened to see this at the store last night." She handed Sam a bag with a satisfied smile.

"Thanks." Sam took the bag reluctantly and knew what it was the moment she touched it. She pulled out a copy of the *Reader's Digest Complete Do-It-Yourself Manual.*

"Now that you have your own copy," Fiona said, "you can take the library's copy back before they make a public spectacle of you."

"Uh-oh. Now you've done it," Sam said. "I purposely left my impending fine off my list of debts on the loan application form."

"I'll pretend I didn't hear," Kevin told her, with the trace of a smile.

"And I'll be on my way," Fiona said and went back downstairs.

Sam put the book down and led Kevin out into the hall. "Come on, I'll show you the larger suites."

"Okay," he said.

Their footsteps echoed on the bare wood floor, making a cold, lonely sound. She stopped at the first doorway and let him precede her. He had picked up a tuft of Toby's hair somehow; it was stuck on the seat of his pants. She wanted to reach out and pull it off, but her hand froze at her side as if it didn't dare touch those tight buns. As if it might not stop at plucking off the cat hair, but slide into a caress. This was crazy. Where had that thought come from?

She cleared her throat. "These suites are also missing wallpaper and drapes," she warned him. "All that stuff's on order."

"I did assume you weren't going to rent out the rooms with newspaper on the windows," he said and made some notes on his pad.

Her erratic heart had better fall into line. This man wasn't her type at all. So why, then, was her heart suddenly trembling from being close to him, from watching the way his pulse beat at the base of his neck? She took a deep breath and turned away.

"That it?" he asked.

She was about to say yes—her mouth was open ready to agree—but perversely a different word came out. "No. One more thing."

She led him back down the stairs to the kitchen and then out the back door, stopping only to grab up the bag of bread crusts she kept in the refrigerator.

He gave her a questioning look as they walked down the gently sloping back lawn, but she said nothing until they stopped at a wall of bushes alongside the path. She pushed the bushes aside and stepped into the tiny alcove they formed at the water's edge.

"What—"

But then two majestic figures glided into view. "This is Romeo and Juliet," Sam said.

Kevin turned to frown at her. "You're kidding."

"Hey, I didn't name them," she protested, and tossed some bread out onto the water. The swans moved in closer to pick up the pieces. "Those have been their names for as long as I've known them."

She held out the bag of bread, telling herself it hardly mattered if he wanted to feed the swans or not, yet her heart smiled when he reached into the bag. He broke the slice into pieces and tossed them slowly onto the water.

"You make it sound like they're old friends," he said.

"I guess they are. My sisters and I were at a day camp on the other side of the lake when I was six. We first met them then."

He whistled softly. "That must make them fairly old in bird years."

"I guess." She wanted to tell him about the rescue, but was suddenly afraid of letting him know too much about her. She was supposed to be concentrating on making the bed-and-breakfast a success, not making eyes at the banker. She probably shouldn't have brought him down to this secluded spot; not to the swan's favorite feeding spot.

"Well, that's about it," she said as she turned to push the bushes out of the way so he could get back on the path. She stopped suddenly and glanced at him. "Why Sam and not Samantha?" she asked.

He turned to face her. The warmth of the summer scene was in his eyes and she felt like dry tinder ready to ignite at his slightest touch.

She swallowed hard, sorry that she'd let the question fly out of her mouth. "You know. You said before you'd rather call me Sam than Samantha and I wondered why."

He looked uncertain for a moment—trapped? "It's easier to remember," he said with a shrug. "You know. It's shorter."

She felt stupid for making a big deal of it. What had she thought he would say? What had she wanted him to say?

Nothing, she told herself. Maybe the air out here was too thin. Or maybe it was the swans. Maybe seeing Romeo and Juliet with Kevin nearby had awoken in her heart that old woman's weird promise about finding love.

Except that love was the last thing she was looking for right now.

She turned to duck through the bushes, a sudden need to hurry back to the house nipping at her heels, when she tripped over an exposed root. She tottered sideways for what seemed an eternity, then suddenly she wasn't falling—at least, not in actuality. But she was in Kevin's arms and staring up into his stormy eyes.

She saw all sorts of emotions there—loneliness and fear, desire and longing, and mostly confusion. As if the strength of the storm in his heart had taken him by surprise.

Or was she looking into a mirror and seeing her own reflection there? She needed him with a heat that had never burned her before. Her soul seemed seared and scorched from the touch of his hands on her and she yearned to lie closer in his arms, to feel the touch of his lips on hers; to let her heart taste the joy of his nearness.

They broke apart suddenly and Sam stepped back against the bushes, her legs weakened and her soul trembling. She felt Kevin turn and heard his ragged breathing, but she needed a deep breath, then another before her voice had the strength to speak. She couldn't be so affected by him. He wasn't her type.

"Maybe we'd better go inside," she said, needing an oasis to regroup.

"Sounds like a wise thought."

He pushed aside the bushes and she ducked through them, her legs luckily finding the power to walk. She could just see herself if they hadn't: an untidy heap in the middle of the yard. Kevin would stop to stare at her. She would just smile politely and ask him to explain to her father that she'd fallen apart from Kevin's touch and needed those old crutches in the garage to get back to the house.

"Everything seems in order," Kevin said as he walked behind her.

She stared ahead. Just what might not be in order?

"It's just a matter of filling out a report on my visit and getting the approval of the other officers."

She stopped to glance over her shoulder at him. "Oh. The loan," she said lamely as she opened the back door, then smiled in relief at the sound of footsteps approaching. "The cavalry." And it was needed this time.

Her sister-in-law Diane appeared in the hallway. "Oh, there you are, Sam. Oops, sorry. I didn't know you had a guest."

Right. As if the Scott telegraph system hadn't alerted the whole city. "My banker," Sam said with a wave of her hand at Kevin. She didn't mean to be rude, but introducing him would involve looking his way and that might involve meeting his gaze and that would definitely involve collapsing into that untidy heap on the floor.

"Oh," Diane said with a bright smile in Kevin's direction before turning a sisterly frown on Sam. "I just wanted to tell you I've got the laundry. I'll bring it back tomorrow."

"Okay." Sam didn't have the strength to argue. "Thanks."

They followed Diane back into the living room. Right foot, left foot. Her eyes closed. Lordy, his shoulders were broad. It had been heaven to be in his arms. She opened her eyes and concentrated on walking. Much safer. By the time they got to the other room, Sam had found enough strength to smile a businesslike smile.

"We never looked at my business plan," she reminded.

"That's all right. I've got a preliminary copy here." He stopped to pick up a book lying on the table near the door. The library's copy of the *Complete Do-It-Yourself Manual.* "I'll drop this off at the library. I'm driving right past it."

All her wobbliness faded faster than the river's mist in the hot summer sun. "You will not!" she cried and tried to grab the book from his hands.

His eyes warred with hers briefly as their hands warred over the book. The anger in his gaze this time wasn't cool and distant; it was raging hot, but she stared him down.

"Caveman," she hissed.

He frowned and let go of the book. "Scarlett O'Hara."

"She survived the burning of Atlanta," Sam declared, hugging the book to her chest.

"And cavemen survived the Ice Age."

He picked up his folder and slammed out the door before Sam could ask him what in the world that was supposed to mean. She turned to walk into the kitchen.

"Did you ask your friend to stay to lunch?" Diane asked. "No."

"Did you ask him to the Las Vegas Night?" her father wanted to know.

"For goodness' sake," she snapped. "He's my banker, that's all."

Sam shoved the unwrapped hamburger in Cassie's face. "Look at that," Sam demanded. After her little discussion with Larry in front of the library, Sam was in no mood for compromise. "This is the last straw."

"Yeah?" Cassie looked cautiously at the sandwich and then back at Sam. "What is?"

"Pickles," Sam hissed through her clenched teeth. "You know how I hate pickles."

"Pick them out."

Sam sighed and dropped her head on Cassie's desk. After leaving Larry, Sam had wanted to go off and kick something or somebody. Instead she'd come over to join Cassie for lunch, stopping at a fast-food drive-through on her way over.

"You want me to pick them out for you?" Cassie offered.

"No." Sam sat up and picked out the pickle slices, flinging each one down onto the paper sandwich wrapper. "You know, if I wanted reasonable and sympathetic, I could have had lunch with Fiona."

"Sorry," Cassie replied as she bit into her sandwich.

"Cassie," Sam wailed. "Just look at yourself. You're getting to be so genteel and ladylike that pretty soon I won't be able to tell the difference between you and Fiona."

"I don't think there's any danger of that."

"Oh, yeah? When's the last time you hit somebody?"

Cassie smiled, looking almost like a sixth grader after her first kiss. Sam pushed aside the sense that something was missing from her life—something that Cassie had found. That was crazy, Sam assured herself. Her life was full. She didn't need anything or anybody else in it.

"There are other ways to get what you want," Cassie said. "Ways that are more fun."

Sam felt a little shiver of concern ripple through her body. She could always get a rise out of Cassie. Or at least, she used to be able to. But not anymore. Pregnancy and her impending marriage had turned her sister into an angel. All the foundations of Sam's world were crumbling.

"Are you going to finish your french fries?" Sam asked.

"Boy." Cassie pushed the package of fries toward her. "You sure got a burr up your saddle today."

Sam made a slight face as she continued eating. She couldn't hide anything from her sisters. Both of them knew that Sam went on eating binges when she was upset. "You know where I can get myself a good hit man?" she asked.

"Which one of the boys do you want to eliminate?" Cassie asked.

"Larry," Sam replied with a glare. "Although Bobby and Adam are just as deserving."

"Who's he trying to fix you up with now?"

"I don't know." Sam slurped up the last of her strawberry shake, almost hoping that Cassie would bop her on the head for making such a disgusting noise. But her sister just sat there, smiling sympathetically. Sam slammed the empty drink container into the wastebasket. "Someone he works with."

She watched as Cassie cleaned up the rest of the garbage from her desk. "Actually, I don't care who it is or where he comes from," Sam said. "I just don't want any of the boys butting into my life."

"You're the only one who can fix that," Cassie said.

"Right. That's why I want to hire a hit man."

"Get serious, Sam."

Sam slouched back in her chair. The hit man didn't have to kill them. He could just kidnap all three brothers and drop them off in the middle of the ocean or deep in the jungles of South America. By the time they found their way home, she would have her life under control. Maybe.

"You've got to take charge, Sam. Show them that you don't need their interference."

"Wow," Sam replied. "Why didn't I think of that?"

"You must have taken some science classes to get your degree in library science." Cassie was obviously ignoring her sarcasm. "Didn't you learn that nature abhors a vacuum?"

Sam nodded and shrugged at the same time. She'd never been a science whiz but she did remember how air, or something, always rushed in to fill a vacuum.

"Well, our brothers are the same way," Cassie said. "They can't stand it when they see us alone. So they have to rush out and find us a boyfriend."

"So, in order to keep them out of my life, I have to get a boyfriend?"

"Not a real boyfriend," Cassie said. "But you have to fill that vacuum."

"Maybe I should go out and buy one of those male mannequins. You know, the kind women put in the passenger seat when they drive around alone at night."

"I think you need something that walks and talks."

Sam made a face and looked around Cassie's cluttered little office. Both her sisters had everything they wanted in their lives. They had their men and they had their careers. Sam wanted to get her life in order before she went looking for a man of her own.

Trouble was, she wasn't sure what getting her life in order meant. Mom had thought she would be a great children's librarian, and Sam hadn't had any other ideas, so that was what she'd studied in school. Dad wanted to run a bed-and-breakfast and couldn't do it alone, so Sam jumped in to help. She enjoyed all of it, but none of it ever seemed to satisfy her soul.

Kevin's statement about following everyone else's dreams nagged at her like a pesky mosquito. But what was wrong with helping others reach a dream, when she didn't have one of her own to reach for?

"Find someone who doesn't want to get serious," Cassie advised. "Someone who's safe."

"You mean, like a married man?"

"Not in the married-to-a-wife sense," Cassie said. "But maybe somebody who's married to his job. Or married to his past. Someone who'd like some fun but no commitment.''

Sam grunted. According to Cassie, all of her previous relationships would qualify.

Chapter Three

Kevin pulled the car up to the curb in front of the old house late Friday morning and took a deep breath as he turned the motor off. He didn't know why he was doing this. A vision of Sam—soft, warm, womanly—filled his mind and he corrected himself. All right, he knew damn well why he was doing it, but he also knew that he shouldn't be doing it. That woman was dangerous to the peace and well-being of his mind.

He picked up his leather-bound folder and got out of the car. He'd hoped that once the loan process was over, she would step out of his life and stop haunting him; that there would be no more reason for him to see her, and all further transactions would be done through the mail or handled by the bank's clerical staff.

Except that the loan committee was concerned. The loan was large; the Scotts were inexperienced. There would have to be periodic inspections, at least for the first year. And it would be Kevin's job to make them.

The front door, looking freshly painted, was standing slightly open so Kevin squeezed inside. "Hello?" he called out. "Anybody here?"

Toby jumped down from his sun-drenched window seat and glared at Kevin.

"Hey, I just need to get some papers signed. Then I'm gone, at least for a while." Kevin paused for a moment to trade stares with His Royal Highness. A noise from the kitchen drew his attention and he pushed open the door. "Hello?"

Sam was at the sink, washing paintbrushes, and looked up. A smile bathed her face in sunshine. "Hi. What are you doing here? Need to see my business plan, after all?"

"Nope." He put his folder down on the kitchen table and pulled out a stack of papers and a pen. "Just need you and your dad's signatures in a few places and the money will be deposited in your account."

"Just like that?" She wiped her hands on a towel as she came over to the table. "Wow. It hasn't even been a week since you looked at the house."

"Well, it's not quite that simple," he said. Her light brown hair was catching the sunlight so that it sparkled with gold. He could run his fingers through it and be richer than he'd ever dreamed.

"Oh?"

He dragged himself back to reality. "The bank wants me to make periodic inspections for the first year, at least."

"And if we don't pass, they'll revoke the loan?"

He shook his head quickly. "No, nothing like that. If I spot any problems, we'll advise you on what you should do or steer you to someone who can help." He put on his banker voice. "We like to think of ourselves as partners with our clients. We want to help you succeed."

"I see." She looked down at the papers he'd taken out of his folder. "So where do I sign?"

He handed her the pen. "Here." He pointed to a spot. "And here, here and here."

In a matter of moments, it was done. Her signature was in all the right places.

"My dad's not here," she said as she handed his pen back. "Can you leave the papers or do you need to come back?"

His heart said he would like to come back but his head said he didn't need to. Not quite so soon. "He can sign it without me. Just have someone other than you witness it and then you can mail the papers back to me." He slipped his pen back into his pocket. "I'll be stopping in every couple of weeks, but feel free to call if you should have any questions sooner. Your new payment book will be mailed to you about a week after we get the signed papers."

"This feels too simple," she said with a laugh. "You can't rush off right away or I'll figure I dreamed the whole thing."

Her mouth was soft with laughter but he was sure that passion danced just below the surface. Oh, baby. His own passions were starting to burn like a teenager's. Time for him to hit the road. And the sooner, the better.

"At least, you have to stay for lunch," Sam said. "I heat up a mean can of soup."

"I should be getting back," he replied. To work, golf, go out and buy an ice-cream cone. As long as it was out of here.

"You have to eat. How about a bacon, lettuce and tomato sandwich?"

"You have enough to do around here without serving lunch." His argument sounded weak even to himself. It was all due to those damn eyes. A gentle blue, so calm but fringed with laughter. He glanced at them again. Unfortunately, they seemed to glow with more than laughter.

"Dad's having lunch with some other bed-and-breakfast owners, but I have to eat myself," she said. "A few more slices of bacon means more work for the microwave, not me."

"All right. But only if you let me help." He did have to eat, and what difference would a few more minutes of her company make?

None, he told himself. Absolutely none. Sure, she was a beautiful little enchantress. But, hell. It wasn't like she was the only one in the world. His own bank was full of attractive young ladies. They didn't upset his equilibrium. No reason why Sam should.

"How about if you handle the soup and I'll do the sandwiches?" She opened a cabinet of canned goods. "Take your pick. I like anything that's there."

Kevin shook his head. He'd been doing that a lot, lately. Hang around with Sam long enough and he could sell his head for a rattle. Setting his face in a businesslike frown, he walked over to the pantry and checked out the array. Everything from consommé to split pea. "You're easy to please."

"You go hungry if you're too picky in a big family." He heard her bustling about behind him, opening the refrigerator door. "Want rye, wheat or white bread?"

"Rye."

"Toasted or not?"

"Toasted."

He took out a can of chicken noodle and studied the label. "They shouldn't put the noodles in with the soup. They just get soggy."

She took the can from his hand and replaced it with a can of chicken vegetable. "Then heat this up and cook your own noodles. Pasta's on the shelf above the soup, and pots are in the cabinet to the right of the stove."

He got the water started for the noodles and put the soup on a low flame. It was surprising how comfortable it felt working with Sam in the kitchen. He'd thought that his domestic urges had died with Debbie.

"The soup'll never get warm turned down that low," Sam said as she slid the bacon plate into the microwave.

"Hey, you assigned this area to me, so let me take care of it. If I fail, let me fail on my own."

"I thought that was my song," she said with a laugh.

Smiling, he gave the now boiling pasta a few stirs and then turned his attention to the soup. "You're a bit on the bossy side for a younger sibling, aren't you?"

Sam's laughter was louder, filling the kitchen with its teasing sound.

"Inside every youngest child there's a control freak waiting to burst out."

"I didn't know that," he replied.

"We get bossed around a good part of our lives. When we get our chance, we make the most of it."

Still smiling, he turned down the heat under the pasta pot. For a moment the kitchen was filled with the sound of running water and then there was silence. A silence that softly crackled with an unnamed tension. A yearning.

"Did you know your wife a long time before you got married?" Sam asked. "No, that's none of my business and Fiona would tell me I'm being rude."

"I don't mind the question," he said and surprisingly he didn't. He watched the pasta water slow to a soft boil before turning to lean on the counter, facing Sam. "We grew up together. I was in fourth grade when she was in first and I was supposed to walk her to and from school each day. I thought no kid had ever been so put upon."

She smiled, making him feel that this sharing of his past was something special. "Did she make life miserable for you?"

Kevin shook his head as he stared down that portion of his memory lane. "No, that wasn't Debbie. She'd just look at me with her big brown eyes and make me feel like a rat."

"When did you decide she wasn't a pest?"

"Probably somewhere around sixth grade, when I was at the losing end of a fight. She came flying into the middle of it, her Rocky and Bullwinkle lunch box swinging right and left. They had glass thermoses back then, and those things were heavy. Hers broke, but we won.''

"And became friends.''

"Or at least no longer enemies. We sort of took our time about going from one stage to the next. When her parents moved across the country right after we started college, we decided to get married and make our own home.''

The noodles were done and so was the bacon, so Kevin was able to retreat into himself as they served up the food. But surprisingly, he didn't really feel the need to pull back. As they sat down to eat, an aura of comfort settled around them. The attraction he'd felt for Sam was exciting but it was nice to be able to relax with her, too.

"Did you ever date anyone else?'' Sam asked. "Before you were married, I mean.''

Kevin laughed. "Not successfully. I had a date now and then with someone else in high school, but it never felt right. You know how it is when you just don't mesh. It was always Debbie for me.''

"And still is?'' she asked.

"No. Not really.'' He dragged his spoon slowly through his soup, watching the noodles trail in the spoon's wake. "Oh, I go out some. But I'm not interested in marrying again or even having a close relationship with anyone else. But it's not because I haven't let go of Debbie.''

They ate in silence for a time, but it was a comfortable silence and he watched her hands as she ate. Her fingers were slender, yet he sensed a strength in them that belied their delicacy. Those hands worked hard, as the scratched knuckles attested to, but they could still inspire some interesting daydreams. His breath caught at the idea of those hands on him, and he had to look away. Cool Kevin did not let his emotions take charge.

"So, what about you?'' he said after a moment. "I know you said the other day you weren't about to reel someone in, but I can't believe that you don't have anybody special in your life.''

"I have a lot of special people in my life.''

But not that one special someone. That surprised him; pleased him, for some crazy reason. "Don't worry," he said. "Someday your prince will come.''

"For all I know, he may already have come by. I've been pretty busy lately.''

"Don't be too busy.''

"Why do you say that?" Sam asked. "You speaking from experience?''

"Not exactly," he said. "Just sort of general logic. But I don't think love is like a train. You know—don't worry if you miss one, another'll be along soon.''

"You believe there's only one person for each of us?''

That stopped him, made his heart quail at the thought. If he believed that, it meant with Debbie gone, he was finished with love. He hadn't been looking for someone else, hadn't even thought about looking for someone else; but did he want to give up all chance that he might find love again?

"I don't know," he finally replied, feeling her eyes on him. He tried to laugh. "I guess I ought to be pretty depressed if there is.''

"Well, I don't believe in one true love," she said sharply as she got to her feet. "I mean, suppose I have a cold and skip the party where I'm supposed to meet my true love. I have to spend my life alone because I took care of my health? You want any more of the soup?''

"Uh?" He looked up, feeling bewildered. "Ah, no. You go ahead. I've had enough.''

He watched her walk over to the stove with quick, sure strides. There was a grace about her, a fluid rhythm that drew his eye and ignited his senses. Yet, despite the strength of her movements, she was all woman, and in his blood a deepening ache grew to match her rhythm. It was time to leave.

"I have to be getting back to the office," he said, picking up his dishes. "Thanks for the lunch and the company." He carried his things to the sink.

"Just leave them there. I'll load up the dishwasher."

She walked with him to the kitchen door. He thought maybe she would stop there, was hoping it, even, he told himself. But he was glad when she came on through the living room with him. There was nothing wrong with eyeballing a beautiful lady. He wasn't a young stud anymore, but he sure wasn't dead.

Sam put her hand on his arm to stop him. "I need a favor. A big favor."

"Okay."

"I mean, a really, really, really big one."

"It's still okay." Actually, it really wasn't. Her hand on his arm was stirring wild feelings in his body. Feelings that he was sure his senses had forgotten. Like a need to crush her young body to his. He really had to run. Although it was doubtful that he could get to his shower fast enough. Maybe he should just jump in the lake out back of the inn.

"You remember my dad mentioning a Las Vegas Night his seniors group was sponsoring?"

"I was aware of it. I saw some ads in the paper."

"Well, everyone's really been bugging me to go, but I don't date much. I mean, it seems like all the guys my age want to settle down and I don't. But since you said you feel the same way, I thought maybe..."

She ended her sentence with a shrug. And Kevin felt the air go out of him. He should have run when he had the chance. Now, since she'd asked him, it would be impolite. He cleared his throat. "You want me to take you?"

She made a face, crinkling up her eyes and pouting her lips into such a tempting frown that he had to fight all the hungers that were washing over him again—a need to laugh, a need to dance, a need to sweep her into his arms.

What he really needed was to leave.

"If you're not already busy tomorrow night." She brushed the fingers of both hands through her hair. "I know it's the last minute, but I just thought it would make things easier. You see, my dad really wants me to go. And my brothers are all hot to find me a date. And—" She shook her head. "Ah, forget it. It was a dumb idea."

He had a choice. He could be wise or he could be foolish. He could dance around the edge of danger or he could play it safe.

"Sure."

"You probably have better things to—" She stared at him for a moment. "Sure?"

"Yeah, sure."

"Are you sure?"

"Suretainly."

She laughed, the sound running over him like a brook trickling over stones and setting them alive.

"You're the first guy I've asked for a date since Jason Rhembold," she said. "I was a freshman in high school and we had this Sadie Hawkins dance. It was just before Halloween. I'm babbling, aren't I?"

"What time do you want me to pick you up?"

"I can drive." She took a deep breath and shook her head. "I'm the one who asked you."

He ignored her. "Eight o'clock all right?"

She raked her hair again. "Yeah, that'll be great."

"Fine." He nodded. "I'll see you at eight tomorrow night."

She took another deep breath. "You know, there's no problem with me driving."

"I couldn't do that," he said, shaking his head. "The Duke wouldn't allow it."

Sam made a face.

"You know," he said. "John Wayne."

"I knew which duke you were talking about."

"Good." She was glaring at him and he was filled with an irresistible urge to sweep her into his arms. The Duke would certainly have approved of that. But he wasn't John Wayne or even a John Wayne wanna-be. He nodded and turned on his heel.

"See you tomorrow," she called after him.

This was not a real date, Sam told herself as she pulled her deep blue silk dress out of the closet the next evening. And there was no reason for her heart to sing as it did while she showered or for her cheeks to glow even before she put any makeup on. It wasn't like she'd never been on a date before.

Luckily, the mortgage money was already in their account. So no matter what kind of fool she made of herself, they couldn't take it back. Or could they? She wasn't too sure about these periodic checks that Kevin was supposed to make. The clock told her that she was pressed for time, though, and had better limit her analysis to which earrings to wear. When she hurried downstairs a few minutes after eight, Kevin was waiting in the living room with her father.

"Look at Cinderella," Dan Scott whistled.

"Very nice," Kevin said.

"Golly, yes," Sam mocked. "All that soot washed off pretty darned good."

Her father snorted in the background, but before he could make any more comments, she kissed him on the cheek. "We'll see you at the hall, Dad."

"I'd better," he said. "I don't want you young folks sneaking off."

Kevin laughed as he opened the door and looked back at her father. "Some of us are not all that young anymore."

"Hey." Sam stopped as she was halfway out the door. "Speak for yourself, fella."

"Yeah, I suppose I should."

Sam could have sworn some of the light went out of his eyes, and she frowned as they walked to his car. Was he sensitive about his age? He couldn't be that many years past thirty—although he was a vice president of the bank. That might mean he was close to thirty-five.

"Sam?"

Startled, she saw that Kevin was holding the car door open for her. Lord, where was her mind going? "Thanks," she said as she slipped into her seat.

He hurried around to the driver's side and, once he'd settled himself, gave her a smile before starting up the car and putting them on the road.

It wasn't a compact car. It was a luxurious sedan with more than enough room for two people, but it felt so close—as if she and Kevin were hand in glove. She could almost feel the tickle of the hairs on the back of his hand. Her body was filled with tension. A sweet kind of tension that could only be satisfied by wrapping herself around him. She quickly directed her attention out the window to the passing scenery.

She had to admit that she was getting to like Kevin a whole lot. He didn't treat her like her siblings did—like a little kid in need of watching and rescuing from imagined dangers—too often. He didn't treat her like a little kid much at all. And that was a danger in itself, but only if she let it get in the way of her goals. Just because she felt a wondrous tightening of her nerves and her heart when he was close, it didn't mean she would compromise who she was and where she was going. Her heart could be weak, but her resolve was not. By the time Kevin pulled into the parking lot at the VFW Hall, Sam had her body and emotions under complete and total control. Almost.

"Looks like there'll be a good-size crowd," he said as he helped her from the car.

"Dad said ticket sales went well." The parking lot was gravel and seemed uneven under her heels so she put her arm through Kevin's for support. "Thank you, kind sir."

"My pleasure," he murmured.

Strange what kind of tricks a person's ears could play on them. If she hadn't known that this was just a onetime kind of thing, she would have thought he really meant it. "You must have had some other role models besides John Wayne," she said. "I didn't think he was known for any kind of sensitivity."

"Hey, the Duke was a very sensitive guy."

"He hid it well," she said.

"Maybe he felt he had to."

"I thought he only did things because he wanted to, not because he had to."

"This could turn into a real argument," he warned.

"I never argue," Sam said. "I'm just telling you how things are."

He opened the door for her. "I know your father is going to be here. How about your brothers and sisters?"

"My brothers are on an Indian Princess camp out with their daughters. You know, that YMCA program for fathers and daughters? Fiona's here with her husband and Cassie's with her fiancé." Sam stopped just inside the doorway. "Oh, Fiona was hoping we would sit with them. Is that okay?"

"Sure. That would be nice."

The lobby had Christmas lights strung over everything so that the room fairly glowed. They each turned in their tickets for a wad of play money and some chips, then worked through the crowd into the main room. The game tables were set around the perimeter while tables for sitting filled the middle. Sam found her hand in Kevin's. A wise precaution, given the people milling around them.

"Is that Fiona?" Kevin asked, nodding toward a figure waving at them.

"You have a good memory."

"Not really. She reminds me of you in little ways."

"She does?" Sam hadn't thought any of the three of them resembled each other.

"Hi, guys." Fiona had come up to meet them. "How are you?"

"I'm just fine and dandy." Sam pulled Kevin slightly forward. "You remember Kevin? He's giving us the money for our bed-and-breakfast."

"Lending," Kevin said with a chuckle. "We'll want it back, you know."

Sam gave him a pained look.

"Sorry." He flashed his heartbreaker smile. "Banker humor."

"I didn't know there was such a thing," Sam said. "I thought bankers and humor were mutually exclusive."

"Ah, a math major."

"No way," Sam replied. "I had to take a statistics course for my library science major." She stopped at the table and introduced Kevin to Fiona's husband, Alex, and then their middle sister, Cassie, Cassie's fiancé, Jack, and his aunt Hattie.

"You look sort of familiar," Kevin said as he shook Jack's hand. "Aren't you—"

"Yes," Sam interrupted. "He's a famous ex-football player turned lawyer, but he's very modest so we don't talk about it."

"Actually, I was going to make a remark about lawyers," Kevin said.

"A banker telling lawyer jokes." Jack snorted. "That's really a case of the pot calling the kettle black."

"Behave, you two." Sam turned to Cassie. "So have you guys looked around? There any games here I have a chance of winning?"

Fiona just groaned, then looked at Kevin. "Sam is the most incredibly lucky person I know. She always wins stuff."

"I do not," Sam protested. She thought about all the times she'd argued that she could do something herself, and lost. All the times she'd fought against her brothers' fix-up dates and lost. All the times she'd wondered if this guy might be the one...

But then she'd stopped looking, so that wasn't really a loss.

Her sisters weren't thinking along those lines, though. "What about that raffle in high school when you won the stereo?" Cassie asked.

"Or the radio contest last year?" Fiona added.

"Or all the games we played as a kid, when we were afraid you'd cry if you lost?"

"I would not have," Sam protested, but everyone just laughed. Boy, was she glad that she and Kevin had stopped by. "Come on," she said to him. "Let's go lose our junk money."

"Save some prizes for the rest of us," Cassie called out as they left.

Sam didn't deign to reply, but took Kevin's hand as they wandered through the crowd to the nearest game table. It held a roulette wheel.

"Want to try this?" Kevin asked. "Or should we give other people a chance before you sweep all the prizes?"

"Boy, I thought you would be on my side," she said and took her hand from his, but only to put a small stack of chips on the number six. "I'm not any luckier than anyone else. I bet you've won your share of contests and games."

"Not me." Kevin put a small stack of his own next to hers.

She just frowned at him slightly. Even though her siblings joked that she always won, they never followed her lead. Never. They were always too busy hoping she'd be wrong and they'd be right. It was a strange feeling to have someone actually look up to her. Figuratively speaking, that is.

Somehow it seemed more personal, more intimate than holding his hand and having their shoulders brush as they went through the crowd. She just looked away, staring down at the wheel, though not really seeing it. Dealing with that, coupled with her attraction to Kevin, she felt like she was walking a tightrope. Playing with matches. Daring to walk the rapids.

And she liked the rush that swept over her.

"Number six!" the man running the game called out. "We have two winners."

Their piles of chips doubled in size and Sam laughed. What a pair she and Kevin made! Her siblings would be sorry they weren't along.

"Well, what now?" Kevin asked. "Do we let it ride? Pick another number or move on to a new game?"

"You pick," she said.

He picked up half the chips, handing her her share. "I'm not that brave," he said and moved the others onto the red square. "This is my first meeting with good luck. I don't want to push it."

"'Faint heart never won fair maiden,'" she quoted, and put the chips he'd handed back with the others. "I can tell you've got a lucky streak just waiting to burst out."

"You think so?"

His eyes caught hers and all sorts of dreams danced in the air between them. There was fear lurking in his soul, and hope wanting to burst free. A shadow was hanging over his heart—a shadow that he wanted to push aside so that he could grasp at life again. But that fear kept getting in the way.

She wanted to help him break free. She wanted to help him learn to laugh and dance and feel the magic of the stars. She wanted to help him come alive.

"And we have another winner!"

The man's voice broke the spell and they both turned to look at the wheel. They'd won again!

"You see?" Sam said with a laugh and threw her arms around Kevin. "Didn't I say you were lucky?"

His eyes looked startled, but only for a moment before his arms came around her. He swung her slightly, laughing, and let the joy surround them. She could feel his body relax—the hard muscles seeming to let go of tension—and open itself up to happiness. Or at least to the possibility of it.

"We make a great team," Sam said as he let go of her. "Nobody can beat us."

"We'll win every prize," Kevin agreed.

"We'll be the envy of everyone here."

"We'll be generous and play another game for a while."

She laughed again and helped him gather up their chips, dropping them into the pocket of his suit coat when her hands couldn't hold them all. Then, as they moved on, he let his arm slip around her shoulders.

Ever so slowly, like an ember growing into a flame, she felt a rising heat where his hand rested. The fire spread, winding over her shoulders and easing into her heart. A longing began to expand, seeping into every inch of her being, every shadowy hidden corner of her soul. A need to belong, a sudden certainty that life could hold so much more.

Her heart—and her resolve—began to waver. She was no longer quite so sure that her feet were on the right road.

"Poker's over there and bingo's this way," Kevin was saying. "And I think there's a blackjack table back there."

It would be fine, she told herself. She could enjoy his company and enjoy life. She didn't need to think everything through a million ways just because she was having fun one evening.

"Let's do poker, then bingo," she said. "We'll save blackjack for last."

Laughing, they went from one game to another, arm in arm. They won more than they lost, but mostly Sam was just having a good time. Kevin was so easy to be with, so ready to laugh at her jokes and share her silences.

Little by little he was opening up to her, too. She found out he had two kids—one about to be a college freshman and one a sophomore—who had lived mainly with their grandparents once his wife had gotten ill. She sensed there was distance between him and his kids—more than just the hundred or so miles down to Purdue; a distance he didn't know how to cross.

When the evening was winding down and prizes were being awarded to those turning in the most play money, she was conscious only of a sense of disappointment that it was over.

"Look at this!" Fiona cried, joining Sam and Kevin at the table where they were turning in their money. "I won a door prize." She held up an autographed football.

"Cool, Fi," Sam said. "Prissy and Elvis will love it."

"Prissy and Elvis?" Kevin asked.

"Her cats." Sam turned back to her sister. "I guess I'm not the only lucky one in the family."

"I always thought I was the lucky one," Alex said, coming up behind Fiona and slipping his arms around her.

"You just want my football," Fiona teased, but her eyes grew soft with obvious love.

Sam just looked away, conscious of a real burning in her heart. A yearning, for just a moment, to be the center of someone's existence. It would come someday, she told herself. She just had other things to do first.

"Ladies and gentlemen," a man on the stage called out. "We've totaled up the big money winners for the evening and we have some prizes to give away."

The crowd shifted to get a better view and Sam found herself standing in front of Kevin, leaning up against him while his arms lightly encircled her. It was just a temporary encircling, she thought. Just for this evening, she would let herself be the captive of his eyes.

"The prize for the third most money won tonight goes to Miss Hattie Merrill."

"All right, Aunt Hattie!" Cassie called out as the older woman walked up to the stage.

"We have a gift certificate from Reader's Paradise for this lucky lady."

"Way to go, Aunt Hattie," Sam cried, then looked up over her shoulder at Kevin. "Aunt Hattie's been taking care of Cassie's fiancé's twins since they were babies. She's really the nicest lady."

"What's she going to do once Cassie and Jack marry?"

"She says she's moving out and finding a job. Cassie says she's staying right there."

Kevin smiled. "So all you Scott women are rather pugnacious."

Sam gave him an offended look. "All but me."

He chuckled and tightened his hold. It felt too good.

"Second prize for the evening's winnings goes to Mickey Baylor." There were some cheers and catcalling from the other side of the room as an older man climbed up onto the stage. "Mickey gets a gift certificate from Bobick's Golf Shop."

Once Mickey had left the stage, the emcee frowned at the paper in his hands. "It seems we have a tie for first place. Our book of ten dinner coupons from Michiana-area restaurants was won by Samantha Scott and Kevin Delaney."

Sam felt her cheeks go fiery. They'd won ten dinners together! Her family crowded around her, laughing and calling teasing remarks.

"I'm not sure how this happened," the emcee said. "Perhaps we can split the prize. Give them each five dinners."

"Or they can just share the ten," Cassie cried out.

"Cassie!" Sam hissed at her, even as hands were pushing her and Kevin up onto the stage. "This is ridiculous," she said to Kevin.

"Hey, no big deal," he said lightly. "It was your good luck. You can have them."

"No, we both won them," she insisted.

"Here you go," the emcee said. "Are you two going to fight over the prize?"

"Not at all," Kevin replied. "The lady can invite anybody she chooses to share her dinners."

The emcee winked broadly at him before turning to the audience. "Anyone as long as it's you, eh?"

Everyone laughed, even Kevin, but Sam was finding it hard to breathe. It wasn't the idea of winning, but that the idea of spending ten romantic dinners with Kevin was becoming obsessively appealing. Ten whole dinners alone together at some of the area's best restaurants; long hours to talk and get to know each other.

"And you said you weren't lucky," Fiona mocked.

Sam started, realizing they'd come off the stage and were making their way toward the door. A few people were starting to clean up the games, but most of the crowd was on their way out.

"Nice job, Sam," someone said.

"Lucky dogs," someone else called out.

Sam just stuck the gift certificates in her purse. "We'll argue this out some other time," she told Kevin.

"Nothing to argue. It's yours."

"You can have half, you know."

The ceiling lights were on in the lobby, all the pretend neon was lost in the glare. The magic was over with, the evening was done.

It was just as well, Sam reflected as they walked in silence across the parking lot. This kind of explosive attraction was rife with problems and complications that she didn't want right now, she kept reminding herself as Kevin drove her home. And besides, they hardly knew each other. So then, why did her heart feel heavy, as if Santa had skipped their house?

"It was a nice evening," she said, when he pulled his car to a stop in front of her house.

"Yes, it was."

Sam turned to stare out the window. There were no hidden meanings in Kevin's words. Sparks didn't fly, threatening to engulf them. Whatever enchantment had almost captured them earlier was gone now.

"Want to take a walk?" she asked him.

"Sure," he said.

"Just let me run in and change my shoes."

Kevin waited on the porch, and she was back in a moment, ready for a pleasant end to a nice evening.

Kevin took her hand and they walked down toward the lake. The air had a sharpness to it that made the stars seem more distant, more forbidding. They turned onto the path that ran alongside the shore, and followed it until they came to a dock a few hundred yards from the inn. They walked out onto the pier and leaned on the wooden rail at the end, staring down into the dark, still waters.

"There's something about the lake," Sam said after a long silence. "It's so peaceful. I've been feeling more like a river these days."

"That's just how I've been feeling lately," he said. "Like I'm rushing headlong into danger without a life preserver."

There was a new tremor in his voice, a hint of that earlier passion. She turned to find him watching her.

He reached out, brushing back a curl from her face with infinite slowness. She took his hand before he could pull it away, and held it against her cheek, needing his touch but not having the words to say so. Her eyes met his. The intake of his breath was sharp and fast as he moved suddenly to pull her into his arms.

Their lips met in a blinding flash of passion. The air that had caressed her cheeks with its warmth was chilly compared to the blazing heat that surrounded them. Sam couldn't hold him close enough, couldn't kiss him deep enough. Their tongues pushed and probed, pulsing to a basic rhythm that was echoed in Sam's pounding heart. It was as if the world had come to a halt, as if all life was suspended for the moment except their needs and passions.

They pulled apart slowly, uncertainly. Their gazes were locked, their chests heaving. Her heart slowed enough so that the nighttime song of the crickets could be heard. But all she knew was the whirlpool depths of Kevin's eyes. She was drawn to them, wanted to drown in their raying turmoil. Kevin turned to face the lake, gripping the wooden railing as if it was his lifeline.

"So, Scarlett, think you can survive another burning of Atlanta?" he asked.

Sam tried to steady her breathing. Consciously she paused between breaths until she could speak. "I don't want this to be happening between us." Her voice was uneven, light enough to be carried away on the breeze.

"So we ignore it," he said.

"How?" She watched him in the pale light thrown from the houses across the way. He was holding himself rigidly in control, his hands still gripping the railing.

"Just not see each other," he said.

His words were a quick stabbing of her heart, and a silent wail of pain rose from deep in her soul, even as she agreed it might be best. "What about those periodic checks you have to make on the inn?" she asked.

He turned then, his shadowed eyes on her. "I forgot about those visits." His gaze seemed to search her face, seeking the answer to some question she couldn't put into words. He returned his gaze to the water as a car pulled into a driveway nearby. The sound of the motor died away. He sighed. "That makes it all the more complicated."

"Why?"

"It just does," he said. "We're in business together, so to speak. If we went out socially, it could look like harassment or coercion."

"To who?" She wished she could see his eyes, really see into them and know what his heart was trying to say.

"I don't know," he said. His voice was weary. "To me. To anybody. It would just make everything awkward."

"And it isn't now?"

He grabbed her hand and brought it to his lips, setting the sparks off again. But this time, she didn't fly into his embrace and he didn't sweep her into his arms. They just looked at each other, stared into the shadowy depths of the other's soul as sparks singed the air between them.

"We'd better go back," Kevin said, and led her along to the path.

Once they got to her yard, he dropped her arm. Although their shoulders were brushing, he made no move to touch her. Sam wrapped her arms around herself and trudged at his side. Her body was afire, wanting his touch, but not wanting it. She didn't know how to sort out this craziness.

He took her arm as they went up to her back porch. "I guess I was a bit of a caveman back there," he said.

She shrugged.

Kevin stopped walking and turned her to face him. "Are you okay?"

Her eyes stung and she blinked back sudden moisture. "Yes," she finally said, then seemed to collapse into a sigh. "I don't understand any of this. I'm not looking for a relationship. I don't have time for one. But if I'm so damned uninvolved, why is my heart racing so?"

He put his arms around her, holding her close to him but somehow keeping the fires at bay. "We need to think about all this someplace where thought is possible. And that's not out here in the dark alone with you."

She sighed into his chest. "I don't see what there is to think about."

"This thing between us is too hot to play around with."

"Let's be honest," she said. "Neither of us want love, but obviously we're attracted to each other. Aren't we adult enough to enjoy the passion and avoid the entanglements?"

"Love isn't something you dictate. Your only defense against it is to avoid situations where it's likely to grow."

Sam looked at him and saw his stubbornness. She kissed his cheek quickly, then stepped back before she could be caught in his spell again.

"We need time," she said. "I'll call you in a couple of days."

She didn't wait for his reply, but sped into the house. When his car had pulled away and the night was once more bathed in silence, she walked slowly up the stairs to the third floor. The room was drenched in moonlight as she stepped over to the windows and stared thoughtfully down at the lake.

Chapter Four

Kevin slowed the car and pulled onto State Road 17. It was a gorgeous August day—sunny and warm, with only a hint of fall. But he just frowned into the glare.

He hadn't slept much last night. Every time he'd drifted off, he'd felt the wonderful softness of Sam in his arms. Then he would jerk awake only to find that his lips were aching for her. Or that he longed to breathe in her gentle scent. Being awake didn't help at all.

In the middle of the night, with only the silent blinking of the clock for company, he and Sam seemed so possible. Not just possible, but right and necessary and the only sane course of action. Why was he hesitating? He was attracted to a beautiful young woman who was attracted to him.

No rational man would think twice. No rational man would worry or question. What was twelve years' difference? Or even thirteen? What mattered was a person's spirit. His zest for life.

Ah, there lay the problem. Did he still have the same zest for life he'd once had? Or had life and all its pain made him cautious and careful? An observer rather than a participant?

He had lain awake most of the night, seeking answers in the breezes that rustled the leaves of the trees. Morning had been the only thing that had come.

But somewhere around mid-morning, or maybe it was when he was heating up a can of soup for lunch, he'd suddenly known there could be no Sam and Kevin. It just wouldn't be fair to her. She'd said she had too much to accomplish before she settled down, but if the right man came along, she would learn she could do both. But how would she recognize the right man if her attention was focused on *him?*

He was glad that he had this barbecue to go to this afternoon, although it would awaken painful memories. But they were familiar memories, ones that belonged to him. And if he wasn't particularly comfortable with them, at least he knew how to deal with them; knew their place in his life. And they helped him remember his place in the whole scheme of things.

A sign came up. Plymouth—nine miles. Kevin just sighed and let the past wash over him.

That summer six years ago had started on such a high. Everything had been going great. Stacy had been about to start high school in the fall and couldn't wait; was planning her wardrobe and schedule and activities. Jon wasn't all that excited about eighth grade, but he'd gotten a mountain bike for his birthday and was going to spend his free time exploring the county parks with his friends.

It had started as a great summer for Debbie, too. She'd been accepted into the university's creative-writing program and was anxious for the fall semester to begin.

Then everything went down in flames. Just a few days before the Fourth of July, Debbie had gone in for a routine checkup.

They all went into a state of shock when the diagnosis was dropped in their midst. Lymphoma. Cancer of the lymph glands.

Kevin couldn't believe it. He tried not to believe it. He wanted to take the whole family and run off to some tropical island in the South Pacific, as if putting distance between Debbie and the diagnosis would save her. But reality set in and he knew that their only chance was to start treatment immediately.

The kids had wanted to stay and help, but Debbie couldn't take that. She'd always been the strong one in the family, the one who'd taken care of everyone else. Having to endure radiation treatments and chemotherapy was hard enough, but appearing helpless in the eyes of her children was more than Debbie could bear.

So the kids spent the summer with Debbie's parents in Plymouth. It was less than an hour's drive from their house; near enough to visit often but far enough to give Debbie the space she needed. And they would be back together in the fall when school started.

Fall came quickly but so did more treatments, and it didn't seem right to bring the kids home. So Stacy and Jon started school in Plymouth.

It seemed there was always something. The days were filled with one crisis after another, and there was barely enough time to breathe. By the time Debbie died, Stacy was a junior and sports editor on the school paper, in the glee club and drama club, and on the softball team. Jon was a sophomore, and the track and basketball teams, the only sophomore on the varsity squad. It didn't seem right to pull them out of what had become their community. Besides, Kevin needed some time to heal himself.

As it turned out, the time had never been right to transfer the kids to South Bend, and both of them graduated from Plymouth High School. Stacy had been the valedictorian of her class and Jon had received the Kiwanas award for outstanding student athlete in his senior year. Debbie would have been proud.

Kevin sighed as he turned into his in-laws' neighborhood, an old tree-lined area on the west side of downtown Plymouth. He had hoped that the kids could spend this summer with him—kind of a last thing before they really went off on their own, to give them all a chance to catch up with each other. Stacy was going into her sophomore year at Purdue University and Jon would be a freshman there.

But Stacy got a chance to work with a summer-theater group at the university and Jon, along with a part-time job in the athletic department, wanted to go to summer school. Kevin wasn't going to stand in their way.

So now all they had was a day. One afternoon—before school started—to get caught up with their lives.

Maybe that was why he'd been mopey these past few weeks, he thought. His kids were almost grown and had lives of their own. Lives in which he was only a peripheral player, at most.

Kevin parked at the curb and slowly made his way to the back of the house. Debbie's parents lived in one of the newer homes on the street, a sprawling ranch built back in the early sixties. The trees and bushes were all mature and a profusion of color provided a testimonial to his mother-in-law's green thumb.

Laughter and good cheer echoed from the backyard, which meant there would be other guests besides Kevin and his kids, but that was normal. His father-in-law's barbecues were famous in three counties.

Kevin paused at the corner of the house, letting his eyes scan over the guests. He hoped that his mother-in-law didn't have a free "young lady" around, one who "happened" to be in the neighborhood. He just wanted to visit with his kids.

"Daddy." Stacy dropped her badminton racquet and came running toward him.

His breath caught as he stared at her. Damn. His little girl was a woman. A beautiful woman.

"Daddy," she said again as she hugged him fiercely.

He swung her around, happy with her greeting. But then Stacy had always been a cheerful, bouncy sort. It was his son that he was really worried about. He had his mother's eyes but his father's reticent nature.

"Hey, Dad. What's happening?"

Kevin stared. Jon had only been gone a couple of months, but it was almost a different person standing before him. Jon had gone away a boy and come back a man. Kevin tentatively extended his hand. His son just as slowly put his own out.

"So," Kevin said as they shook hands. "How are things going?"

"Pretty good," Jon replied. "Pretty good."

"Oh, for heaven's sake," Stacy said. "You guys look like an insurance salesman meeting with a customer. Hug each other, you dummies. You're father and son. Remember?"

Embarrassed, they took each other in their arms, stiffly.

"Oh, that's swell," Stacy said. "You want I should search you guys for weapons first?"

Laughing, they tried again. This time they were relaxed—pretty much.

"That's better."

He and Jon exchanged put-upon looks as they separated. Stacy looked a lot like Kevin but there was no doubt she was Debbie's daughter.

"Man. All summer I have to look after him," she said, shaking her head and pointing at Jon. "And now I have to take care of the two of you." She looked pointedly at Kevin. "I hope I get some help soon."

It was just as well she didn't know about Samantha, he thought, as he walked with them toward the people sitting on the deck. He quickly eyeballed the group as they drew near. There were some younger children, kids Jon and Stacy's age, and a handful his in-laws' age. No thirtyish ladies, sitting off to themselves. Kevin let out a quiet sigh of relief.

"Don't worry," Stacy murmured. "Grandma didn't get you a date today. She said you've been kind of grumpy lately."

"I have not." Maybe it was just as well that his daughter was living away at school. His mother-in-law was bad enough. He hated to imagine what his life would be like if the woman had help from Stacy.

"She said you're really early for male menopause but things sometimes happen that way when you've been under a strain."

"Give me a break," he muttered.

"Hey, Kevin." His father-in-law came toward him, hand extended. "You're looking good."

"Hi, Barney," he replied. "You're looking chipper yourself."

"Hello, Kevin." His mother-in-law came up and gave him a hug. "How about something cool to drink?"

"Thank you, Mabel. I'll have some lemonade."

He had a few bones to pick with his mother-in-law but he didn't want to give her any ammunition for her "Kevin is grumpy" analysis. So he put on a big, big smile and found himself a place to sit down.

"Boy," Kevin said. "Sure has been hot this year."

"We've had more ninety-degree days this year than any summer in the last seventy-five years."

"And so humid. There are days you can barely breathe."

"I wonder how people stand it without air-conditioning."

Kevin smiled as he took his drink and murmured a thank-you. He really appreciated Midwestern weather. Once folks got started, it preempted all other topics of conversation. Let's see you try steering things toward my lack of dating, he wanted to say to his mother-in-law. But he satisfied himself with giving Mabel a bland look as she settled herself in a lawn chair.

"Chow's on," Barney shouted before they could get the weather conversation restarted. Kevin looked around for a place to put his drink but his kids were already at his side.

"We'll get your food, Daddy," Stacy said.

"Yeah," Jon added. "Can't have you old folks running around in this hot sun."

He wanted to give his daughter a smile but instead he glared at his son. The kid hadn't even started college yet and already he was an obnoxious smart aleck. But Kevin's frown had no more effect now than it had when Jon was ten. His kids hustled off to the serving table where Mabel was now helping Barney pass out the food.

They brought him an overflowing plate, another glass of lemonade, and no smart-ass remarks. Thanking Providence for small favors, Kevin bit into his barbecued chicken leg. A couple of bites of chicken and some potato salad and he would toss out another few remarks about the weather. If people got tired of that, he could always bring up the Silver Hawks, the area's minor-league baseball team that was doing quite well this year.

"How did you enjoy the Las Vegas Night?"

The chicken in his mouth turned to sand. Kevin glanced over at one of Mabel's lady friends and swallowed hard. He would never be able to look Jon in the eye if he let some little old lady in blue hair and pink Bermudas push him around.

"Okay," he replied.

"My friend Annie went. She said it was a lot of fun."

Kevin nodded slowly. "Yeah, the folks running it did a good job."

"She said you went with one of the Scott girls."

The woman might as well have fired a cannon. The air went dead quiet as everyone turned to stare at him. His kids and Mabel looked especially interested.

"One of the Scott girls?" Mabel asked her friend.

"Yes." Kevin jumped with the answer. "She's one of my customers."

"That's such a nice family."

"Which one of the girls was he with?"

Hey! They were talking as if he weren't there. Maybe he should jump up on his chair, pound his chest and give a Tarzan yell.

"Annie said it was Samantha."

"Oh, it can't be Samantha. Why, that girl's no more than a child."

"Had to be her. Fiona's married and Cassie's engaged."

"Well, how old is Samantha?"

"Twenty-seven," Kevin said.

The people chattering all turned to look at him. His children had never taken their eyes off him. No one said anything.

"That's what she indicated on her mortgage application form," Kevin added. "So I'm sure it must be true."

The silence hung in the air like the smoke from Barney's barbecue. Then, as if swept away by a gust of wind, it dissipated.

"Boy, how time flies."

"I remember when those girls were in high school."

"They've all gone to college."

"My, my."

"I just went as a favor to her," Kevin said.

"Here I was worried you were lonely," Stacy mocked. "And now I find out you've got this humanitarian service you provide to the unattached females of South Bend."

Everyone burst out laughing.

Kevin glared at them but it didn't slow their laughter one bit. Mabel gave him a wink. Damn. Why hadn't he remembered that Plymouth was shouting distance from South Bend?

"Good morning, Kevin."

"Morning, Cindy."

Kevin hurried into his office, hoping his secretary would read the message in his clipped tones. She liked to start the week by sitting down with him and chatting for a while. Normal' / he didn't mind, but not today.

The weekend hadn't gone as he'd planned. He'd had a nice time with Sam. All right, a great time. But that had been Saturday night. And so what, if he thought about her most of Sunday? He'd decided they were not going to date. No way. Never. They would be business associates and that was all.

Spending time with his kids was supposed to drive away the image of her smile, but it hadn't worked out that way. They'd split their time between him and their grandparents and then gone off with some high-school friends who had dropped over.

When he'd gotten home, the house had seemed especially empty. Even the cats had other interests, barely giving him a glance while they watched fireflies flitting about in the backyard.

For a moment he was tempted to call Samantha. Tell her about the people who still thought she was a kid; who hadn't realized that she'd graduated from college. Share a laugh with her.

But that would hardly be keeping their relationship businesslike. Besides, she probably wouldn't be home. A pleasant weekend, with no rain, was a rare treasure this year. She would have been with her friends—probably out on one of the many beaches lining the eastern shore of Lake Michigan.

So he hadn't talked to anybody. He'd finished out the evening watching some show on TV. All in all, he'd felt a good grump coming on. And for him, those things always had to run their course. Like a cold or the flu.

"Busy?" Cindy asked.

Damn. People always said women were the sensitive ones, the ones who could read others' feelings. That was bull. A lot of times they didn't have a clue as to how a person felt inside. Kevin slowly forced his head up.

Cindy had a smile on her face—the kind women wore when they were going to do something for you; something that did not contain mutually-agreed-upon benefits. Great.

"Actually, I am busy." Kevin indicated the piles of papers on his desk. "I have all these—"

"I won't be long."

His secretary sat down and let him bask in the warmth of her smile. He took a deep breath, slumped back into his chair, and waited.

"Mr. Cartwright's party is this weekend," Cindy said.

Kevin just stared.

"Like in Chairman of the Board Mr. Cartwright," she said.

"Yes, I know." Kevin nodded as he worked up to a good, hard glare. "This Friday night."

"You must also know, those things are much more fun if you go with someone."

Apparently Cindy had work backed up, too. She usually liked to beat around the bush for thirty or forty seconds, take her time getting to the point.

"Are you trying to organize a car pool?" Kevin asked, twisting his lips into a smile of his own.

Cindy made a face at him. "Anyway, we got together and made a list."

The smile dropped off his face like a snowslide down a cliff. He could have asked, Who got together? Why? And what kind of list? But he knew that he didn't want to know any of the answers.

"I'm glad you're making good use of your free time," Kevin said, picking up a stack of loan applications that his staff had preapproved. "But I really need to—"

"There are a lot of nice women on our list," Cindy said. "Any one of whom would enjoy the Cartwright party."

"I enjoyed it last year."

"You went alone."

"I enjoyed it very much," Kevin said. "So much so that I can't imagine making any changes to my modus operandi."

"You were the only one who came alone."

"Which made me the center of attention." Kevin smiled. "And you know how I love that."

His secretary's lips tightened into a straight line and her fingers, tapping on the arm of her chair, went from waltz time to a country-and-western line-dance beat. Kevin could feel a lecture coming on. It was best to head it off now, before both of them became angry. Spending several days not speaking to each other would take a big nick out of his productivity.

"These items need to be reviewed by me and approved or disapproved by eleven this morning. And, as much as I'm enjoying our little chat, I really have to get to work."

Cindy slowly stood. "I'll check with you later in the week."

"Great." He didn't try doing anything with his tone. Cindy was one of those women who were totally impervious to sarcasm.

"How about Wednesday?"

"Wednesday would be terrific. Want to shut the door on your way out?"

Cindy left. She could have used some lessons on the difference between shutting and slamming, but the door was closed. And that was all that mattered. He forced his attention to the forms before him.

The morning went by reasonably fast. There were a number of things that needed his attention and years of discipline had taught him how to concentrate on the task at hand; how to keep stray, extraneous thoughts out of his head. Such as Samantha, who would be a nice date for Cartwright's party. But that idea was quickly dismissed. They'd just done the one thing together. And that was only because she'd needed someone to fill in an empty space; someone to keep her brothers off her back. Even though they both had enjoyed themselves, they were not going to pursue the matter.

Along toward noon, he leaned back from his finished work and stretched. Fortunately, there was a knock on his door before his mind had a chance to drift.

"Got a minute?" William—not Bill—Cartwright looked in the door.

"Sure," Kevin said as the chairman came in. "Something wrong?"

"Ah, no." Mr. Cartwright shook his head. "Not at all."

"Good."

"Everything's great."

"Super."

They shared a long silence. His manager was not a man to be hurried, so Kevin slouched back and waited. Finally Mr. Cartwright cleared his throat. Ah, a pronouncement was coming. Kevin sat up and leaned forward.

"Are you coming to our party this Friday?"

"Yes, I am."

Cartwright nodded his head for several moments. "Good, good. Marcella will be pleased to hear that."

There were going to be two hundred people at the party. Kevin couldn't imagine why Mr. Cartwright's wife cared whether or not he came. He silently waited for further enlightenment.

"You know," Cartwright said, pursing his lips. "Women are different from us."

"I've heard that," Kevin replied dryly.

His boss didn't even glance at him, maintaining eye contact with the window on the far wall. "Now take Marcella, for instance."

Kevin considered saying no, you take Marcella, she's your wife. But he decided that, for the moment, anyway, discretion would be the better part of valor. So he said nothing.

"She's a fine woman," Mr. Cartwright said.

Kevin nodded.

"But she has this thing about symmetry."

"Symmetry?"

"Yeah, you know. Equal here." He indicated with both hands to his left. "And equal there." Cartwright swiveled toward his right. "Balanced." His boss bounced his hands in opposition to each other, indicating weighing something on a balance scale. "You get my drift?"

In normal circumstances Kevin would have pretended that he didn't understand. But he was pretty damn sick of this whole thing, himself. It was bad enough having his daughter, his mother-in-law and secretary trying to manipulate him. But now his own boss. A guy like himself. It was enough to make a grown man cry.

"I presume you're talking about a boy-girl, boy-girl kind of balance."

"Yeah, yeah." For the first time, Cartwright smiled. "You got it."

Oh, he had it, all right. Like a bad case of the stomach flu. It took all of Kevin's effort to stay civil.

Cartwright cleared his throat and Kevin held his breath. "Marcella knows a lot of people."

"I'm sure she does," Kevin replied.

Marcella and William Cartwright gave a party every year around this time for the employees of the savings and loan, but also for Michiana's high society—such as it was. With catered delicacies and a string quartet from the South Bend Symphony Orchestra, the party was held on the Cartwright's spacious grounds on a bluff above the St. Joseph River. Dress was formal.

"I was wondering, Bill."

His manager's face hardened, but only a person who knew Cartwright well would have noticed. By calling him Bill, Kevin had indicated a smart-ass remark was coming.

"Should I wear my green loincloth or the red one?"

"Aw, come on, Kevin. Be a sport."

"Me?" Kevin laid a hand on his chest. "I'm supposed to be a sport? Am I the one butting in on other people's lives?"

"Now don't go blowing a gasket."

Kevin turned slightly so he could glare out his window.

"You know this picnic thing is important to Marcella."

Yeah, he knew. She spent her time schmoozing at it, raising a lot of money for the symphony orchestra. It served as the start of the year's social season in the area. Kevin didn't say anything.

"So she's got this thing about symmetry," Cartwright said. "You've got to admit she does a lot for the city."

Yes, she did. The Cartwrights had no children and Marcella didn't need a job, so she was a professional do-gooder and fund-raiser for just about every charity in Michiana.

"You want me to talk to Marcella?" Cartwright asked.

"I'll take care of it," Kevin muttered, the words slipping out the spaces between his clenched teeth.

"Good." Cartwright nodded and bounced up from his chair. "Great."

"Yeah, great."

"Well." His boss looked at his watch. "Gotta run. Lunch with the mayor." He turned to leave but paused at the door. "See you Friday?"

For a moment, Kevin thought of telling Cartwright to go to hell. Of telling him that by Friday he would have a bad case of typhoid. Maybe leprosy. But he didn't. It wasn't that he was a coward. He was just tired of this nonsense.

"Yeah, sure," he replied, as he turned toward his window.

He heard the door shut quietly behind him. Damn. He sighed, fighting back that image of Sam that came dancing unbidden into his thoughts once more. He was a loner. He'd had his chance at love and it had ended early. So now he was no longer part of a couple. Why couldn't people accept that?

Another, stronger vision of Sam came into his heart. Her laughter, her warmth, her beauty tried to grab hold of his gloom and smash it apart. The light of her smile was blinding, rushing into the shadowy corners of his soul and sending his demons fleeing. She could set his feet to dancing again. She could remind his lips how to smile and his eyes how to glow.

And teach his heart how to break once more if he let it start to care again.

He looked at his own watch. Time for lunch. He forced his reluctant body out of the chair and out of the bank. Once outside, his feet took him to an Amish sandwich place where he usually ate when alone, but the line was on the long side. Kevin went on past the shop.

He wasn't very hungry. Maybe he should walk around for an hour or so. Do something that would clear his head and get the cobwebs out. He was getting too gloomy lately. It was partly being with Sam and being teased with what life could offer, and partly the memories of what he'd had.

He stopped in front of the library. Why not? He could peruse the new magazines. Maybe find an interesting article or two and read in the pleasant cool of the old building.

The new magazines were in long racks on the second floor and Kevin climbed the curving stairs, trying to decide whether he should search out his favorites or just start at *A* and work his way to—

"Hi."

The voice banished all traces of the black cloud that wanted to hang over his head. He turned to find Sam smiling at him. She worked here. How had he forgotten that? Or had he forgotten it?

"Hi. How are you?"

"Just fine."

She was dressed in culottes, a sleeveless blouse, and sandals. It was obvious that Mabel's friend hadn't seen Sam in a long time. There was no way that someone could mistake her for a child. A lively, good-looking woman, yes. But definitely not a child.

"What are you doing here?" she asked.

"Checking out your magazine collection," he replied, indicating the long racks to their side.

"I thought you business types were more likely to use our research department."

"I was just going to browse." He shrugged. "It's my lunch hour."

"Mine, too."

They stood there, the noise of library quiet swirling around them—the clink of a coin slipped into a copying machine, a mother hushing her child, the clunk of books being stacked. He'd forgotten how really comfortable it was to be with her.

"I was going to grab a sandwich," he said. "I like that little Amish place over on Michigan."

"Oh. Me, too. That's one of my favorite lunch places."

She had such a way about her, such a burst of energy in everything she did. She was like champagne just freshly opened—all bubbly and bright. But there was more to her than that. There was a depth that called to him, that promised peace and safety, that promised he could lay his head down and rest. Kevin would have been glad to miss lunch and just stare at Sam, drinking in everything about her.

But he knew better. He'd made his decision. "Want to come with me?"

"Let me get my stuff," she said. "I'll be right back."

He watched as she hurried up the stairs, not breathing until she was out of his sight. It was all right. This was just two friends having lunch. That wouldn't betray their banker-client relationship. And the age difference wouldn't matter when they were just having lunch. He was so out of step with the world in every way, he'd forgotten how to have a friendship.

"All set."

Sam was back with her smile and a fanny pack. He couldn't help noticing the smile. No more than he could help noticing her fanny, which was just below her fanny pack.

"Boy, here it is, almost September," she said as they stepped outside into the summer air. "And still ninety degrees."

"Yeah," he agreed. "And the humidity's been awful. I almost wish I had a pair of gills so I could breathe easier."

The weather discussed and dismissed, they walked quietly toward the Amish sandwich shop. He took her arm as they crossed the street and there seemed little reason to drop it once they were across. He savored her joyful silence as they continued on, hand in hand.

"You know," Sam said, "I've been thinking."

He knew it was presumptuous to assume he'd lingered in her thoughts as she'd lingered in his, but he didn't ask what she'd been thinking about.

"My dad plays golf with his doctor."

For a moment, Kevin was lost. "Oh?"

"And he plays bridge with our accountant. None of them argue that they can't be friends because they've got a business relationship already."

He sighed. "I'm not sure we were heading toward friendship," he said.

"How do you know what we were heading toward? You backed off." She stopped outside the sandwich shop and turned to face him. "Look, your bank has already approved the loan. You said you aren't taking it back even if you're making these periodic checks. So that makes you just like the guy that sold us the riding mower who's coming over to give us some pointers on how to cut near the lake."

"I guess." Her logic sounded too...too...logical.

"Would anyone say anything if I went out with him?"

A sudden fear gripped his heart. "Do you want to?"

Sam laughed and the sun came out again. "No, I don't want to. But I could without compromising our lawn-mowing relationship. The transaction is over, just like ours. We can be friends. We can date. We can make mad passionate love down by the lake and no one would care."

Her last image stuck with him, stealing his breath and causing his heart to race double time. "They might if it was high noon," he countered.

She just stared at him.

"Making love by the lake," he said, his doubts seeming to disappear. "Have you forgotten already? I can't say that I'm flattered."

Sam just laughed again, chasing the last vestiges of gloom away as she took hold of his arm and pulled him toward the sandwich shop. "So what do you say we grab some lunch?"

"My treat," Kevin said.

"No." She shook her head. "Besides, I owe you for Saturday."

"I know a better way for you to repay me," he told her. "You see, I have to ask this really, really big favor...."

Chapter Five

"Do you want to dance, mingle some more, or walk around?" Kevin asked as he handed Sam a crystal glass of some kind of champagne punch.

"This is your shindig," she just said. "Whatever you want."

"I know you don't like cavemen," he said. "So I was trying to get you involved in the decision process."

"Nice try," she said and sipped the punch, letting the bubbles tickle her nose as she looked over the glass at him.

He was a handsome man any day of the week, but tonight he looked absolutely gorgeous in his white jacket and black tie. Lucky thing that as they'd been mingling among the other guests, she had been standing next to Kevin, not across from him. Too much watching him and her coherency level would plummet. Her determination that this relationship was just for fun might also get lost.

"That's a very pretty dress," Kevin said.

Sam looked down at the green silk. "It's Fiona's. One of the major advantages of having a sister is a larger wardrobe without paying for it."

"I have a sister but it doesn't do a thing for my wardrobe."

Sam laughed and looked around them. They were standing amid a crowd of other formally dressed people on a patio at the back of a large brick mansion with formal gardens laid out in the English-manor style—straight walkways with everything neatly trimmed and in place. It was very nice but a little too formal for her tastes. Somewhere amid the shrubbery, a string quartet was playing show tunes.

"Kevin, good to see you," some hefty older man said in passing.

"Mark." Kevin nodded at the man.

"Sweets?"

A young lady with a tray of exquisite-looking little pastries stopped by them. Sam took one with nuts and chocolate and bit into it.

"Oh, this is too good for words," she said with a sigh. "And to think mere mortals made it."

"Ah, but did they?" Kevin asked as he took another one and gave it to Sam before taking one for himself. "Marcella has connections, you know. They could reach beyond South Bend and Mishawaka. Past Osceola, even."

Sam nibbled at the pastry Kevin had given her, trying to savor the ecstasy. "If I could bake things like this, it's all I'd ever eat."

"I think you'd get tired of chocolate after a while."

"Not me. When I like something, I like it forever."

"Forever's a long time."

"Not to me."

"What if something better comes along? Something newer?"

Sam just laughed and popped the last of the pastry into her mouth. "Something better than chocolate? You're kidding."

His eyes had taken on shadows. "You never know. These things happen."

"Not with me." She took his arm. He was always worrying. "What now? Dancing, mingling or exploring?"

"Whatever you—"

"Oh, no," she said with a laugh. "I'm not making a decision. This is your party."

"Actually, it's Marcella Cartwright's party," Kevin said.

"Should we ask her what to do?" Sam looked up into Kevin's face, a teasing smile on her lips.

The shadows were still lurking in the far corners of his eyes. He looked for all the world like a little boy who had gotten what he'd asked for from Santa, but was sure it was a mistake. And one that would be rectified soon.

She felt an ache growing in her heart, a need to banish those shadows forever. She wanted to see him laugh and believe. She wanted to see hope lingering there in those eyes, and hear the certainty in his voice that life was good.

But the longer her eyes searched his, the more her soul met his in sweet communion and all other thoughts seemed to fade. She found her lips aching for the touch of his. She found her hands itching to feel the steel beneath his skin. She found her body yearning to press close to him, closer enough to feel the rhythm of his heart next to hers.

"Kevin, how nice to see you."

Whatever spell had been weaving its magic between Sam and Kevin was suddenly gone. But like dreams disappearing in the sunlight, the memory of it lingered just below the surface. She had to ignore it, she told herself. She wasn't looking for a relationship. She had things to do, places to see, as it were. She looked over at the couple who had stopped by them.

"Hello, Cindy," Kevin said as he slipped his arm around Sam's shoulders, his voice holding a thread of tension. Or was it just in his touch?

"I'd like you to meet Samantha Scott," he was saying. "Sam, this is my secretary, Cindy, and her husband, Joe."

"Hi." Sam shook their hands.

"It's so nice to see you again," Cindy said, her eyes eager. "I had no idea when you came to the bank the other day that you and Kevin were seeing each other."

Sam just stared at her.

"Not that it matters," Kevin said quickly. "But Sam and I are just friends."

"I didn't mean anything," Cindy said. "I was just glad to see you. I was afraid you weren't going to make it."

"Even without your car pool, I made it."

"Car pool?" Cindy's husband looked as confused as Sam was. "We didn't come in a car pool," he said.

"Nope," Kevin said lightly. "Turns out we didn't need one, after all."

"Well, I'm glad," Cindy said brightly. "Now, we ought to go over and say hi to the Cartwrights, so if you'll excuse us..."

Sam just watched the couple make their way through the crowd, wondering what all of that was about.

"I'm tired of mingling," Kevin said. "Let's take a walk."

"Okay." She took his hand and they strolled along the walkway that led toward the river. "That was an unusual exchange with your secretary."

He sighed. "Cindy means well."

They reached a bend in the path and the crowd on the patio disappeared behind the bushes. A gentle breeze rustled the leaves, a soft song sung by the summer evening. The shadows were long, stretching out before them with the promise of silence.

She liked being alone here with Kevin, liked the sense of wonder as to what would be around the next bend. And she knew it wasn't just the path she was thinking of.

"Were we supposed to be having a torrid romance?" Sam asked after a moment.

"No. Cindy just wanted the gory details."

"I didn't think there were any. I suppose I could have made some up, but I don't always think fast enough on my feet."

"I'm sure you'll get another chance."

Sam said nothing, just pondered what that meant. Was he assuming they would run into Cindy again at the dinner? Or was he assuming they would go out again and run into her somewhere else?

The path led them to a small gazebo set among the trees and overlooking the river. "Oh, this is perfect," Sam said. "If I lived in that house, I'd be here all the time."

"Eating your chocolate pastries."

She grinned at him as she stepped onto the wooden floor. "You betcha."

She walked over to the rail, leaned on it and looked down at the water coursing below them. Both banks were heavily wooded so their view of the river was obscured, but somehow that made it better. More mysterious. More special.

"It is nice here," Kevin agreed, at her side.

She turned to find his eyes on her and suddenly his words took on a different meaning. A deeper meaning. A more personal one. If she moved forward just a hair, she would be in his arms. The fire that had tried to consume her last Saturday would come rushing back.

But maybe it was time to let her head be in charge for a while. She moved, but it was to turn back to the river. She gazed at the sky, drinking in the reddish orange of the setting sun.

"How many kids were in your family?" she asked.

"Just me and my sister," he replied.

"Lucky." She flashed him a brief grin. "You never had to share your room with anybody."

"Nope." He shook his head. "College was the first time I had a roommate."

"And was it a shock?"

"We got along just fine," Kevin said. "I am very easy to get along with."

"Would Cindy agree?"

"Whew. You like to play tough, don't you?"

His tone was teasing, echoing hers, and she couldn't help but turn back to face him. Once she'd done that, she couldn't help but take that tiny step forward. And then she was in his arms.

It was better than the gazebo and the chocolate pastries put together. His lips came down on hers as his hands spread out over her back, pulling her closer and closer into his embrace. She felt a sweet inertia claim her, a hypnotic languor seep through her blood. Her heart cried out to lie in his arms forever, her soul begged to feel his strength until the end of time.

Her mouth moved against his, and the languor disappeared in a rush. Fire took its place—a seeking, hungry fire that wanted to consume them both in ecstasy. Her hands roamed over his back, pulling him closer so that she could feel his heart racing next to hers; so that she could feel his ragged breath echo hers. It was time standing still. It was heaven come down to earth to bless them. It was—

"Is the river up ahead?"

A voice from somewhere down the path shattered their seclusion. The evening became just a summer evening once again. She pulled from Kevin's arms and tried to steady her faltering composure.

"So how's the inn business going?" Kevin said after a moment.

His voice was none too steady, but she appreciated his attempt at normality. Especially as several people had reached the gazebo and were oohing and ahing over it. Kevin took her arm and steered her past the others, nodding at them.

"Any new developments?" he asked.

"Not really." She sounded like she'd just run a marathon, but at least her brain was semifunctioning. "We've decided to go ahead and have the boiler replaced, so we've got a stack of estimates to go through."

"Sounds like the kind of thing I probably should take a look at," he said.

"That'd be fine." She was feeling steadier by the minute. "We think all the firms we contacted have good reputations, but your input would be appreciated."

Once they'd turned onto the path and were alone again, he let go of her arm. She felt relief rather than rejection. Breathing was almost possible when he wasn't touching her.

"Maybe I'll stop by one evening next week," he said. "Unless you'd rather I come during the day."

She smiled at him and felt her heart flutter like a bird caught in a cage. "No, evening is fine. I'm working during the day most of the week. Except for Monday, of course. I'm off since it's Labor Day."

"Great. Next week, then."

The shadows were longer now, longer and deeper, as if they wanted to pull her into their darkness. But she just skipped lightly through them, certain that there was light up ahead. There was no reason to avoid Kevin or to pretend that they weren't drawn to each other.

She had her priorities in order. She knew her goals. There would be no straying from them just because her heart raced when he was near. She had everything under control.

"I don't want to keep you, Stacy," Kevin said into the phone. "I know you must have plans for Labor Day."

"Yeah, I was just on my way out when you called," she said. "But it was great to hear from you. What've you got on your agenda? Going to some hot picnic?"

"Uh, no," he admitted.

"Dad." That one word held about ten volumes of scolding. "You can't just sit at home all the time. What about that lady everybody was talking about at Grandma and Grandpa's? Why aren't you taking her to the beach or the park or someplace?"

Because she probably had a whole horde of young guys swarming around. But he wasn't about to admit that to Stacy.

"Just because I said I wasn't going to a picnic, it didn't mean I was staying home," he said briskly. "I'll have you know that I'm going out with some friends of mine."

"Really?" She sounded so delighted that he winced. "Well, have a great time."

"Yeah. You, too."

After he hung up the phone, Kevin just frowned out the window at the sunshine. There was just the slightest of breezes and not a cloud in the sky. It was a perfect day for a picnic or a trip to the beach or just sitting around with friends.

He fought back a sudden vision of himself with Sam and turned from the windows, his gaze finding his two cats, curled up asleep on the sofa.

"I don't suppose you guys want to go for a walk, do you?" Kevin asked. "You know, keep me from being a total liar."

Duke didn't even bother to acknowledge Kevin's existence, while Duchess barely let one eye flicker open, but only for a moment. The two Himalayan cats were curled into a single fuzzy ball and were certainly not in any mood to help him battle his conscience.

"I'm sorry," Kevin said. "I realize going for a walk is a dog thing, but I thought you guys would welcome a little adventure."

Neither of the cats stirred, seeing his pitiful argument for what it was. "Well, I think I'll step out myself," he told the cats. "Catch a breath of fresh air."

They responded just as he'd known they would—by ignoring him. He went into the kitchen and was about to grab his car keys when he stopped. He hadn't driven the Jeep in ages. It wasn't good to let a car sit for too long.

Maybe it wasn't good to let a heart sit too long, either, he thought. Maybe that was why his thoughts kept straying to Sam. He would take a drive, maybe stop at Leeper Park and watch the people canoeing on the river.

He went outside and took a deep breath. A cooling breeze was coming in from the northwest and the TV weatherman was talking about temperatures falling back into the normal range for early September. Maybe when it got cooler and the humidity disappeared, he would be able to fight off the attraction better.

Sure. And maybe Chicken Little and the Easter bunny were going to open an omelet house.

He took a deep breath, told himself he was old enough to control his wayward feelings. He backed out the drive. The wind ruffled his hair as if it were trying to set his soul free.

Debbie used to tell him he was too hidebound, too afraid to try something new. It had been at her urging that he'd bought the Jeep three years ago. His tastes ran to more sedate sedans—"banker cars," Debbie called them. But he wasn't just a banker, she used to tell him; somewhere deep down inside him, he wanted to run free.

Kevin hadn't been too sure of that, but he'd been willing to give it a shot. Anything to bring a light into Debbie's eyes.

After she'd died, the Jeep had pretty much just sat around unless one of the kids borrowed it. He was thinking he ought to just be done with it and sell it. No reason to have a car around that nobody drove.

Kevin drove aimlessly. He could have headed toward the university; classes had started this week and the campus would be lively. But instead, he headed for the edge of the city.

Once past the more developed areas, Kevin leaned back and took a deep, deep breath. It was a beautiful day, with bright sun shining and a light breeze. A day to savor. Especially for someone who worked indoors.

Suddenly the surroundings looked familiar. "Damn!" he exclaimed. "What the heck am I doing here?" Shaking his head, he drove on past Sam's bed-and-breakfast, intending to go around to the other side of the lake.

But he frowned as he stopped at the crossroads just beyond the house. This was silly, him just driving past the place. Hadn't he said he would drop by this week and review those boiler estimates? He was in the neighborhood, and it would only take a few minutes. That is, assuming anyone was home. Sam probably wouldn't be. Not on a gorgeous day like this.

After checking for traffic in all directions, Kevin put the Jeep into a wide U-turn. This would save him a trip later in the week. Make him more productive.

Sam came around the corner of the house just as he turned off the motor. She was wearing shorts and a T-shirt, carrying a garden trowel and overflowing with vigor and vitality. It almost hurt to look at her, to feel her energy calling to him.

"Hi, stranger," she said. "What are you doing out here in the country?"

He had to fight to breathe, had to concentrate to make the words come out.

"I was just in the neighborhood," Kevin replied. "So I thought I'd drop in and see if you guys were home."

"You want to see how much money we have left?"

He wasn't sure it was safe to join in her teasing. He wasn't sure his heart knew when to stop. "If this is a bad time, I can come later in the week."

"No, this is a fine time. I was looking for a reason to get out of work, anyway."

Her lips said one thing but the mischievous gleam in her eyes said a lot of other things. It said that her joy was enough to swallow them both up. It said that he should take a chance, that he should be brave and daring and venturesome. That she would keep him safe. He had definitely better not play along.

"Hello, Mr. Delaney." Dan Scott came around the corner of the house, carrying a potted mum in each hand. "Getting worried about your money?"

"Man." Kevin shook his head. "This is a tough crew."

"Kevin came out to see how we're doing," Sam said.

"We spent all the money," Dan said, grinning.

"Dad! He's just trying to help us."

"He can help us plant these mums."

Sam laughed—a soft tinkling sound that spread comfort across the inn's spacious front yard. "He wants to see the boiler quotes and make sure they're reasonable and from good companies."

"Then he can help us eat that concoction you've got in the fridge for our dinner."

"It's not a concoction. It's a seven-layer salad."

"It's rabbit food," Dan said to Kevin. "She's trying to poison me. It's your duty as a fellow male to stay and protect me."

"I sure don't want to shirk my duty," Kevin said slowly. They did it so easily, made him feel at home and welcome. Not just welcome. Wanted.

"You guys are so brave," Sam mocked and turned to Kevin. "Come around back and I'll show you the quotes."

They walked around the house, along the gravel driveway and past the side garden where Sam and her father had been planting rows of red and gold chrysanthemums. It was a riot of color that reminded him of laughter and sunshine.

"The place is looking good," he told her.

"Yeah," Sam agreed. "We needed to get some color in fast because Cassie and Jack's wedding is going to be here in three weeks, but next spring, we'll plan things out a bit more. I want to put in more variety and color. Especially day lilies. I really love them."

"They were Debbie's favorite flower, too."

"A lot of people like them." She smiled brightly at him, letting innocence ride her lips while a dusky mystery filled her eyes.

"Yeah." Sam was right. Day lilies were a popular perennial. "Right."

They went around the back of the house. There were more mums here, in among the plants that had already been in the flower beds. It felt very safe, very solid here. As if time was a friend.

He let his feet take him down to the water's edge. A few ducks in the middle of the lake changed course and headed toward him.

"Do you have a garden?" Sam asked.

He shrugged. "I guess I technically still do, but it hasn't been tended in a few years."

He looked out across the water, waiting for the familiar pain to grip him in its vise. He took a deep breath to steel himself, then another. But the pain was only a slow ache, more a healing bruise than a fresh wound.

He turned back to Sam. "Debbie loved to garden and I helped her some. When she got sick, I tried to keep it up because it made her happy. Once she died, I just let it go. It didn't seem worth the effort."

Sam just shook her head, smiling gently. "It's always worth the effort," she said. "To bring a garden back to life again is a healing process."

"Maybe." He smiled, a strangely easy thing to do, even with ghosts hanging in the air. "Thinning out my day lilies, though, would definitely not be. That'd be more likely to send me to the hospital with a strained back. They're one huge clump."

"I can help you thin them," Sam replied. "Pay you back for all your help."

Her offer took him by surprise. And while his heart urged him to accept, his head was wiser. "No, there's no need for you to do that. I've just been doing my job."

"Sure. And what else—" But before she could finish her sentence, a car pulled into the drive. "It's Fiona and Alex," Sam said, walking up the slight slope to the drive.

By the time the car stopped and Fiona and Alex had gotten out, Dan was up by the car, also.

"Something wrong, honey?" he asked.

Fiona nodded. "We have to go to St. Louis. Alex's cousin was in some kind of accident. It sounds serious."

"Oh, how awful." Sam took Fiona's hand. "I hope everything's all right."

"Was it someone you were close to?" Dan asked.

"I don't even know her," Alex said. "But my mother knew her father real well. We're picking Mom up in Chicago, then heading down together."

"I was hoping you'd look after Elvis and Prissy," Fiona said to Sam. "I already fed them this evening, but if you could keep an eye on them . . ."

"Sure, don't worry about anything."

"Thanks, hon." Fiona gave her sister a quick hug, then she and Alex got back in the car.

Sam, Kevin and Dan watched as the car disappeared down the driveway. "Hope things turn out okay," Dan said with a sigh, then went back to his planting. Sam and Kevin ventured toward the back porch.

"That's a long drive," Kevin said, as they climbed the steps.

"It's family," Sam replied. "It's what you do."

He suddenly felt a twinge of envy for the Scotts with all their siblings. He came from a small, not-very-close family. And he wasn't the type to hang on to anybody. But there had been times, especially during Debbie's illness, when he would have welcomed a helping hand.

And there were times now, when his loneliness threatened to overwhelm him, that Sam seemed to offer that hand to him. Maybe it was time he got brave enough to reach out for it.

Sam rang the front doorbell, then stood back. She'd lived in the northern Indiana area all her life but wasn't familiar with this little stretch of homes along the St. Joseph River in Mishawaka. Edgewater Drive was a brick-paved street with a line of fine old homes on one side and the river on the other. It appeared to be just one block long. She was about to push the button again when the door opened.

"Sam," Kevin said, flashing a smile. "What a pleasant surprise."

His offhand manner took her aback. She'd never seen him this lighthearted. She liked the change, but then she liked a whole lot about him—the shorts and knit shirt that showed off his rangy, lean build. The way his eyes mirrored his thoughts. The way his lips felt, pressed against hers.

Maybe it was best not to let her thoughts travel down that road.

"What brings you to my neighborhood?" he asked.

She started, suddenly realizing that she had been standing there, staring at him. Her cheeks felt warm. "What brings me here?" she said gruffly as she held out the piece of fax paper. "Are you saying you know nothing of this?"

He took the note from her hand and gravely studied it.

Our conditions are deplorable. Our children have no room to grow and are unable to reach their full potential. Please help us. Take us to a new land where our families will have space to grow.

The serious look on Kevin's face was there only because he hadn't read aloud the last lines of the note. "Sincerely, The Day lilies of 117 Edgewater Drive." The note had been faxed to the main desk of the library so that all the world could see it. And from all the teasing Sam had gotten, all the world apparently had.

"Well, it is true. They are very crowded and, because of that, have not been blooming very well."

She didn't know where this new Kevin had come from. The shadows in his eyes weren't totally gone, but he was obviously trying to keep them at bay. She was willing to help him. It didn't mean she was straying from her convictions,

"Then why are we standing around here?" Sam raised the bucket—filled with paper bags and a small shovel—she held in her left hand. "I'm ready to go."

"Let's do it."

He stood back to let her in and she stepped onto the slate-covered floor of the foyer. The walls were painted white and the molding was thick and heavy looking, stained a very dark shade. The interior of the house had a Southwestern feel to it. The furniture was an eclectic mixture of modern, traditional, and masculine. She felt she was getting a glimpse into his soul, and the idea made her both anxious and eager.

"Very nice," Sam observed.

"Debbie was the decorator," he said with a shrug. "I haven't changed much of anything. Just too lazy, I guess."

"As long as you're comfortable."

"And that's Duchess and the Duke." He indicated two cats sitting on the window seat and glaring at her. "Duchess is the one with the lighter coat."

Sam waved. "Hi, guys."

Like true cats, they barely acknowledged her existence. Blinking once, they turned their attention back to the outdoors.

"They're not the glad-handing type," Kevin said.

"No self-respecting cat would ever demean themselves so," Sam said.

Kevin guided her down the hall into the kitchen. It was decorated in a European motif, all white with sharp angles and straight lines. She would have preferred something warmer, but maybe this reflected who Debbie was. Or Kevin.

"Would you like something to drink?" he asked.

"Maybe after we're done," she replied.

They went past an island stove, around the refrigerator and out the back door. The yard was a nice size and not totally unkempt, but it was obvious that Kevin's gardening efforts had been purely defensive. Keep things neat and contained but without the effort and care to make it vibrant and pulsing with life.

"The day lilies are along the back fence and in front of the garage," he said, pointing.

"You haven't topped them off," Sam said.

He shrugged. "There's a lot I haven't done."

"Then let's get going." Sam slipped off her shoes and walked down the back stairs into the yard. "You need to take out at least a third of those plants, maybe more."

"Do you always garden in your bare feet?" he asked.

Surprised by the question, Sam just stood there a moment and stared at him. Then she shrugged. "Yeah, I guess." She turned her attention down to her feet and memories flooded in, like the mist on a dark and foggy night. "My first mother always did that. I guess I'm like her in that regard."

"Your first mother?"

"Fiona, Cassie and I are adopted," she explained. "The Scotts adopted us when I was six. I don't remember my first parents much, but Fiona told me stories about our mom. How she liked to garden barefoot. And loved to recite poems and parts of plays and stuff for us. I kind of remember her singing and swinging me around in her arms."

"It's nice that you have a few memories of her," he said. "Stacy and Jon are lucky that way. They were old enough when Debbie died to remember her."

"That is nice. She'll always be real to them then." The mood was growing darker though, even in her own heart, and it was time to lighten things up. "Come on." She pulled at his arm. "I can hear the day-lily people calling."

"I don't hear anything."

"My father—" Sam noticed uncertainty creep into his face and, laughing, she drew herself close to him. "I mean my present father, Daddy Scott. He says you have to listen in order to hear."

"I know how to listen," Kevin said with a frown.

"Do you?" Sam asked. "Or do you just wait to hear what you think is going to be said?"

"That makes me sound very closed-minded. Is that how I seem to you?"

He sounded as if it mattered to him. "We all are in some ways," she said. "And we always expect to hear with our ears. Sometimes we have to listen with our eyes or with our hearts."

Kevin put a thoughtful look on his face. "I hear the day lilies now, real clear."

"Good." But her words were echoing in her own mind, challenging all her comfortable notions.

How often did she listen with her eyes or her heart? Was she now? Kevin was acting like he hadn't a care in the world, yet those shadows lurking in his eyes said otherwise. What did he need from her? How could she help his heart heal?

"Hey," Kevin said. "Are you here to thin the day lilies or talk?"

"Some people can do both, and more." She hurried off to the day-lily patch, promising herself she would chip away at those doubts, little by little, until they were gone. It was the least she could do for a friend, and that was what he was. A friend. Nothing wrong with that. Nothing to threaten her peace of mind.

They worked hard for about an hour or so. Sam tried to get him to talk about himself, or his kids, or anything, but he obviously wasn't a big talker. She filled in the silences with her own chatter, but grew increasingly irritated with herself.

It wasn't any great mystery why Kevin's laughter didn't often reach his eyes. He'd lost his wife and, in essence, his kids. Cracking stupid jokes for him wasn't going to make a lasting difference. Neither was telling him stories about her family. But what was?

Sam bit her lower lip and concentrated hard on the day lily before her. Somehow she had to make Kevin part of his family again. She threw the plant into her bucket and stood, mopping her forehead with the back of her hand.

"Sure is hot."

"You think so?" he asked. "It's warm, but I didn't think it was hot."

Sam turned away and swallowed the laughter that wanted to bubble up. Her mind had been working on solving Kevin's problems, but her body had been busy reacting to his presence. The day may not have been hot, but somebody sure was.

"I guess the temperature is pretty close to normal for this time of the year," Sam agreed.

"Want to stop and have something to drink?"

"Naw. I'm tough. I can take it."

Kevin went back to splitting the day lily he'd dug up and Sam snuck a long glance at him. Was working in Debbie's garden hard for him? Were they keeping it alive for her in his mind, or tearing it apart?

"Oh, hell," Kevin said. "I don't remember what color these things are."

As if in a haze, Sam looked down at the long green leaves. "It doesn't matter."

"You don't know what you're getting."

She laughed, sounding a tad high even to her ears. Wasn't that true in just about everything? "Oh, I don't mind. It's not like I'm a total innocent, you know."

He looked bewildered.

"Hey," she said. "I knew day lilies were done blooming by now, so I was taking potluck. I have no problem with that."

"Oh." His grin spread across his lean face. "That's good."

There was something in his eyes that teased her, awoke longings to take him in her arms and forget all about the day lilies. But a little worm of common sense took over. Throwing herself into his arms was not what she'd come here for.

"Let's get back to work," she said. "We should be done in another half hour at the most."

They started back to their digging. They worked well together, not needing much talk to get the job done. But that didn't mean she was about to forget that he was near. She tried concentrating on—

"How about dinner tomorrow night?"

She forgot whatever it was she'd been concentrating on. "Dinner?" she repeated as if she wasn't sure what that was.

"I know it's short notice," he said. "So I'll take a rain check if you can't make it."

Dinner would be a better place for him to relax. A place where there'd be no lingering memories of Debbie to haunt him. Except . . .

"I'm afraid I can't," she said. "I'm in charge of the kids' summer-theater program at the library. We're putting on our final play tomorrow night."

"Oh."

It didn't have to be one or the other, though. "I'll be done by eight-thirty," she added.

"Eight-thirty?"

Sam tried to keep her disappointment in her stomach and off her face. "Yeah, I know it's late."

"Not at all. It's okay." He put on that grin again. "I get to stay up as late as I want on Wednesday and Saturday."

"Great. We can use the first of our dinner coupons."

"Those are yours to use as you want," he said. "This dinner will be on me."

"They belong to both of us. We just have to decide where to go." She bent back to the task of splitting the day lilies. Over dinner she would find a way to make him open up.

Chapter Six

"Well, a jolly good-morning to you, too," Cindy said to Kevin.

He came to a stop at his office door and took a deep breath, letting it out slowly before turning back toward his secretary. "All I said was good-morning. Just like I do every morning."

"No." Cindy shook her head. "Not like you do every morning. This was brusque."

"It was not."

"Must be my ears," she said stonily and turned her attention to papers on her desk. "George Lewis called in sick this morning."

This quick change of subject indicated that Cindy knew she was right and didn't want to talk about it anymore. Which was fine with him. Just because Kevin was having minor second thoughts about getting involved with Sam, he certainly wasn't letting it affect his general demeanor.

"His allergies acting up again?" Kevin asked.

"Yes. He doesn't think he'll be in until Monday."

"I'm sure things will clear up by then. He's usually not off more than a couple of days." He was about to go into his office but paused. "He didn't have anything pressing, did he?"

"He was scheduled for a commercial-loan subcommittee meeting at the Indiana Bankers' Association headquarters in Indianapolis. You'll have to—"

"I'll go."

"I was going to say that you'll have to send someone else in his place."

"I said, I'll go."

Cindy's face tightened and Kevin steeled himself for another reprimand—something about the inappropriateness of a bank officer at his level and size of bank attending a subcommittee working session. He should send a representative; a representative who was subordinate to him.

Well, Kevin knew all that, but so what? Sometimes an executive had to get out and mingle. Sometimes he had to... had to just get out.

"Get me George's files on his last two meetings," Kevin said, before stepping briskly into his office and shutting the door.

He had a lot of things to do. And now he had a lot less time to do them. That loan-committee approval meeting would have to be rescheduled for Monday. And he would have to—

He was supposed to have dinner with Sam tonight.

He fell heavily into his chair, conscious of the indecision churning about in the pit of his stomach.

Their first two dates had been just for fun, no strings attached. They had shared a few laughs and had a nice time. That had been it. No big deal.

And giving her the day lilies had been fine, also. The plants had needed to be thinned. Sure, he could have thinned them himself or, better yet, hired somebody to do it, but Sam and her father had needed some perennials. So he had actually been helping a client get her small business started. Something, as a bank officer, he was supposed to do anyway.

So since everything had been going along beautifully, why had he gone and spoiled everything? She'd already returned his favor. He'd crossed the line from good business to monkey business.

Time to pick up the phone and give Sam a call. Let her off the hook. Do her a big favor. Give the lady some time of her own so that she could go out and do something she really wanted to do.

Kevin picked up the phone, but instead of dialing Sam's number at the inn, his finger hit the intercom button.

"Yes?"

Cindy's voice was pleasant enough, although Kevin thought he could feel a certain tightness around the edges. "What time does that subcommittee meeting start?"

"Ten o'clock," Cindy replied. "You'll have to leave early in the morning. Around six-thirty."

Six-thirty. He could still go out with Sam. Even having dinner at eight-thirty wouldn't keep him out that late. Except his doubts were still alive and well.

"Make me a reservation at a hotel in Indianapolis for tonight and tomorrow night. I'll leave this evening."

"You can get to the meeting in plenty of time if you leave early in the morning."

Kevin clenched his jaw tight for a moment. "I don't want to chance being late."

"What's wrong with taking a chance once in a while? It puts a little excitement into your life."

He suddenly felt tired. He did plenty of exciting things. Last summer, he'd spent three weeks running white-water rapids in Colorado. The summer before that, he'd gone on a camera safari to Africa. He'd sailed around the cape in a storm. He'd had a lot of excitement in his life.

"Cindy, just get me a room for tonight. Please."

His arm slowly fell and he let the receiver rest in its cradle. He could call Sam but that seemed rather cowardly. It would be better to tell her of his change of plans face-to-face. Tell her the dinner was off. And not discuss an alternate date.

Unfortunately, his day was filled with meetings. And then he had that luncheon with the industrial planning group. There was no way to see Sam until tonight.

Sure, tonight would be rather short notice, but they hadn't planned on anything special. They probably would have just popped down the street for a pizza. She probably wouldn't care that he was canceling.

A slight nagging in the pit of his stomach told him he would care. But still it was for the best.

Kevin grimaced as he caught sight of the clock over the library's main desk. Damn. He'd hoped he would be able to talk to Sam before the play started. He didn't want to wait until it was over. Then it really was last-minute.

"Hey, fella. Watch it."

"I'm sorry." He had been so intent on getting into the auditorium that he'd almost run the woman over. The woman? Hell, everything was running in slow time for him, especially his brain. "Cassie. I'm sorry. I wasn't watching where I was going."

"Boy, you look like you're in a real hurry," Cassie said with a laugh. "What did my little sister promise to get you so excited?"

For the first time in a decade, Kevin felt his cheeks grow warm from embarrassment. What the hell was it about these Scott women that could throw a man off his tracks? They were certainly a dangerous crew.

"Nothing." He shook his head. "Nothing at all."

"Sure." He didn't much care for the smirk on Cassie's face but he wasn't about to encourage it by arguing. "That's why you just about smashed me into the ground. For nothing."

"I wouldn't do that," Kevin protested and glanced around at the number of people that were moving around them into the auditorium. It looked like Sam's show was a popular event. "Anyway, aren't you going the wrong way? Why are you leaving?"

"The doctor told me not to take anything that might upset my stomach."

Kevin looked quizzically at her.

"Just a weak attempt at humor," Cassie explained. "Most of our nieces and nephews are in this play. And there ain't a Scott living, adopted or biological, that's any good as an actor."

"Oh?"

"We're so bad that the only way our kids get into something like this is through nepotism."

"That makes me really anxious to see the show," he said.

"Just don't let Sam talk your bank into backing one of her shows," Cassie told him and waved slightly as she moved away. "I'd better go or Sam'll kill me. She sent me out to get one of the props from her car."

"Bye."

Kevin slipped into the auditorium. The chairs were rapidly being filled up by anxious family members. The sign on the stage proclaimed that *Fractured Fairy Tales* would be performed at seven-thirty. He glanced at his watch. It was almost 7:25.

He hurried over to the side door where stagehands were bringing on scenery. A number of kids were milling about in costume—princesses, witches, ogres and elves. He stepped through them and turned a corner. At the end of the hall was Sam with Cinderella and a fairy godmother.

They were obviously having a last-minute pep talk. And maybe some last-minute instructions. For as Kevin watched, Sam began to recite lines that must be from the play. Her eyes were fiery and intense, her heart on display for all to see.

Right before his eyes, she was transformed into Cinderella—no costume necessary. Then, in the blink of an eye, she became the fairy godmother.

The really amazing thing was her voice. He suspected she could read a grocery list and make it sound exciting. Or scary. Or tragic. He had never seen someone who was so naturally an actress.

Yet Cassie had said they all were terrible on stage. Did Sam freeze and could only act in private?

"Kevin, hi." Sam gave him a robust wave, indicating that he should come over. "I didn't know you were going to come see the show."

"Uh, I needed to talk to you."

"Oh, sure." She took a misshapen set of antlers from a woman who was trying to bend them back into shape. "This is Mrs. Jakosey. She's our costume person and sergeant at arms."

"Hi," the woman said with a quick smile.

"I can take care of this," Sam told her. "Why don't you go help the mice with their whiskers?"

"So, what's up?" Sam asked, as the other woman hurried away to corral some gray-clothed kids.

"This is quite a scene back here," Kevin said.

Sam shrugged. "They're just a little excited, not dangerous. Nothing to worry about."

"I know you're pressed for time, but something's come up." He grimaced slightly. "I was wondering if I could take a rain check on tonight's dinner."

She gazed at him for a moment as he cursed himself internally. Damn it. He wasn't supposed to ask for a rain check. He was supposed to call it off.

"I have to go to Indianapolis tonight," he told her.

"That's just as well." She gave him a quick smile. "The kids want me to go for pizza with them and their parents after the show."

"Oh, that's nice," Kevin replied.

"I didn't find out until I got here tonight."

He smiled. "So they want to stay out and party?"

Sam glanced back at the horde of minipeople behind her. "It sure looks like it." She turned back to Kevin and put a hand on his arm. "And I'm afraid it might get a little wild."

"Probably too wild for a banker."

"Depends on the banker."

Her eyes flashed and for a moment Kevin wondered what they were trying to tell him. But he probably didn't want to know. Or shouldn't know. Or it wasn't worth knowing, anyway. Maybe all of the above.

"So, it's a good thing that I have to go out of town?"

"I don't know if it's a good thing," she said with a shrug. "But it'll probably be a lot easier on your nerves."

"Why don't we get together Friday night?" Damn. He wasn't supposed to do that. "I mean, if I get back in time."

"That would be fine. Give me a call."

She hurried back to her kids and Kevin watched with something that almost felt like jealousy. Did she care that he'd broken the date? Did she hope he would get back early on Friday, or was she just being polite?

He wanted to rush after her and say he'd changed his mind. He wanted to confess that he could leave later, or even in the morning. But he knew that what was best and what he wanted were miles and miles apart.

"Morning, Dad."

Her father lifted his head from his morning paper and gazed up at Sam over the tops of his glasses. "What are you doing up so early? Can't you sleep?"

"I slept quite well." She shuffled over to a chair across from her father and dropped into it.

The early-morning sun was filling their dinette/sunroom with a golden light, as Sam tried to avoid her father's curious gaze. "Goodness," she said, concentrating her attention on a willow down toward the lake. "Some of the leaves are changing color already. It seems too early."

"You look a little peaked around the edges, sweetheart."

Sam curled her bare feet around the chair legs. "You know I've never been a late sleeper."

There was little doubt in her mind that her father was looking at her, but Sam refused to break. She just kept on staring out at that big old willow in their backyard. If she made eye contact with her father, she was a goner.

A grunt from across the table indicated that he'd gone back to reading his paper. Sam let out a slow, silent sigh of relief.

Actually, she had had a very active night. Her dreams had carried her across town to Kevin's house, but it had been surrounded by a high wall. And although she could see him and he would talk to her, he never would come down from the wall.

When she'd finally decided she would have to climb it, she kept slipping down. Finally she was crying and kicking at it like a little kid having a tantrum. But it didn't matter. Kevin kept himself out of reach.

Fortunately, Sam had awoken. Or maybe not so fortunately. She'd lain in a moody tangle of sheets, yearning for someone she'd convinced herself was just a friend. But it was only a dream.

She'd kept telling herself that as she showered. Then, once she was cleaned and dried, Sam had sat by her window and watched the new day come. Watched and wondered what it would bring. It would bring the same thing yesterday had brought and the day before that: everything she needed and wanted. She had a full life.

Well, maybe not everything. But certainly what she could handle. It had been crazy of her to think she could somehow help Kevin. It had been crazy of her to want to get involved.

"You want me to fix you something?" her father asked.

"No." She shook her head. "I have a lot of stuff to do. I'll just have some cereal."

"If you have a lot to do, you should have a good breakfast." He got up from the table. "We have loads of blueberries. I'll make you some crepes and fill them with fruit."

"Dad, you don't have to—"

But he was already moving. Her father wasn't the type to bustle around, but once he put himself in motion, he was hard to stop. Besides, now that she thought about it, blueberry crepes sounded good.

"I'll have some orange juice," she said, getting up to set the table and get her drink.

It was just as well that Kevin had canceled their dinner. Going out with the kids from the play wasn't something she could have backed out of. But at the same time, she wouldn't have felt comfortable bringing him along. Sure, he was a father, but his kids were out of high school. Old enough so that he probably would have forgotten how rambunctious grade-school kids could be.

"Aren't you going to work?" her father asked. "I thought tomorrow was your day off."

Sam had that uncomfortable feeling of being yanked out of a cozy cocoon and had to struggle to keep from frowning. "No, Marla wanted to switch, so I did," she replied. "I'm going to paint and wallpaper our office today."

Her father finished pouring the batter into the frying pan before he spoke again. "I thought Jerry was going to get to that after he finished with the guest rooms."

Sam shrugged and took a sip of her orange juice. She knew that, but she felt so twitchy she had to do something. Something physical. Something that would make her sweat. "I like to do that kind of stuff, Dad."

"That's a big job," he said. "There are ten-foot ceilings in there and you'll have to pull off the old wallpaper."

"I know."

"Hmm," her father grunted as he flipped her crepe out onto a plate and poured the batter for another. "Don't get in over your head."

"Don't worry. I won't." Good advice for a certain aspect of her life. Like Kevin. She sat back down at the table. "I figure since it's not a guest room, it doesn't have to be as professional as Jerry and his guys can do."

Her father turned his attention to filling the crepe with blueberries and rolling it up. A pleasant silence filled their kitchen as Sam watched him. He looked up unexpectedly and caught her watching him.

"You know, this shouldn't become your life," he said gruffly. "The bed-and-breakfast, I mean."

"Who said it is?"

"You're young. You should be spending your day off having fun, not stripping wallpaper off an old wall."

"Maybe I like doing it."

"It's not that I don't love you for all your help," he said. "It's just that this was my dream, not yours. So when your dreams call, I want you to promise you'll follow them."

"What's all this about?" she asked with a laugh. "You trying to get rid of me as your partner?"

"You know I'm not." He brought her crepes over and put them on the table. "So, do you promise?"

"Fine. Yes." She sighed. "I promise to follow my dreams, should one ever surface."

"So," her father said, going back over to the stove. "That banker fella coming around anymore this week to check up on us?"

"No," she replied. "Not this week."

"Oh." Her father picked up the frying pan. "Like I said, I was just wondering."

"He had to go to Indianapolis. He won't be back until late tomorrow."

"Ah." He took the pan and put it in the sink, squirting out some soap as he ran water into it. "Probably be around next week."

"I suppose."

She wasn't holding her breath. Kevin had said he would give her a call when he came back and they would set up another time to go out. But if he didn't, she wasn't going to chase him down. She'd been dreaming when she'd decided she could bring him happiness.

He had to be willing to be led from his loneliness, and she wasn't at all sure he wanted that.

"Oh, I almost forgot to tell you," her father said. "Larry was talking to me after the play last night. Wanted to know if you had a date for Cassie's wedding."

Sam just groaned and closed her eyes for a minute. "Maybe I want to go alone," she said. "Maybe I don't want a date."

"You want to tell him or should I?" her father asked with a laugh.

"Small-business loans are not always that profitable. They require a lot of individual care. But every so often you get one that makes all the rest of them worthwhile."

The words floated way out to the edges. Out to where Kevin's sense of the real butted against his subconscious. Kevin knew the man was talking about money and profitability. But, as a smiling pixie-like face dancing in the misty corners of his mind was pointing out, not all paybacks came in dollars. Sometimes the best currency had nothing to do with silver or paper.

There was no doubt that when the moderator spoke of that one small-business owner who made everything else worthwhile, he wasn't speaking of Samantha Scott. In fact, if Kevin had come to this meeting two weeks ago, he wouldn't have made that connection, either. He shook his head.

Two weeks, hell. It would have been the same thing if he'd come a week ago. Days even.

Kevin refocused on the presentation for a moment and found that it wasn't anything he didn't already know. He beat a hasty retreat to his own thoughts.

When had this momentous change taken place?

And it was momentous. One minute Sam was a customer and the next, she was under consideration for... For what? A good friend? He had a lot of good friends. A very good friend? That didn't quite do it, either. An extremely charming lady friend?

A quiet sigh floated up and out of his lungs. There weren't any precise words to describe Sam. Yes, she was charming. But she was also intelligent, giving, pleasant to look at. Kind of ornery. He shook his head. A lot of ornery.

A smile pulled at his lips. This whole thing was still hard to believe. Heck, Sam almost hadn't made "customer." Not after she'd thrown him out of that old house of theirs.

He really should be paying attention to the presentation but, hell, it wasn't like he was missing anything. Cindy had been right. These sessions were geared for less experienced personnel. He didn't need to be here at all.

But it had been necessary for him to get out of South Bend. He'd needed to be off someplace by himself so he could think.

He'd spent last evening at the downtown hotel Cindy had booked him into, not far from the Indiana Bankers' Association's offices, reveling in his anonymity. Unlike South Bend, no one stopped to talk to him. No one came by his table as he ate his solitary meals. He was faceless. Anonymous like a fish in a school of others just like itself. A perfect environment for thinking and mulling things over.

And that was exactly what he had done. Analyzed. Weighed the pluses and the minuses. After all that, he'd come to a basic simple truth: the only thing he had to fear was fear itself.

This age thing wasn't that big a deal. Yes, he was older than Sam but he was still her contemporary. They shared a lot of the same values and liked some of the same things. Cats. Day lilies. The outdoors. Pizza and wine.

It wasn't as if they'd been soul mates from the beginning of the universe, touching and dancing in a number of past lives. But there certainly was no reason for them not to date.

They had fun together and enjoyed each other's company. What else was there? He looked at his watch. He hoped this damn presentation would be over soon. He wanted to get on home.

Chapter Seven

Sam tossed the last of the bread onto the water. "That's it, guys. End of the handouts for today."

The swans took it well, just turning and gliding back into the growing shadows around the lake. The ducks were harder to convince. They kept pushing and squabbling and looking for more food.

"You're out of luck. Sometimes you just have to accept that things aren't the way you want them."

Sam knew that all too well herself. Take her and Kevin. Obviously, things weren't going the way she wanted them to. He hadn't called like he said he would.

Maybe she should just be glad that her life was still totally hers. No distractions. No reason to wait until eight in the evening to eat dinner. She turned away from the lake and started up the slope to the house. It was getting dark. Time to—

A sedan was pulling into the drive. It stopped and Kevin got out. Her heart did a crazy leap and her feet moved a bit faster, even though she tried to hold them at the same speed.

"Hi," he called over to her.

"Hi."

He was still dressed in his suit, though minus his tie, and his eyes looked weary. She felt an overpowering urge to take care of him.

"You look beat," she said. "You just get in?"

He nodded. "I thought we had a date."

"I thought we had a tentative one," she said and took his hand. "Come on inside. Have you eaten yet?"

"I thought we had a *dinner* date."

"It's almost nine," she reminded. "I assumed you hadn't gotten back or you'd changed your mind or something and eaten ages ago."

He frowned, looking hurt. "It's just past eight-thirty," he said. "And I wouldn't have changed my mind and not let you know."

"Well, it wasn't like it was a definite thing."

"I should have called," he said. "I'm sorry."

"No big deal." They went on into the living room, and then into the kitchen. "The kitchen's a mess. I've been painting the office and I've moved everything into the kitchen. Our banker's here, Dad."

Her father looked up from the papers he was working on on the kitchen table. "Don't bring him in yet," her father said, snatching up the computer printouts and putting them in the cold oven. "I'm not done cooking the books."

"You'll have to excuse him." Sam involuntarily rolled her eyes. "He thinks he's a comedian."

"Maybe I'd better look at your accounts," Kevin said.

"Good idea," Sam replied.

She pulled the computer printouts from the oven and laid them on the table. Kevin pulled out a chair and sat down while Sam leaned back against the kitchen counter.

"Greatness is never appreciated," her father said. "I'll leave you two alone." With a broad wink at Sam, he went out into the living room.

The silence grew louder and louder. "We've got some leftover pot roast," she told Kevin. "Want me to warm it up for you?"

"That would be great."

While he flipped through the pages, she stuck a plate of the pot roast into the microwave. Their accounting system was a standard small-business software package and not all that complex. It wouldn't take Kevin long to do his review.

"You're doing real good controlling your expenses." He put the papers in a neat pile and leaned back. "It looks like you're about fifteen percent under budget so far."

"Yeah, we had a number of good things happen. Like the freezer doesn't have to be replaced like we originally thought it would." She smiled at Kevin. "And a very generous benefactor made a donation of day lilies for our perennial garden. So our landscaping expenses are also way under budget."

He returned her smile and nodded. "Every little bit counts."

"Although that new boiler puts us a little over on our capital equipment budget."

"You're still doing well." He put his hands behind his head and bathed her with his smile. "Actually, you guys are doing very well."

"Thank you." She felt her cheeks warm as her left foot moved over to cover her right. "Now all we need is customers."

"I'm sure you'll do fine. Probably have to beat them off with a club."

"We can always hope."

The kitchen went quiet, filled only with the sounds of the approaching night. The days were still warm in early September, but the evenings were getting cooler. At the moment, a breeze was blowing through the kitchen's open windows. Yet Sam felt all warm and cozy, like a kitten in a muff.

Their eyes met and suddenly the air grew thicker around them, making breathing more of an effort. Sam had pretty much told herself that Kevin was only interested in her as a bed-and-breakfast owner, a loan customer. Nothing else. What else could there be? What else did she want, anyway? Didn't she have everything she wanted already?

The microwave beeped, much to Sam's relief, and she grabbed up some silverware and a napkin. "What can I get you to drink? Iced tea? Milk? Pop? Beer?"

"Iced tea would be great," he said as he went over to the microwave and got his plate out.

"I could have done that," she protested as she poured a glass for each of them.

"I don't need you to wait on me."

"You're my guest."

"I'm not a guest," he argued.

"All right, then. You're my banker."

He frowned at her. She frowned back. Something was flicking in the air between them. There was something raw and wild and elemental charging about. If it had been dark, she would have seen sparks or flashes of lightning. Or fireworks exploding in a cascade of brilliance.

She took a deep breath and looked at the glasses in her hand. "Want to eat in here or out on the porch?" she asked.

"The porch sounds nice." His voice was tight and hoarse.

She grabbed up his silverware and led the way. The sun had almost set, but still painted a spectacular array of colors across the sky. Although dusk was falling, she hated to turn on the porch lights.

"This is great," Kevin said, looking around as he sat down at the picnic table. "Are you going to feed your guests out here?"

"Maybe in the summer. It's not something we're working on until the spring."

He grinned at her. "Like the pipes held together by mineral deposits?"

"You have too good a memory," she grumped. "So how was your trip?"

"Boring." He tasted his dinner. "Very nice. Somebody here makes a mean pot roast."

She just ignored his comment, not wanting to admit for some reason that she'd made it. She didn't think she wanted his compliments for some housewifely skill. And she definitely didn't want to figure out why. She stared out at the lake, trying to find Romeo and Juliet in the shadows, but the light was getting too dim.

"What we need is somebody who's good at muffins and breads and other breakfast stuff. We're only serving breakfast here."

"I'll remember that the next time I'm hungry," he said. "How did your play go?"

She brought her gaze back to him. "Fine. No major catastrophes."

"Cassie says none of you guys can act."

She stared at her glass of iced tea. "Nope. No potential Academy Award winners in our family."

"At least, none that'll admit to it."

She looked up at him, sorry for a moment that the gathering gloom made his eyes indistinct. "What's that mean?"

"I saw you rehearsing with some kids. You were great. A natural actress if I ever saw one."

"Rehearsing isn't acting," she argued.

"No, but it's close," he said. "And you'd have to have one hell of an attack of stage fright to lose all that talent."

"Maybe I'm happy directing the kids' plays."

"Maybe. But why would Cassie say none of you could act?"

Sam pulled back, glad, suddenly, of the shadows that allowed her to hide for the moment. "She's never seen me," she admitted. Sam was certain none of this was his business, but she wasn't certain why she was telling him any of it. "Scotts can't act."

"And so you deny your talent in order to fit in." He'd finished eating and pushed the plate to one side.

"It's not that at all. I've always felt like I fit in. The Scotts were...are wonderful. They wouldn't be upset if I could do something none of the rest could do. They'd be really supportive."

"Your mother was good at this, wasn't she?" he asked. "Your biological mother, I mean. You said she loved to recite stuff."

Sam just shrugged. "She might have been. I don't know. I don't remember her much. The Scotts were much more my parents."

"And using your other mother's talent would be disloyal."

"That's crazy."

"Is it?" He lowered his voice to a harsh whisper. "You're helping your father run the inn *he* wants. You're pretending you don't have a talent that would tie you back to your other parents. And if I knew you better, I probably could list a whole mess of other examples."

His guess had hit too close to home. Although she rarely spelled it out so clearly in her mind, she knew he was right. Partially, anyway.

"It's not that I'd feel disloyal, exactly," she said quietly. "I just want them to be happy. I want everybody to be happy. And I don't care how much Dad says we should remember our other parents if we want, it has to hurt him if we do. It's like he and Mom weren't enough."

"I doubt that he feels that way, and even if he should, you have to be who you are—not who you think will make others happy."

"It's not that easy," she said.

He sighed. "No, and I didn't mean to preach. Goodness knows, the guiding force in my relationships—or lack of them—has been a desire to make the other person happy."

"Isn't that what most relationships are about?"

He didn't say anything for the longest time, then reached across the table to take her hands in his. "I'm better at nonrelationships, I'm afraid. I'm not pushing back into my kids' lives because I figure they're happy the way things are. And I keep avoiding you because I figure you'd be happier with some guy closer to your own age."

"You're sure making a lot of assumptions," she returned. She liked the feel of her hands in his. "Have you ever asked your kids how they feel? And just how much older than me are you, anyway?"

He smiled. She could feel it in the air, even though it was too dark to see it.

"Your loan application said you were twenty-seven," he said. "I'll be forty in three weeks."

"And from the exalted wisdom that comes from that advanced age, you know what's best for everyone."

"Sometimes."

"You're sort of an adviser on emotional loans, too, then. Really an all-purpose banker."

"Well, I—"

He seemed to realize then that she was joking and he stopped. In a moment, he started to laugh. "So, what now?" he asked.

"Now you go home to your pussycats and a good night's sleep," she said, getting to her feet and reluctantly releasing his hands. "Come on over tomorrow if you want and I'll give you a test. You can help me do chores and we'll see if you've got the stamina to keep up with me."

"Are you sure?" he asked, seeming to ignore her attempt at humor. He let go of her hands but took them again once he was on his feet.

"About the chores? Sure. I'll take any help I can get."

"You know that's not what I mean."

He enfolded her in his arms and just held her for the longest moment. She laid her head against him, letting the wondrous night slide over her. An hour ago, she had been lonely and now—suddenly—all the world seemed to lie at her feet. She wanted to laugh and shout and dance. There was nothing to worry about here. She could let her heart have free rein.

Kevin moved slowly away from her. "I guess if I've got a big test tomorrow, I'd better get home and get some rest."

"A wise man, indeed," she teased.

He leaned down and brushed her lips with his. It brought a touch of heaven to the darkened porch, and a brief glimpse of shooting stars and birds singing. Then it was over and he was gone.

Sam just sighed and grabbed up the dishes. Their age difference didn't matter at all to her. She hadn't even given it a thought. But now that she was thinking about it, thirteen years wasn't all that much. It was attitude that counted.

And any man who could kiss like that, had a young attitude.

Sam hurried down the inn's front steps Saturday afternoon, her feet bare and her shoes in one hand. Kevin had just pulled the Jeep up to the house. He got out to meet her on the gravel drive.

"We need to stop at Fiona's house first," she told him. "I have to feed her cats. Then we need to stop at the grocery store, the cleaners and the hardware store."

"I'm exhausted already," he said, then stopped, frowning down at her feet.

"It's still summer, you know," she reminded. "Fall doesn't start for another two weeks. And even then, it won't be all that cold."

"I wasn't thinking about the cold," he replied. "I just can't believe you walk on gravel without any shoes."

"Us small-town girls are tough."

"Well, us big-city boys aren't."

Suddenly he swooped her up in his arms. It felt so right. So natural. Before she knew it, her arms were around his neck.

"You don't have to do this," she said. "It really doesn't hurt a bit to walk on these stones."

He stared at her. It could have been her imagination but Sam thought that his grip on her had tightened. She did know that the look in his eyes had turned dark and dangerous—and that something deep in her soul wanted to respond.

"It might not hurt you," he finally replied, carrying her to his open-topped Jeep. "But it hurts me, watching you."

After he'd set her down in the front passenger seat, she missed the touch of his arms, and her weakness annoyed her.

"Us kids always went barefoot in the summer," she told him. "Our feet are tough."

"Humor me," he said as he got into the driver's seat.

"Why should I?"

"Because I'm your banker."

Sam suddenly found herself glaring at him, her emotions going from soft and cuddly to hard and edgy in the blink of an eye. He certainly was a bossy cuss.

"Seat belt, please."

Sam jerked the belt into its grip at her side of the seat. She hated obeying, but common sense told her that refusing to fasten up would be worse than childish. She promised herself that she would fix him later.

They drove mostly in silence to Fiona and Alex's house. Except for Sam giving Kevin directions, neither said anything. She concentrated on the passing scene as she tried to figure out the sudden change in mood.

Last night he was all laid-back and now he was all pushy. Or was she the cause of everything? Was she responding to him or he to her? Or were they both tuning in to some unknown karma floating about in the atmosphere? He pulled up in front of Fiona and Alex's house.

"I'm just going to put out some food, change their water, and clean their litter box," Sam said as she slipped her feet into her shoes. "I'll be right out."

"I'll go in with you," he said, following her up the front steps.

"You might scare the cats."

"I'll be very careful," he replied, suddenly dropping his voice to a whisper and moving on tiptoe.

Sam growled softly as she unlocked the door. "You're the oldest child, aren't you?"

"How did you know?"

She stepped inside, let Kevin enter and then closed the door behind them. "It's obvious."

"I don't think your attitude can be described as humoring your banker."

"If my banker isn't careful, he's liable to find himself humoring a good swift kick." She stopped and poked him in the chest. "And I don't need shoes to make it hurt."

"Hey," he said, smiling. "There's the cat."

Sam put all thoughts of ravaging his body out of her mind. "That's Elvis." She walked over and patted the cat's dark little head. "Where's Prissy? Huh? Where's your sister?"

The cat just blinked, pushing his head against her hand, demanding more scratching.

"She's probably off sleeping somewhere," Kevin said. "She'll come out when she hears the can opener. That's what my cats do."

"Except that Fiona uses a brand that doesn't require a can opener," Sam said, reaching into the cabinet for a tin of cat food. She tapped the dishes extra hard as she spooned food into them. "Prissy, honey. Din-din."

Elvis rushed over to devour the salmon but still no Prissy. That was unusual. Little Prissy was actually a bit of a pig, always pushing to be first where food was concerned. In fact, since Sam was a little late, Prissy should have been waiting with Elvis.

"I'm going to look around for her," she said. "I'll be back."

"Elvis and I will guard the kitchen," Kevin replied.

Sam went off to find the little red cat. She looked in the bedrooms and the bath, the living and dining rooms and in the basement, before coming back to the kitchen.

"I can't find her," she told Kevin.

He went with her and they looked everywhere all over again. Upstairs, downstairs. In between stairs. Every single place that a cat could go in the house. No Prissy.

Sam took one last look under Fiona and Alex's bed, then sat back against the bed, fighting panic as she petted Elvis. "Where did she go, Elvis?"

"Let's think this out," Kevin said. His voice was so calm and controlled that it made Sam feel slightly better. "We're reasonably certain she couldn't have gotten outside."

"I don't know." Despite her best efforts, Sam's voice was wobbling. "I don't know anymore."

"Well, Elvis is here, so for now, let's assume that she's inside the house, too."

"But we looked everyplace."

Kevin sat down on the edge of the bed, dropping a hand on her shoulder. "Cats are very creative, and you said Prissy's a small cat. There have to be hiding places she knows about and we don't."

Afraid to trust her voice, Sam could only shrug.

"I think we should try the basement again," he suggested. "That's where my cats' favorite hiding places are."

She nodded dumbly and let him pull her to her feet. They returned to the basement, with Elvis trailing along behind them. When they went into the laundry room to search, Elvis climbed from the washer to the sink to the water softener, then sat there staring at them.

"We've turned the place over six or seven times," Sam said. "There's no way Prissy can be down here."

"Maybe we've done too much. Let's just stand back and look around. Pretend we're a little pussycat."

Sam could only nod. Kevin's approach was very logical but it was no use. Tears were starting to form in her eyes. What was she going to tell Fiona? Her sister loved that little cat. And so did she. She blinked repeatedly as she imagined Prissy lying dead in some alley. What if she hadn't been careful when she'd shut the door behind her? Maybe she should have come by more than three times a day to check up on them....

"What's this little door?" Kevin asked, pointing to a door about two feet square in the middle of the far wall. "Where does it go?"

"Oh." She shook her head. "That's to the crawl space under the sunroom. But she can't be in there. It's latched and I never opened it."

He rubbed his chin. "We didn't look there."

"It's all sealed off," Sam said, waving her hand in a half circle to indicate the rafters and supports above them. "She'd have no way to get in there."

Without replying, Kevin walked forward and opened the little door. Sam looked over his shoulder into the opening before turning away.

"It's all full of cobwebs and dust," she said. "Prissy would never go in there. She's much too fastidious."

"Well, hello, there," Kevin said.

Sam spun around in time to see a red feline face looking up at Kevin from inside the crawl space. Apparently satisfied he was a good guy, the little cat jumped through the opening and up onto his shoulders. Kevin brushed cobwebs off the cat's back as she licked her paws.

"Prissy!" Sam screamed.

The cat gave Sam a look of disgust before going back to cleaning her paws.

"Where were you?" She snatched Prissy off Kevin's shoulders and hugged the little cat to herself. Prissy appeared unimpressed, biting at one of her hind feet. "We were looking all over for you."

Kevin poked his head deeper in the windowlike opening. "We need to find the hole and cap it."

"I grew up in this house," Sam said. "We always had cats and we never had one go in there."

"Unless Scotty beamed her in, there's got to be a hole."

"Don't tell me you're a 'Star Trek' fan, too," Sam said. "John Wayne and 'Star Trek.' What a combination."

"A good combination, you mean."

Prissy jumped out of Sam's arms and raced up the stairs. Elvis was following her.

"I hope Elvis ate everything," Sam called out, but Prissy was already disappearing around the edge of the door. Sam turned her attention back to Kevin. He was frowning into the cobweb-festooned crawl space.

"We'd find the hole easiest from inside the crawl space," he said. "The light from in here would spill through it, but I'm not sure I could fit through that opening."

"I guess I could go in." Although the prospect didn't thrill her.

"Let's check things out from here first."

She didn't argue with that and watched as Kevin poked around at the supporting joists along the wall between the crawl space and the basement, proper. With the boiler and its pipes, plus the washer and dryer and their vents and pipes, checking wasn't all that easy. Not to mention the water softener over there in the—

Sam frowned. "Elvis was sitting on the water softener," she said. "Maybe he knew where she'd gone and that was as high as he could climb."

"Worth a shot." Kevin climbed up on a chair and felt around the top of the wall over the water softener. "Here it is."

"I don't believe it," she said.

He jumped off the chair and made a cup with his hands. "I'll give you a boost up and you can feel for yourself. It's right above that big pipe."

Sam hesitated. Sticking her hand in some black hole didn't exactly thrill her.

"Don't be such a scaredy-cat. If you lose your hand, I'll buy you a new one."

Clenching her jaw, Sam put her foot in his hand and pulled herself up the wall. "Remind me to kick you in the head when I'm back down on the floor," she muttered.

Once she knew where to look, the hole was easy enough to find and Sam put her hand all the way through it.

"You can feel the other side of this wall, right?"

"Yeah." She removed her hand and, with Kevin's help, slid back down to the floor. "But it's so small. Barely bigger than my hand."

"Big enough for a cat Prissy's size to squeeze herself through," Kevin said. "We need to seal it off."

"How can we do that?" Sam asked. "With wood somehow?"

Kevin just shook his head. "Poster board nailed or stapled across the opening should do it for now. I don't think she'd chew her way through."

Sam just smiled at him. "I'm sure Fiona must have some poster board someplace around here. You guard the hole while I go look." She started toward the stairs.

"Sam." Kevin's voice stopped her and she turned. "How am I doing on my test so far?" he asked.

"Not bad," she told him. "Not bad at all."

* * *

"Here's to new adventures," Kevin said, raising his wine in a toast.

Once they'd secured the hole to the crawl space and double-checked to make sure all closets were closed and the house was as safe as they could make it, they'd started in on Sam's other chores. It had made for a full afternoon, so a nice quiet dinner at an out-of-the-way restaurant had seemed in order.

"Uh-uh." Sam shook her head but raised her glass anyway. "My heart can't take more excitement."

"And I thought I was the one being tested for fuddy-duddiness."

He couldn't help smiling as she sipped her wine. Sam's heart might have been bothered by the cat's temporary disappearance but she sure didn't look any worse for the wear. Her cheeks had a glow to them and her eyes were soft and sparkling, like distant stars.

"I could have murdered her," Sam said, running her fingers through her hair. "That little creep. I bet I'll be all gray by morning."

"She looks like she's part Abyssinian. They're a curious breed."

"I don't care." Sam took a healthy sip of her wine. Obviously her nerves had not yet returned to normal. "I'm still mad at her."

"It's in her genes." He took a drink from his own glass. "We are what we are. All of us."

Sam made a face and looked out at the quiet city street. Kevin sat quietly and watched her, then took her hand in both of his. "Prissy wasn't trying to be mean. She was just being who she is."

"I know," Sam replied.

"Curiosity is just a part of who she is. She inherited it from her ancestors."

"I know."

"Like you inherited your acting ability from your biological parents." Judging from the lines forming at the corners of Sam's mouth, her agitation was growing, but Kevin went on, anyway. "Fiona doesn't expect Elvis to be Prissy or Prissy to be Elvis. She lets each cat be themselves. Sort of like the story of the Ugly Duckling."

She frowned at him. Not a friendly frown, either.

"You know, the story where the baby swan is in among the ducklings," he explained.

"I know what it is," she snapped. "It was my favorite story when I was a kid."

"Then you must know that the swan was happiest when it was true to its nature."

"Maybe," Sam said. "But what about the mother duck? Nobody ever worries about her and her feelings."

"How do you know the swan didn't come back to visit sometimes?"

"You're as know-it-all as my brothers," she grumped.

"I just know that regret can be a bitter pill to swallow."

"Right now, I'm regretting letting you do chores with me." Her face fell, then. "Though I never would have found Prissy without you."

Much as he wanted to take credit for the rescue, he couldn't. "Prissy would have gotten out by herself," Kevin said. "I doubt that that was the first time she'd gotten in there."

"I wouldn't have wanted to take that chance."

"No, I agree."

"Sam?" a woman coming down the aisle toward them called out.

Sam looked up, then sprang from her seat. "Angie!" Sam cried. The two women hugged briefly.

A flicker of irritation rippled through Kevin's gut as he watched a tall blonde, her escort, and another couple advance on their table. Mid-twentysomething. Sam's age.

Thirteen years younger than him. He forced a pleasant expression onto his face.

"You still at the library?" the woman was asking Sam.

"Yeah. And I'm helping my father open up a bed-and-breakfast over on Clements Lake. You still selling cars?"

"Sure am."

Sam turned to the others. "So what are you guys up to?"

"Starving."

Sam's eyes darted around the room, obviously seeing that all the tables were filled. Then her gaze returned to their large, mostly empty table. It was easy to see what she was thinking.

"We have a lot of room," Kevin offered. "If you don't mind, we'd be happy to have you join us. Right, Sam?"

"Oh, yeah." She flashed him a quick smile before turning to her peers. "Okay with you guys?"

"Are you kidding?" Angie said as, laughing, she and her group quickly occupied the empty chairs. "Hungry as I am, I'd sit on the floor."

"We ordered a cheese-and-sausage pizza," Sam said, as Kevin signaled their server. "That should be here soon. Why don't we all share that and then order more?"

Introductions were made all around and then everyone settled into a moment of quiet as they waited for their drinks and the first pizza to arrive.

"Say, weren't you in the 10K stampede up in Cass County last month?" Angie's date asked.

Kevin nodded.

"You were in the top five, right?"

"Third," Kevin murmured.

"Are you running in the Blueberry Stomp in Plymouth at the end of the month?"

Kevin nodded.

"Rats," the man exclaimed. "I need to get about three or four of you top guys to drop out before I make the top five."

Everyone laughed.

"Do you run?" Angie asked Sam.

"No way," Sam replied.

"I don't, either," the other woman said. "I like a purpose to my running. Like scoring a goal in soccer or basketball."

The discussion quickly turned to whether exercising was goal enough. Kevin leaned back and smiled. He didn't feel out of place with Sam's friends at all. As a matter of fact, he'd had these kinds of discussions many times. There really wasn't much of a difference between his friends and Sam's.

He smiled across the table at her. He had a feeling he was going to pass her test with flying colors. And his own test, too.

Chapter Eight

Duchess turned from her dish and glared at Sam, looking as fierce as a lion in the wild. "Boy." Sam pulled her hand away from Kevin's cats. "For a little fuzzball you certainly look mean."

"They can be pretty grumpy at times," Kevin said with a chuckle.

Sam stepped back and watched the two cats eat their canned food. She and Kevin had finished their own dinner—spaghetti with Kevin's homemade sauce—and had cleaned up the dishes before he fed his cats. It was a very comfortable—homey—atmosphere.

Sam leaned against the stove. "Well, at least they don't give the people who take care of them heart attacks."

"What are you going to do?" Kevin asked. "Hold a grudge against Prissy forever?"

"Sure. I'm the youngest," Sam replied. "Family babies hold grudges the longest."

"Sounds like you guys are maladjusted."

"Older siblings are always insensitive."

Kevin shook his head. "And where did this little nugget of information come from? The Youngest Siblings Society?"

"Something like that."

Outside of the scare with Prissy yesterday, Sam had had a wonderful time with Kevin. And the age difference that he'd seemed so concerned about had been unnoticeable. When her friends had joined them for dinner last night, he had fit in perfectly—like he had gone to high school with them all. She would like to keep on seeing him.

But how did he feel about things? Certainly his inviting her over this evening for dinner had to mean something positive.

Sam picked up the open can of cat food and divided the remains equally between the two cats. "Poor little guys," she said. "They were starving."

"They had dry food," he replied.

"See?" Sam wagged a finger at Kevin. "What did I tell you? You're the oldest kid in your family and look at your attitude."

"There were only two of us," Kevin protested. "And my sister is the bossy one."

"Doesn't matter. You're still the oldest."

"Guilty as charged," he admitted. "Want some more wine?"

"Okay." She picked up her glass and held it for Kevin to refill. Duchess glanced over her shoulder, glaring at Sam with dislike. "Maybe I should wait in the other room."

Kevin shook his head. "You're going to let a little six-pound tyrant kick you out?"

"Sure." She just laughed and, taking her glass of wine, wandered into a small office off the living room. Bookshelves covered one wall of the room and she let her eyes dance over the titles, curious about Kevin's reading habits.

But her gaze stopped almost immediately on the two portraits—one of a young woman and one of a young man. Stacy and Jon? Sam thought she could faintly see Kevin in the young people's faces.

"Where'd you go?" Kevin called out, then appeared in the doorway. "You can take the lady out of the library, but not the library out of the lady."

"Very funny." She nodded at the pictures. "Jon and Stacy?"

"Yep."

"They're good-looking kids," she said. "You must miss them."

He just shrugged. "They have their own lives. That's how it is when your kids grow up."

"Are they coming in for your birthday?"

"No. They're too busy."

"Have you asked them to?"

"I'm not a birthday person," he said and turned toward the living room. "Want to watch a movie? I've got a lot of videos."

"Sure." She followed Kevin into the living room. "How about if you choose? I'll pick the next time."

"Okay."

As she sat down on the sofa, Kevin went to the shelf of videos. Sam was sure that he would choose some John Wayne flick, but she really didn't care. She was more interested in the fact that he'd accepted her reference to a "next time."

"How about *Fantasia?*" he suggested. "I enjoy the musical score."

Flabbergasted, Sam could only blink for a moment before replying. "Sure."

Kevin loaded the video and sat by her side. She pulled her bare feet under herself, leaning against him. He was not only attractive, but he was also nice. A potent combination. She took a sip of her wine, then put the glass on the end table near her.

"It's not too late, you know," she told him.

He frowned at her. "For what?"

"To be a part of your kids' lives again," she said. "But if you keep pushing them away, it'll be harder and harder."

"I'm not pushing them away."

"Are you pulling them closer?"

"They aren't at an age where they want to be close to a parent," he said. His voice sounded tense, on edge.

But Sam didn't care. "How do you know? They've gone through a lot in the last few years. Even if you don't think you need to be part of their lives, they may need to be part of yours. Kids need to be secure in their roots."

"That seems strange, coming from you," he snapped. "Considering you're denying one set of your roots."

She pulled away from him. "I'm not denying anybody."

"Are you accepting that both sets of parents had a role in who you are?"

"Of course, not that it takes me very far," she replied, a little terse herself. "What I know about my biological parents would fill a half sheet of paper—even in large print. And that's adding what Fiona and Cassie remember."

"Have you ever thought of looking for more? There have to be people out there who remember them."

"I couldn't do that to Dad."

Kevin just sighed—long and loud. "What if your parents had family that are still around? If you found them, you'd be giving a piece of your parents back to them. Think of how happy they'd be."

It was something she hadn't thought about before. Not quite like that, anyway. "My mother doesn't have any family left," she said slowly. "She grew up in South Bend and we looked, but I have no idea if my father has family around. He never talked about his past or his family, not even his friends."

"So find out." He took her hand in his. "You know where he came from?"

"An Indian reservation in South Dakota."

"Then check it out. Don't put it off." His grip on her hand tightened and his eyes drew hers to his. Their look was soft. Gentle. Kind. "Debbie's death taught me that we don't have forever. It's easy to put things off, but sometimes you put them off until it's too late."

"I know...."

She let her words trail off, as the air around her grew stuffy, filling with a growing tension. His eyes looked so serious and solemn. It would be so easy to get lost in those eyes, to rest there and follow his lead. But this was about more than herself.

"It's good advice for you, too," she told him.

"I suppose."

He sighed and, letting go of her hand, leaned his head back against the top of the sofa. "Have I been acting like John Wayne?"

"A little."

"And I've probably flunked my test, right?"

"Did you want to?" she asked. "I'm willing to grade on a curve."

He sat up, his eyes serious. "What are you saying? Are we going to give it a try?"

"Why not?" she countered, her heart suddenly in her throat, making it hard to breathe. "Just for fun."

"Sure," he said. "Just for fun."

But then she was in his arms and his lips on hers felt like anything but light, carefree fun. There were sparks in his touch and somehow the promise of freedom. She was soaring into the treetops, gliding on the night breezes even as her soul was on fire.

She wanted his embrace to go on forever, to last as long as the stars. She wasn't afraid to let her heart trust him. She wasn't worried about tomorrow or her goals or making everyone happy. There was only here and now and Kevin. Music swirled around her, like a thousand violins bursting into song. The beating of her heart tried to match the crescendo.

They pulled apart, both breathing hard. Their eyes were locked on each other, but still the music filled the air. Suddenly Sam began to laugh as she turned to the TV. *Fantasia* had started and was providing the musical accompaniment.

"I think we missed half the movie," she said.

"We can do it again."

The movie or the kiss? She just smiled at him and cuddled up to his side. "Sure." If they were to take a vote, hers would go for repeating the kiss. "Cassie's wedding is next Saturday. Would you like to come with me?"

"The brothers threatening to find you a date again?"

"Does the sun set in the west?"

He laughed and reached over to kiss the tip of her nose. "I'd love to come with you," he said.

"I really appreciate you helping with this," Cassie said as she carried a stack of boxes up the steps. Her fiancé's aunt Hattie was just behind her with another box. "I can't believe how much last-minute stuff there is to do before a wedding."

Sam held the front door open for the two of them, grabbing Toby out of their way. "You could have eloped," she replied. "No fuss. No muss."

"And half the world wouldn't speak to her again," Aunt Hattie said.

"I didn't think she would've cared."

"At this point, I don't think I would have." Cassie put the boxes on the entryway floor. "That's just a dent in the pile. There must be millions of silk flowers out there."

"Millions?" Sam repeated with a laugh. "Is it too late to back out now? How about if I remember I was supposed to work today?"

"You do, and you're dead meat."

Aunt Hattie just shook her head. "She's been like that all day."

Sam just laughed some more. "Boy, and here I was afraid love and pregnancy was mellowing her."

They carried in the rest of the boxes. Then, while Sam and Cassie spread the silk flowers out over the living-room floor, Aunt Hattie went into the kitchen. She brought back a glass of iced tea and a glass of milk, plus a plate of muffins that smelled wonderful.

"Milk?" Cassie protested when Aunt Hattie handed her that glass. "I don't even like milk."

"Don't matter none," Aunt Hattie said. "Your baby does."

Cassie just made a face and turned to Sam. "She does that to me all the time. I'm waiting for her to say the baby wants me to clean out my refrigerator or do the laundry."

Sam just laughed and helped herself to one of the muffins. They were still warm from the oven. "I think it's great, Aunt Hattie. We never could make her do anything she didn't want to do, so I say go for it."

"What I'm going to go for is the kitchen," Aunt Hattie said. "If you're still sure it's okay for me to bake the cookies here."

"Sure," Sam told her and nodded at the muffin. "For another one of these, you can have the kitchen."

Aunt Hattie just smiled and went back through the swinging door.

"It was really nice of you to let her use your kitchen," Cassie said. "I guess these little wedding cookies are some tradition in Jack's family, but she wants them to be a surprise."

"I think that's sweet." Sam pulled over a pile of silk flowers and began to wind the flowers into garlands that would decorate the house on Saturday for the wedding. "So, are you excited?"

"Yes."

Cassie's smile was soft and secretive—and awoke longings in Sam to feel that way about someone. She plucked another rose from the pile.

"Fiona called last night," Sam said. "Alex's cousin died. She said they'd be back Thursday. Said I should tell you not to worry. She wouldn't miss your wedding."

"It was too bad about Alex's cousin."

"Yes."

They worked in silence for a while, the garlands growing longer and longer. And growing larger and larger in Sam's mind were questions she'd never even thought to ask.

"Do you ever feel funny talking about our first parents?" Sam asked suddenly.

"Funny?" Cassie just frowned at her.

"You know." Sam shrugged. "Like you were being disloyal to the Scotts."

"Not really." Cassie finished up one thirty-foot length and coiled it along the far wall. "Dad always seemed to feel if we'd be happier knowing, then we should try to find out."

"I guess." Sam stared down at the flowers in her lap. "There's not much to know, though, is there? I mean, Mom didn't have any family but us and we don't know much of anything about Dad."

"Except where he was from."

"Yes." Sam twisted one of the roses around her finger like a ring. "Did you ever think he might have family somewhere other than the reservation?"

Cassie frowned. "I suppose he might. I hadn't thought much about the possibility of relatives."

"Do you think they knew he was killed?"

"I don't know. I don't think so. If there were relatives to notify, wouldn't you think we would have been sent to them?"

"True."

Sam slid her rose ring off her finger and leaned back against the sofa. Toby had come over to sniff at the fake flowers. The idea of a family—parents, even—waiting forever for some news of her dad nagged at her.

Since Cassie had recently found out that their father had changed his name when he'd left home, it sounded like he had wanted to cut all ties with his past. Did that mean his family too? But had they wanted to cut ties with him? Even if they had, they deserved to know he had died. And that he had a family.

"I was thinking of trying to find out if there are still relatives of his around," Sam said.

"I think that's great," Cassie replied. "Have you told Dad or Fiona?"

"Nope. Just you."

"How will you start?"

"Maybe with copies of the information Jack got for you about where our father was from."

"Sure. And Fiona's got a copy of the accident report from when Mom and Dad were killed."

"I'll ask her for it when she gets back." Sam picked up another silk rose and began entwining them again. Maybe she wouldn't tell Dad just yet. After all, she might not find anything and he would be hurt for no reason.

"So, how are things with you and your banker?" Cassie asked.

"Fine."

"You bringing him to the wedding?"

"Yes."

"To keep Larry from fixing you up with somebody?"

Sam paused like a diver about to plunge off the high board. "Nope," she admitted carefully. "Because I wanted to bring him."

Larry had nothing to do with her invitation, Sam realized. She'd asked Kevin simply because she wanted to share the event with him.

"Sounds serious," Cassie teased.

Sam just twisted some more flowers together.

"Why don't you let me go up?" Kevin asked as Sam scampered up the stepladder, curtains draped over one arm. "I'm taller."

"Isn't that the whole purpose of ladders?" she teased. "To sort of even out the height advantage?"

"I wouldn't have to climb as high."

"I'm not afraid of heights."

"Were you always this stubborn?"

She glared down at him. "How often have you hung drapes?"

"I see. This is guy discrimination."

"No, it's drape-hanging discrimination," she said as she slipped the hooks into the carrier slides. "I've hung enough drapes to block out the sun from the Northern Hemisphere. I could do it in my sleep."

"If you're sleepy, climbing ladders is dangerous."

She slipped the last hooks into the master slide and leaned back against the top of the ladder, not even bothering to answer him. He'd been dropping by after work every few days, and spending the evening with her. It was fine with her. She liked having him around.

"Want to try closing the drapes?" she asked.

He went to the other end of the rod and pulled the cord. The drapes closed neatly, fitting just right. "Okay, you can open them again."

When she climbed down the ladder, he was there to steady it for her.

"You know, I was up and down this ladder all day without once tipping it over," she said.

"Then you're lucky I'm here," he told her. "The law of averages says you're due."

She just groaned. "I guess I should be grateful to you for saving my life, then."

"You should be," he said and moved a step closer. "The question is, just how grateful are you?"

She grinned. "Grateful enough to let you carry the ladder back downstairs?"

He shook his head. "Not good enough."

"How about letting you pick which window we do first in the dining room?"

"You don't have the hang of this being-grateful business, do you?"

"I take it you have a suggestion?"

"As a matter of fact, I do." He slid his arms around her and pulled her close. His lips came down on hers, and it was the sweetest kiss she'd ever had, full of laughter and lightness and the smiles in their hearts. It was like sunshine in the garden with the birds singing and the fragrance of the flowers dancing in the air. It was like being on top of the Ferris wheel with all the world at your feet.

But then the pressure of his lips changed. The wild beating of her heart made her breath catch and made all sorts of sparks go off in the pit of her stomach. Kevin's hands pulled her closer, pressing her up against his hard, muscled body.

She could feel his hunger in his lips and in his restless hands. She could feel her own needs eating away at her common sense until all she knew was the wonder of him next to her. The thin fabric of her blouse must have melted away from the heat of his touch. The fire was spreading, working its way over—

Suddenly, the noise of a car horn outside broke through and they pulled apart. Feeling like she'd just woken up from a deep sleep, Sam took a deep breath, then looked out the window.

"It's Fiona and Alex," she said, her voice ragged. "They're back."

"Sam!" Her father's voice came up the back stairs.

"We're coming!" she called back.

She and Kevin came down the stairs and hurried out the front door, her father following. Fiona was already out of their car, but instead of rushing to meet them, she opened the back door; and then stood aside to let two beautiful children—a girl about five and a boy who appeared to be about three—step out. The two kids were tightly clutching each other's hand. The look in their eyes was one Sam was all too familiar with from her own childhood.

"Everybody." Fiona knelt down and put her arms around the children. "This is Jennifer and Michael. They've agreed to come live with Alex and me and be our kids."

Their kids? Sam almost screeched out the question but didn't say a single word, didn't even flick an eyelash. Instead, she moved forward and squatted down before the two little ones. "Hi, guys. Welcome to the family."

The children murmured soft greetings but, after a quick glance at Sam, looked over at her father, their new grandfather.

"So, Dad," Fiona was saying. "Think you got room for two new grandchildren?"

"Always. You can never have enough."

The children, especially the girl, seemed to relax noticeably.

Sam's father smiled at the two kids. "You guys like chocolate-chip cookies?"

"Yes, sir," Jennifer replied.

"How about you, young man?" her father asked the little boy.

"Yes, sir," his sister answered for him. "He does, too."

"Then let's get in the house and have some before these—" he indicated the others with a flip of his head "—big kids do. They'll eat everything if you don't watch them."

Sam watched the three of them walk hand in hand toward the house. The kids seemed happy and relaxed in her father's presence. He had that kind of effect on children, she thought, remembering back to the first time they'd met.

A lump rose in her throat. He'd offered Cassie, Fiona and herself chocolate-chip cookies, too.

Sam knew they would love his cookies. Dan Scott's cookies were the greatest. He said they were a special recipe for calming a little kid's worries. Her eyes clouded up. They didn't work too badly for big kids either. Why in the world should she want to find out about her biological father when she already had the best father in the world? She shook her head and turned toward Fiona and Alex.

"So," she said briskly. "What in the world is going on?"

Fiona and Alex looked at each other. Sam stared in wonderment as they reached out to hug each other.

"We have a family," Fiona said.

"I gathered that." Sam went over to their car and leaned against it. "Are these your cousin's kids?" she asked Alex.

Alex nodded. "There were no other relatives who could take them."

"It must be tough for them, losing their parents and moving to a new home," Kevin said slowly. His arms slipped around Sam's shoulders. "But I guess you guys know what they're going through."

"Actually they only lost their mother," Fiona said slowly. "But their father has cancer. He's been spending more time in the hospital than out of it and knows he doesn't have much time left. He thought it would be better if they went with us now."

"Wow," Sam murmured. "That must have been tough for him." She leaned back into Kevin's arms, needing his security around her.

"He loves them so much," Fiona said, her voice cracking with emotion. "He wanted them to start healing and said they'd be much better off with us."

Alex nodded. "He's hoping to see the kids when he's able."

"The kids'll need it as much he will. And then his parents want to stay in touch, too. So we'll be taking them back there for visits."

They had it all worked out, Sam thought. Everyone was so willing to share the kids, so willing to give them everything they needed.

"Do the kids know what happened?" Sam asked.

"We told them," Alex replied. "Although we're not sure how much of all this Michael is comprehending. He's not quite three yet."

They fell silent and Sam thought back to her own childhood. She didn't know what Michael would remember, but she was sure that Jennifer would remember enough to be bothered by the things she couldn't recall.

"Well, let's see how our troop is faring," Alex said and took Fiona's hand.

She laughed. "You just want some of those chocolate-chip cookies," she teased, but allowed herself to be led up to the house.

Sam just watched them for a long moment, not moving out of Kevin's arms. Something was happening inside her that she didn't understand. She felt she was four years old again and her parents had just died. She felt a rush of that old fear that nothing would last, that even the strongest of foundations was only made of sand.

"You okay?" Kevin asked.

She forced herself to pull away from him and smile. "Sure, why not? I just got myself a new niece and nephew! Everything's great."

Chapter Nine

"They want to take pictures of the bridal party now," Sam told Kevin. "Why don't you stay here with my brothers?"

They were in the bed-and-breakfast's backyard. Tables were set up across the expanse of lawn while the house was bedecked with garlands of white roses. Cassie and Jack had been married a few minutes ago in a remarkably touching ceremony.

Kevin had never been quite so moved by someone else's wedding, and he'd been to a number of them over the past twenty years. Cassie and Jack were obviously in love, and their family was so happy for them, that Kevin couldn't help but see again just what a precious gift love was.

After the birdseed had been thrown and well wishes had been given, Sam took him over to the table where her three brothers were sitting. He'd met them and their wives earlier, but the women were all off somewhere and the men were just sitting back and relaxing, nursing their beers.

"You know everybody here, right?" she asked.

"Yes, I know everybody."

"This is Bobby, he's the oldest," Sam said as if he hadn't spoken. "This here is Adam. And that's Larry."

Did she know him well enough to know that he had gotten the names mixed up in his head? Scary thought. "Is there going to be a test?" he just asked.

She made a face at him. "I have to go. I just want to make sure you'll be all right."

"Oh, for heaven's sake, Sam." It was Bobby who spoke. "Don't worry. We'll take care of him."

"Yeah, if anyone tries to kidnap him, we'll pound on them."

"You guys are a barrel of laughs," Sam grumbled. "I don't see how your wives can stand you."

"On account we're so purty."

The brothers laughed heartily and Kevin had to smile as he sat down. It was a perfect wedding in a lot of ways—the weather, the love, and the relaxed, friendly atmosphere that pulled even a stranger like himself into the family.

"I'll be right back."

She patted him on the shoulder, then was charging off to be photographed. His eyes followed her across the yard, unable to deprive his heart of the joy of watching her. She was so full of life. So full of energy and wonder that it splashed onto everyone nearby, like the warm waters of a Hawaiian waterfall.

"You know, she's really a nice kid." This time it was Larry talking. "But there are times when she can drive a person flat out of his gourd."

"Hey, hey. Let's have none of that," Bobby said.

"We'll never get Sam married off with that kind of talk."

Kevin just smiled, seeing what Sam meant about her older siblings wanting to manage her life. "I'm not sure if Sam wants to get married off," he said.

"All women want to get married." The other brothers murmured agreement.

Kevin said nothing. Certainly many—maybe most—women wanted to get married. But he was sure that they wanted to choose the time and man. Not leave it up to their brothers.

"Beautiful day," Kevin said, trying to steer the conversation onto a more innocuous track.

"I'll say," Bobby agreed. "We're lucky the rain held off."

Kevin took a deep breath and savored the late summer day. A few of the leaves had colored but it would be another couple of weeks before they came into their full glory. Still, it was beautiful.

"This is a nice place for a wedding," he said. "Nice big lawn. Pleasant view."

"Yeah, Fiona got married here, too."

"Well, not really here," Adam corrected. "On the other side of the lake, in Clements Woods."

"Oh." Kevin nodded. "Well, that's a nice—"

"Yeah," Bobby said. "If you can't bring the swans to the wedding, then you bring the wedding to the swans."

"The swans?" Kevin stared dumbly at the brothers as they chuckled knowingly. "I don't understand."

"You mean Sam hasn't told you the great swan story yet?" Larry asked.

"Yeah," Adam added. "They saved their lives."

"Who saved whose life?" Kevin asked.

"The girls saved the swans' lives. One of them—the female, I think—was stuck in some trash in the lake. The girls cut them free."

"Yeah, and now they're responsible for them."

Kevin looked quizzically from one brother to the other.

"Don't worry, she'll tell you."

"Unless she doesn't want to."

"Well, that's how we'll know if he's in."

"Hey, that's right." Bobby turned toward him, smiling. "Once you hear the swan story, you might as well set the date."

Kevin wasn't sure that he cared for the direction the conversation was going in—again. He and Sam did not want that kind of relationship. He leaned back and let his eyes take in the yard. He could see where Sam had planted the day lilies. Come next spring, they would provide a nice swatch of color in all that surrounding green.

"Sam says you went to Indiana University."

Kevin brought himself back to the table and turned toward the trio of brothers. "Yes, I did."

"What part of Indiana are you from?" Larry asked.

"Actually, I'm from Illinois," Kevin replied. "The Chicago area. But my late wife wanted to go to IU, so that's where I went. Besides, they gave me a track scholarship."

"You've been married before?"

Kevin nodded. "Yes, my wife died a couple of years ago." The three of them murmured condolences.

"What was it—an accident?"

"No." He shook his head. "Cancer."

"That's tough."

"For a young woman to go like that."

"It's tough at any age," Kevin said.

A silence fell on them. Normal, when a conversation turned to such topics, so Kevin just let it ride out. The laughter coming from the wedding party as they posed for pictures made them turn in that direction. Cassie's husband had twin daughters who had also been in the wedding party and the girls seemed prone to fits of giggling. Fiona's new additions—Jennifer and Michael—were off to one side, but giggling along with the twins. Obviously, they were all sharing some secret joke.

The photo group appeared to be dissolving and Sam was now hurrying over in Kevin's direction. He smiled. She had the ability to light up the darkest night. How was it that she bothered with him?

"I'm a Purdue grad, myself." It was Adam who spoke. "But my boss graduated from IU."

Kevin nodded, his attention still on Sam. Her dress was a deep red, like the leaves on that old oak in his backyard would be in another few weeks. But there was nothing of autumn about her. Her glow was all springtime and life.

"What year did you graduate?"

Sam was drawing closer and Kevin could feel his smile growing—as well as a certain tension that made his senses seem sharper and his hungers deeper. He only barely heard Larry's question.

"I was in the class of '78," Kevin replied.

"Nineteen seventy-eight!"

Kevin turned from watching Sam and looked at her brothers as she stepped into their midst.

"Hi, all."

"Hi," Kevin replied.

"You guys been behaving?" she asked.

"Oh, sure."

But the brothers said nothing. Slowly, it dawned on Kevin. They were doing the subtracting and didn't like the answer. Having their "baby" sister going out with an "older" man obviously was not to their liking.

"Boy," Sam said, "am I hungry."

"Hungry enough to eat a horse?" Kevin asked.

"Not really," she replied. "But I'm ready for some chicken."

Kevin looked around and noticed that her brothers still seemed rather tight around the edges. Well, that was too bad. Sam was a big girl and she could make decisions on her own. And if they wanted to start anything, that was just fine and dandy with him.

"Doesn't Cassie look pretty?" Sam asked. "She's just glowing."

Not nearly as brightly as Sam, Kevin thought. She outshone every woman at the wedding.

"We need a meeting," Bobby said to his brothers as the last of the wedding guests pulled out of the driveway.

Cassie and Jack had left hours ago and Kevin had just departed, so it was only family remaining. Jack's twins were playing with Jennifer and Michael while Aunt Hattie was sitting down near the lake, keeping an eye on them. Fiona and Alex were putting the wedding gifts in the house while the brothers' wives were helping Dad package up the remains the caterer had left. The brothers themselves were stacking the folding chairs in the rack the rental service had provided.

Sam had kicked off her shoes and was taking the garlands off the porch rail near where the boys were working. She was tired. It had been a long couple of weeks, and the last thing she wanted was a serious discussion on anything. And judging from her oldest brother's voice, he was definitely thinking serious. Big time.

Sam stretched her legs out and wiggled her feet. "What do we need a family meeting for?" she asked. "Fiona's taking care of Cassie's dog. And if something comes up, we'll go over and get Ollie."

"This has nothing to do with Cassie's dog."

Lord, Bobby could be so annoying at times. She didn't care what was bothering him. She was relaxing this evening, even if she had to bash a few heads and kick some butts to do it.

"Well, we don't have to do anything with her store," Sam said. "Burt's in charge while Cassie is gone."

"Damn it, Sam," Larry protested. "This has nothing to do with Cassie. She's married."

She looked from one solemn face to another and her tiredness faded away as anger flared. "Back off, you big lugs. My life is my own. So stay out of it."

Their faces tightened up, like the three of them were controlled by the same string.

"I mean it," she said. "I can manage my own life."

"Do you know how old that banker fella is?" Bobby demanded.

That banker fella? Didn't they know Kevin had a name?

"What's Kevin's age got to do with anything?" she asked. "He's a very competent banker."

"He's a lot older than you are," Adam replied.

"Hasn't hurt his banking any." And she doubted it hurt anything he did, but she thought it wiser not to get into that right now.

Although she was tempted. Sam could feel her ears grow hot as her anger grew. Too bad Cassie had left so soon. She'd always been better when it came to beating up on their brothers.

"He's fourteen years older than you," Larry said.

"Thirteen," Sam snapped.

She had no sooner spat the word out than her whole face felt on fire. She felt like some stupid little kid, arguing about something that was none of anybody's business but her own.

"Fiona and I have to go over and pick Ollie up," she said, standing. "He's probably chewing the house up by now."

"Sam, please listen."

Bobby had swapped his mad look for a sincere one, but Sam was still irritated. These guys had always been butting into her life. She didn't need it. She didn't want it. And she wasn't going to have it.

"The meeting's over, Bobby."

She was about to slip her shoes back on but decided the hell with them. Her feet hurt enough already. The people cleaning up the yard could just take them and throw them out.

"Sam."

"It's really none of your business who I go out with!" She caught herself, suddenly aware that she'd been shouting. A few more words and their father would be coming over. There was no need for that. This had been a happy day for him as well as Cassie, and Sam wasn't going to spoil it.

"I can take care of myself," she said quietly.

"Sam!"

She wanted to get away but Bobby's voice was so loud that she was sure Dad would think something was wrong. So she paused, but she didn't turn to look at her brothers.

"He'll be fifty years old when you're just thirty-six."

Sam spun on her heel. "Kevin's wife didn't make it to thirty-six."

They stared at her.

"No one knows what's going to happen in the future," she said. "So it's rather stupid to pretend that it's all cast in stone."

"Look, Sam," Larry said. "I know we're not talking absolutes, here. But the probability of—"

"Mom was nine years younger than Dad," Sam said softly. "And now he's all alone."

She waited for a reply. She dared them to say anything. But nobody did. Sam turned and stomped away from them.

God, this was one of those times when she wished she were an only child. Were her brothers' own lives so dull that they had nothing better to do than meddle in hers?

"The wedding was really nice," Kevin said.

Sam paused, her sandwich half in her mouth, and searched his eyes for any hidden meanings. She saw none.

"Yeah, it was," she said. Maybe her brothers hadn't said anything to him. Hard as that was to believe, it was a possibility.

"Cassie and Jack are lucky to have found each other."

"I think they know it," Sam agreed.

"That is what makes it so special," he said.

They ate in silence for a time. Sam was surprised by his insight; most men that she knew would have talked about the food or the weather or the college football games they were missing. But then Kevin was not like most of the other men she knew. The more time she spent with him, the more she realized that.

"Want a refill on your iced tea?" he asked.

"Nope, I'm fine."

He took his own glass and went back inside the little Amish sandwich shop. They'd been having lunch here together on an almost-regular basis now, even claiming this outside table as their own. Although that would change once the weather did. Autumn was here and then winter would be—

"Place is crowded lately," Kevin said, coming back to their table. "Want to try that new Chinese restaurant tomorrow?"

She shook her head. "I'm taking the rest of the week off. The bed-and-breakfast is opening Friday and there's still a mountain of things to do."

"Need help?" he asked. "I've got some vacation days left—"

"No, don't be silly," she said quickly, even though she would have loved to have him at her side. "Save it to do something fun. Something with your kids."

He frowned at her. "They're in school."

"Don't they get a fall break? They certainly get Thanksgiving and Christmas off."

"And they probably already have plans for them," he said. He drank down his iced tea and gathered up the remains of his lunch. "It's not like we don't spend some time together over the holidays, but they always have set up plans with their friends."

"Maybe because you have nothing set up."

He got to his feet. "Are you done with your lunch?" he asked and picked up her scraps along with his.

She took her cup and the napkins to the trash with him. "I bet they'd love to take a trip someplace before classes start up again after Christmas. That way you could still have Christmas Day with your in-laws and time with the kids."

He bent down suddenly, as if offering her a good view of his hair. "Want to just pull me across the countryside and be done with it?" he asked.

"Huh?" What was he talking about?

He straightened. "Isn't that what you said John Wayne did in one of his hated movies—dragged some woman across the countryside?"

"I wasn't being John Wayne," she protested, then frowned at him. "Was I?"

"Just a little." He took her arm and led her down the block. "Want to walk around a little before we go back to work?"

"Sure." She fell in step next to him, letting her hand find his. "I didn't mean to sound officious."

"I know." They crossed the street and wandered into a little park area with fountains. "So, have you done anything about looking for your father's family?" he asked.

"What's this—tit for tat?" she asked with a laugh.

"Well, if you get to play John Wayne, don't I get a turn, too?" They sat on a bench that surrounded the largest of the fountains. "It only seems fair."

She leaned back, letting the midday sun spill over her face. A gentle spray of water from the fountain hit her back. "As a matter of fact, I made some calls," she admitted.

"Really?"

It was strange. If it had been any of her siblings asking if she'd followed one of their suggestions, she would have put them off; refused to admit that she had taken their advice. But she didn't mind making such a confession to Kevin. She didn't feel like she had anything to prove to him.

"There's some sort of tribal council that keeps records for the reservation," she told him. "But even if his family didn't live there, they might have a record of them. Depends on how active they were in tribal activities and rituals.''

"Sounds promising.''

She just shrugged. "It has potential, but I'm not getting my hopes up at all.''

"Did you call them?''

She shook her head. "I wrote. They want all inquiries in writing.''

"So you have to wait it out.''

"It's not so bad," she admitted. "I have lots to do in the meantime with the inn.''

"My offer still holds.''

Sam laughed and got to her feet. "I've got to get back to work. Thanks for lunch.''

"Thanks for the company.'' He got to his feet also and took a step closer to her. "I suppose I should also thank you for the advice—''

"That you won't take.''

"I think it's really sweet of you to offer.''

"I haven't been accused of being sweet in a long time.''

"Well, I think you are.'' He slipped his arms around her, pulling her into a light embrace. "And I have to admit that I like someone bossing me around once in a while.''

"I'm available anytime," she said. Her arms went around his waist. "You feel the need to be bossed, you just call me.''

"I'll remember that.''

His mouth came down to meet hers, bringing a feather-light touch of heaven. She felt all the joy of Christmas and birthdays and laughter swirl around her. The sun was no match for the warmth that was bursting forth from her heart. She wanted it to engulf both of them. She wanted it to draw them closer and closer until their souls felt no fear.

But they were in downtown South Bend, at high noon, and Kevin was already pulling away. Her lips ached to feel his longer, stronger, deeper.

"Dinner tonight?'' he asked.

She shook her head, her heart suddenly heavy. "I don't think I can spare an evening this week. We've got lots of help," she quickly added. "But I need to be there."

"I think it's getting to be time for the bank to do another checkup, don't you?" he asked.

"As long as 'the bank' isn't using its vacation time to do so."

"The bank is not to be questioned."

"The bank is not above my scrutiny."

"You are a tough critic."

She reached up to plant a quick kiss on his lips. "Nope. I have it on good authority that I'm sweet." She grinned at him. "See ya."

She hurried off, back to work, conscious that his eyes were following her. And conscious that somehow her heart was lingering behind in the sweetness of his gaze. She turned the corner with a mixture of longing and relief.

Chapter Ten

"Darn nice of the boys to bring some extra hands along," Sam's father said. "Now we're sure to be in good shape for tomorrow."

She and her father were standing in the hall looking into the kitchen, where Sam's brothers and some of their friends were sipping coffee and munching on sweet rolls. And, as coincidence would have it, each friend looked to be in his late twenties or early thirties. It was just too much. Sam felt her jaw muscles go tight.

"And on a Thursday evening, too," her father continued. "They've all got work tomorrow."

Her father might be taken in but she wasn't ready to anoint anybody into sainthood. "I'm not so sure it's all that great," Sam said. "We'll have to wait and see if they're able to get off their duffs and do any work."

"Sam, it's only right to feed the boys first. After all, they are donating their muscle."

"We don't have much left to do that requires muscle," Sam observed.

He stood there and looked at her for a long moment. Sam would have loved to stare her father down but there wasn't even a trace of irritation in his soft, loving eyes. She quickly turned away.

"Sam," he said gently. "This isn't like you. Don't you feel good?"

"I feel fine," she said briskly as she forced a smile onto her face. "I think I'll start making the beds."

"I'll see if the boys want anything else," he said with a quick nod and a smile. "And then I'll put them to work."

"Dad, I didn't mean—"

But he was gone before she could finish. Maybe that was just as well. She went upstairs and got the linen cart out of the storage closet.

In order to keep peace in the family, Sam figured that it would be best to stay away from her brothers and their friends. She went into the two-room suite in the southwest corner of the house to begin making up the beds. All the furniture was in place and there was no need for any testosterone-fueled muscle. She slipped earphones onto her head and turned on her tape player before getting to work.

This nonsense with her brothers and their friends was really stupid. What was she supposed to do? Pick one of the three friends and send the others home?

"I pick bachelor number two," she muttered under her breath and briskly snapped a sheet out over the bed. "Yeah, right."

What was really funny was that she didn't know the men her brothers had brought along. Apparently they'd decided to bring in some new blood, figuring that she had already rejected the friends she'd previously met.

That was really stupid. It wasn't like she'd rejected anybody. She'd just had other things in her life. And still did. It wasn't that she and Kevin were super serious about their relationship. He was just a nice guy and she enjoyed his company. No more, no less.

Suddenly there was a light touch on her arm and she screamed, almost jumping out of her skin. "Why are you sneaking up on me like that?" she shouted at Larry.

"I wasn't sneaking up on you," her brother protested. "You probably have your tape player turned up too loud."

"I do not." She glared at him.

Larry rolled his eyes up at the ceiling and shook his head. "I just wanted to introduce you to Clark."

"Clark?"

"Clark Wiggins," the man at Larry's side said. "Not Clark Kent."

Sam looked at him. Clark was a blond, blue-eyed almost-hunk. Nice looking, in a boyish sort of way. "That's good," she said. "Because we don't have any phone booths."

"Phone booths?"

Both men uttered the words, looking bewildered, but Clark smiled first. "Oh, I get it," he said.

Score one for old Clark Wiggins who, at the moment, seemed a little swifter than her brother Larry. But nowhere near as swift as Kevin.

The words had barely began to echo in her mind when Sam felt ashamed. That wasn't fair. She and Kevin were beginning to get to know each other. Their minds seemed to travel on the same wavelengths. Plus, Kevin had never been pushed on her by her brothers. There was no way that Clark What's-His-Name could compete.

"What do you guys want?" Sam suddenly felt very tired. "I have a lot of work to do."

"That's why we're here, Sam," Larry said. "We want to help you."

Yeah, right. Help her get a date so that she'd never have to go out with that old graybeard, Kevin Delaney.

"Fine." She felt her tone growing sharp but figured, the heck with it. She didn't start any of this. "Take some sheets and make the beds in the suite across the hall."

"Darn it, Sam. Why don't—"

"Come on, Larry," Clark said. "We can do that."

Clark didn't sound like too bad a guy. He was probably even a nice guy. Or maybe he just sounded good compared to her brother.

"Just go—"

"Hi, sis." Bobby stepped into the room with his prize. "How're things going?"

Before Sam had a chance to groan, Adam and his buddy came in, too. The six of them were all standing there, staring at her. The weariness in Sam's body was being pushed out by a growing irritation. She wasn't thinking of groaning anymore; she wanted to scream.

"Get out of here. All of you."

For a moment, six pairs of eyes stared at her. Then her brother Bobby spoke up. "It's okay. She's been working hard lately. And she's been getting a little tense."

She glared at him. Yelling wasn't very nice. Besides, it wasn't doing any good. She would be better off wringing his neck.

"And you know—" Bobby shrugged and lowered his voice "—it's probably that time of the month."

He was going to die. Right here and now. Her eyes searched the room for something heavy enough to bash in his skull with, but light enough for her to lift.

"Hello." Kevin stood in the doorway to the suite, holding a big bunch of yellow roses.

"Jiggers, guys," Bobby said. "It's the banker."

Kevin's eyes calmly swept the room while her brothers glared at him and their buddies exchanged puzzled glances. Sam wondered how much her brothers had told their companions. Based on her own experience, she figured whatever they'd said was too much.

Kevin turned his attention back to Sam. "I just dropped by to see how things were going."

"Oh, yeah?" Bobby sneered. "Are you sure you didn't just come by to evict our sister? You know, like foreclose on her mortgage."

Sam went over and took Kevin's hand, pulling him over to her side of the room. "Don't pay attention to him. He's just a little on edge today." She let her voice drop down to a hoarse stage whisper. "It's that time of the month."

A smile peeked around the corners of Kevin's mouth, warming Sam's heart. Unfortunately, Bobby's face was also getting red. That meant trouble ahead. Big trouble.

"Bobby," she said. "You guys go downstairs and find something useful to do."

"Who died and made you boss?" Bobby retorted loudly.

"What are you folks up to?"

Her father's voice was soft and gentle but brought instant quiet. His eyes swept around everyone, then settled on Bobby, the eldest.

"I need a few of you fellas to move some boxes into the storage closet up here. A couple more can trim the grass around our sign." Then he turned to Sam. "You have enough help up here with the beds?"

"Yes, sir."

She suddenly felt eight years old; somewhat in awe of that stern but gentle voice. And also glad to see her brothers get their comeuppance.

"How many flowers you got there?" her father asked, turning to Kevin. "A dozen?"

Kevin nodded.

"You know," her father said, "one of those roses in each room would be nice."

"I don't think we have enough vases," Sam told him.

Her father stepped out into the hall, giving her a quick wink before hurrying away. "Adam, we need a dozen bud vases, all the same kind."

The rest of the conversation drifted away as her father went after her brother. Her father liked Kevin. She was sure of it. Not that it mattered any. And not that it should matter. But it was nice to see.

"So where do you want me to start?" Kevin asked.

"Is this that bank checkup you mentioned?"

"Yep." He bent down as if checking the tautness of the sheet she'd spread over the bed. "We want to make sure you're handling things all right."

"And how are my bed-making skills?"

"Adequate."

"Just adequate?"

He stood and was somehow right next to her. Close enough for her to hear the racing of his heart. Close enough to feel the tension in his gaze.

"We have very strict standards at the bank," he said, his eyes imprisoning hers.

His voice was so low that it seemed only her heart could hear him. And how her heart ached to answer. She wanted to let her lips touch his and whisper words of love and longing into his soul. She wanted her hands to feel the wonder and strength of him. She wanted to breathe in that faint scent of mint that surrounded him, the heat that vibrated in the air around them.

"And can I ever measure up?"

"I'm sure," he said softly. "With the right guidance."

"Hands-on training?"

"Of course."

"We should start soon."

"Before bad habits creep in."

"Come on, Larry," a male voice from the hallway snapped. "Hold that end up."

"I am," Larry snapped back.

Sam practically jumped away from Kevin, then grinned ruefully at him. "I don't know why I did that," she said. "I don't care if my brothers see us together."

"We could arrange that," he said, his eyes gleaming.

But she shook her head. "Then we'll never get this place ready to open."

His sigh was long and loud. "So, what do you want me to do? Start with the pillows?"

Sam went back to the bed, snapping another sheet over the first one. "You don't really have to do anything."

"Haven't I ever told you? I never do anything I have to."

Sam laughed. "What are you, the James Dean of the banking world?"

"He was from Indiana, you know."

"Yes, I know," she replied. "But so what?"

He stepped close to her, very close. His hand went behind her as he bent near. "So we have something in common."

Suddenly it was hard to breathe. Hard to even think. Maybe it wasn't such a good idea for Kevin to stay up here, helping her make the beds.

"Here are some extra towels," Sam said as she patted the pile on the dresser. "And there are extra blankets in the closet. Just call if you need anything else."

"Thank you," the older man said. "I'm sure we'll be just fine."

"Oh, Gene, come look!" his wife called to him from the window. "There are swans down in the lake. Come look."

Sam just smiled and shut the bedroom door on her way out. The place was humming today. She'd never seen the windows shine so or the woodwork look so rich. The rooms seemed cozy and warm, the halls seemed filled with sunshine. With all the guests arriving, it was as if the house was coming alive.

Sam smiled at the thought. Like *she* had come alive since knowing Kevin. She seemed to laugh more, seemed to skip through each day. Seemed to have this urge to burst into song. Her smile turned into a grin. Now, that would startle the customers.

She hurried down the stairs to find her dad refilling the big coffee urn in the dining room. She snuck a cookie off the tray.

"Romeo and Juliet are doing their part," she told him. "That's the third couple that's been at the windows oohing and ahing over them."

"How much bread did you have to hide along the shore to get them to come out?" her father teased.

"None at all," she said. "Maybe they're finally just paying me back for my part in the rescue."

Her father shook his head. "I thought they were supposed to help you fight for your love, not put on a show for overnight guests."

Sam heard some voices in the living room, as if guests were arriving, and grabbed another cookie as she started toward the door. "I'll settle for the show."

"That's your problem," her father muttered after her. "You're too willing to settle for less than you deserve. Ask your banker friend. He'll tell you it ain't good business."

She just laughed and hurried out. Kevin was greeting a young couple and winked at her as she slipped around him into the office. It was great of him to come over to help out. She put the extra cookie by his chair when he turned back to the couple.

"Now, if you'll just sign here . . ." he said and pointed to the form. "And here."

"This is really a lovely place," the woman was saying. "I can't believe that we're so close to town."

"Now, if you'll just guarantee that the University will win the football game tomorrow . . ." the man said.

Kevin just laughed. "I'm afraid that all we can do is guarantee you a room for the weekend. The team'll have to win on its own."

They all laughed as Kevin handed them their receipt. Sam selected a room key.

"If you'll come this way," she said, "I'll show you to your room."

The man picked up the luggage while Sam led the way down the far hall. The woman was at her side.

"You and your husband just open this place?" the woman asked.

Sam blinked. "Husband?"

"Yes, the—" Suddenly the woman laughed. "Ah, sorry. Let me rephrase that. You guys just opened this place, huh?"

Now Sam found herself laughing as she opened the door to their suite. "He's my banker."

The woman came to a complete stop, her eyes opening wide. "Banker? Oh, wow. How did you get a banker like that?"

"I beg your pardon?" Sam felt that she and her guest were talking on two different frequencies. "What do you mean 'get'? And like what?"

"Well, I mean— Oh, God." The woman rolled her eyes heavenward. "This isn't coming out right at all." She cleared her throat. "He doesn't look like a banker."

"Oh." Sam nodded. "He usually dresses more formally, but he was over here helping out. So he dressed down." She shrugged. "You know. Slacks. No tie. Comfortable shoes."

"Ah, yes." The woman took a step and then stopped again. "Honey, you couldn't hide all that testosterone under a tent." Then, waggling her fingers, she hurried into the suite with her husband trailing behind.

Sam managed to smother her laughter until she was back in the living room. But the woman was right—Kevin couldn't hide his manliness, even with a tent.

His eyebrows went up as she came toward him, still chuckling. "They find their room funny?" he asked.

She shook her head. "Nope. We were just discussing camping equipment."

He looked puzzled but let it pass. "Well, that was the last of the reservations," he said. "Guess you're not going to have any no-shows."

"Great." She sat on the wide worktable along the far wall.

He dropped down into a chair across from her and leaned forward on his elbows, exuding the calm of a lion. The kind where the person knew they were the strongest so they didn't have to show off. Her breath was suddenly hard to come by, her heart was suddenly racing.

She looked away and tried to think calming thoughts. "It's nice to know we're filled through the weekend."

"Your guests have paid for the weekend," Kevin corrected. "Most of them probably won't stay all three nights. In fact, if the University team loses, most of them will be heading back right after tomorrow's game."

Sam made a small face and picked up the credit-card receipts. "I know."

"That shouldn't be a problem," he said. "You had all of them pay for three nights up front, right?"

"Yes." She slipped the receipts into the cash box and put it into a drawer. "I know that's the way it is on game weekends, but I feel guilty charging people for something they might not use."

"That's okay," he said. "Feel guilty. It looks good on you."

She looked at him then, quickly snapping a frown in place.

"I mean, it's cute."

"Lean over a little closer," she said, shaking a fist at Kevin. "And I'll show you 'cute.'"

"Oh, what's this?" He took her wrist as he leaned closer and squinted at her fist. "I think I need glasses. I'm having a hard time making the shape out."

"Ha, ha. Ho, ho."

He covered her fist with his other hand, so much larger than hers, and looked into her eyes, smiling softly. "Now I don't see anything at all."

The touch of his hand was doing crazy things to the air in the room. Crazy things to her ability to think. But strangely it didn't change her ability to feel. "You may not see it," she said, "but you're sure going to feel it."

"Big talker," he murmured.

"Hey," she replied. "When you're my size, you take 'big' where you can find it."

His hand caressed hers as his eyes caressed her soul. He leaned forward slightly, somehow pulling her closer as he did so. There was no escaping him, even if she had wanted to. Which Sam didn't.

He owned the air she breathed, the light she saw by, the sounds that bombarded her. She could only move as he willed her to, only feel what he allowed her to feel. Only sing the songs of happiness that he placed on her lips.

Ever so slowly she slid into his arms. His mouth took possession of hers, drawing from the very depths of her soul all her dreams and hopes and wild wishes. With a magic that came only from his touch, he brought the stars down to lie at her feet and grant her every wish. But she wanted only for those same stars to dance around him; to bring the light back into his eyes and the fire back into his heart.

She wanted to see him laugh with a laughter free of memories. She wanted to see him smile without any shadows of yesterday lurking in his eyes. She wanted to erase not his past, but his pain. She wanted him to take joy in what he'd had but also in what he was having. She wanted him to believe in the future.

What was happening to her? How had her hopes and dreams gotten so tangled up with him?

"Excuse me." Her father's voice came between them, splitting them apart. "Hate to barge in here like this, but I wondered how we were doing."

Sam only loosened her hold on Kevin, not able to break the bond completely. "Everybody's here," she said.

"Then why don't you two take off?" he suggested. "Between me and Beth and Melanie, we can manage anything that comes up."

"Beth and Melanie?" Kevin repeated. "Someone else bring back some kids?"

Sam just laughed and lay back in his arms. "They're the two teenagers we hired to help out," she said, then turned back to her father. "Are you sure you don't need any more help?"

"Like the kind you were just giving each other?" he asked. "Naw, I think I can manage without it."

Sam slipped from Kevin's arms, but took his hand in hers. "Well, if you're sure."

She needed to be alone with Kevin; her heart had to explore the new directions it was taking. It wasn't frightening, this new frontier ahead of her, but knowing there was someone else on her horizon did take some getting used to.

"We'll grab some dinner and I'll have her back early," Kevin told her father.

"Don't hurry her back on my account," he replied. "She needs to let the swans work their magic."

"Dad!" Sam scolded, even as she gave him a quick kiss in passing. "See you later."

"What was that all about?" Kevin asked as they got into the Jeep.

"Old family joke," she said. "You know the kind. They aren't the slightest bit funny except to a parent."

"I see." But his voice said he was still curious.

Not that it would make her tell him. The only magic she wanted from the swans was what they'd done today—enchanted the guests so that they would be back for future visits.

"Are you sure you don't want to go out?" Kevin asked, his refrigerator door standing open. "I haven't got much in here."

"I'm not that hungry," she said and slipped around him to look inside. "Hot dogs. Eggs. Pickles. Celery. We could make a really weird omelet."

He just laughed as he pushed the door shut, then let his arms slide around her from the back, pulling her up against the length of him. She cuddled closer, but found it was not nearly enough. She turned in his arms, wrapping hers around his waist and laying her head against his chest.

She remembered his first few visits to the house, when she'd worried that his magic male rays would zap her into submission. Well, they had. They'd zapped her good and hard, and she thought it was the best thing that had happened to her in ages.

"I do have some frozen microwave dinners," he said. "A reasonable selection, in fact."

"Is that all you can think about?" she teased. "You have a beautiful young woman in your arms and you're thinking frozen dinner?"

He looked down into her eyes with a steady gaze that sent fire into her blood. "That's *why* I'm thinking dinner," he replied. "I can't afford to go weak at the wrong moment. She might trade me in on a newer model."

"Never," she said and reached up to brush his lips with hers. "I like quality, not flash."

He frowned. "I might have some flash left in me, you know."

"Wow," she teased. "Quality and flash. I certainly am a lucky lady."

"You certainly are."

When his lips took hers, all joking disappeared. There was a fever in the air, a hunger that consumed them both. A need to be one that could not be denied any longer. His mouth was hot and demanding, asking for a sweetness that would bring him peace and joy. His hands slid over her back, then slipped under her shirt. They felt hot and fiery against her skin, but wonderfully so.

She opened her mouth to his pressure and their tongues danced and dueled. Needs blended into a throbbing pulse that warmed all her parts. Thoughts faded into nothingness along with time and sanity as her heart took control. She was a foggy night, drifting and gliding with the darkness. She was him and he was her; each uncertain where one began and the other left off. Their needs were one, as were their hearts.

He pulled back slightly. His dark eyes glowed and gleamed, their sparks hot enough to singe even the bravest of souls.

"Maybe we ought to take a look at those frozen dinners," he said.

"If you want to risk it."

He looked confused and she laughed.

"We're liable to melt everything in the freezer," she said.

He slowly let her go, his reluctance obvious. "I'll risk it. Maybe the cold air will bring some sanity."

"Do we want it?"

"I don't know." His eyes searched hers like a drowning man searching for rescue. "Do we?"

She reached up, tracing the outline of his lips with her finger. Her touch was light, barely there at all, yet she could feel the quiver go right through him. The charge from her gentle caress had touched his soul.

"I don't want to be alone tonight," she said simply. "I want to be held and touched and loved. You don't have to promise me forever. Just tonight."

He captured her hand, bringing it to his lips as if he couldn't bear not to be touching some part of her. "I'm not a one-night-stand type of guy," he said.

"Well, I'm not a one-night-stand type of woman," she said.

"I thought we were in this just for fun."

She let her gaze capture his, let her eyes tell him all the things that her lips couldn't say. Let her heart speak to his without their words getting in the way. She wanted to tell him how alive she felt with him, how he made her feel whole. How she'd always seemed to drift, not certain what she wanted. Until now.

She couldn't say the things that lay deepest in her heart— that he had become her world and she hadn't even known it until this very moment. That standing here in his arms, she realized just how much he'd come to mean to her. That his happiness was her lifeblood and his smile her sunshine. That she was no longer in it for fun, but for keeps.

Instead, she just pulled back away from him. Maybe they were moving too fast. She was no great expert at relationships.

"All right," she said. "So let's look at this great collection of frozen meals you have."

"I didn't say they were great," he corrected. "I said I had a reasonable number of them."

"Sure, change your story now," she mocked. "Cover your tracks. Qualify everything."

He opened the freezer section and took out a few boxes. "Chicken Parmesan. Turkey divan. Spaghetti and meatballs. Spinach lasagne."

She peered over his shoulder. There was nothing else in the freezer but a loaf of bread and a carton of ice cream. Nothing else besides about a dozen of these frozen dinners.

"Don't you ever cook?" she asked.

"Sure. I cook these," he replied.

"I mean really cook."

He shook his head. "Not just for myself. These are fine. Easier."

She took the packages from his hands and tossed them back into the freezer. "But they have no soul. It's like eating cardboard night after night."

"They aren't so bad."

"They're terrible," she said and for some reason, her eyes got all teary. "You need good meals. Real meals."

"These are real meals." He pulled one from the freezer. "Look, they're even healthy."

"They're still not good for you."

He must have noticed the quiver in her voice, for he tossed the frozen dinner on the counter and pulled her closer. With his hands on her upper arms, he peered into her face.

"What's the matter?" he asked. "You're not going to cry over these frozen dinners, are you?"

She sniffed back the wetness. "Of course not," she insisted. "I just always get weepy when I'm offered horrible, soulless food."

She couldn't tell him the truth. How they made him seem so alone. So resigned to being alone that she couldn't bear it. She wanted to hold him and never let go. She wanted him to feel that he belonged, that he wasn't alone anymore and never would be again.

"We can order a pizza if that'll make you happier," he suggested. "Or we can call that dine-in service that'll deliver meals from real restaurants."

"That's okay. I'm just being silly."

"I think you're being sweet," he said and bent down to brush her lips with his.

It was a mistake, like tossing a lit match into a pile of dried leaves. For as soon as his mouth was on hers, all her hungers came rushing back. The frozen dinners were forgotten, dinner itself was unwanted. She needed nothing more than Kevin, nothing more than to rest in his arms and taste the wonder of his love.

The growing pressure of his lips, the heat of his touch said he felt the same way. His hands moved over her as if driven by some desperate longing, some craving deep in his soul that only she could satisfy. His arms pulled her ever tighter, as if they could become one by merging their souls. They were kindling, set on fire by the heat of their desires. They'd been sleeping and were brought to life by each other's touch.

"This isn't what I'd planned," Kevin whispered, his breath so soft against her skin that it was a caress in itself.

"I know."

"We can stop and have dinner."

"Can we?"

"Or we can have dinner later."

"We could."

His lips came back to hers as if exhausted by all the talking. They drank of hers, pulling sustenance from her very soul. She felt drained and exhilarated. She felt slow and sensuous. She felt alive and strong. Her hands moved over his back. He felt so good, so male. She tugged at his shirt and let her hands slide beneath it.

His skin was as hot as his kiss. As fiery as his lips. As trembling as her own heart. She let her hands roam over his back, delighting in the smooth hard muscles, then slid them lower. Her fingers eased down below his belt and the heat of his kiss grew.

His touch grew more demanding, more urgent. His hands moved around to her chest, cupping her breasts and teasing the nipples until she could hardly breathe. Her body was afire, her heart was aflame. There was nothing but the feel of his hands on her, the need for his lips to be on hers. The hunger for them to be truly one.

"If we're going to stop, we'd better do it now." His voice was hoarse.

"I think it's too late." Hers was, too.

"It was too late about a month ago."

She frowned at him. "What?"

His only reply was to brush her lips with the gentlest of kisses. "Are you sure?" he asked. "Is this what you want?"

His eyes held only concern for her, only a need to please her. "Actually, I'd prefer another room," she teased. "Nice though your tile floor seems—"

But before she could even finish speaking, he was sweeping her up in his arms. "How's this for flash?" he asked.

"Impressive," she whispered, but her lips didn't want to speak. They wanted only his mouth and found it again.

She was vaguely aware that they went through the living room and up the stairs. He laid her on a bed, soft and warm and safe. She had an impression of warm colors and shadows before he lay down beside her.

With slow, teasing hands, he unbuttoned her shirt and ran his hands over her skin. He took the tips of her breasts in his mouth, tugging and teasing until the fire in her wanted to explode. Then he loosened the closure of her slacks enough to let his hand slide down to the warmth that was her womanhood.

She needed him with an urgency unknown to her, with a hunger that was beyond imagining. She tugged at his shirt and pulled it over his head, then ran her fingers through the light mat of hair covering his chest. She wanted to feel every inch of him, to stroke and delight every part of his body, but her hands were already trembling with need. She shrugged out of her shirt and he helped her push her slacks to the floor, then her underwear.

"Oh, my sweet Samantha," he said. "You are so beautiful."

"And you are still so dressed," she murmured, working at the fastening of his pants. She pushed them off, along with his briefs, so that she could admire him also.

But she got only a quick glimpse before she felt him pressed against her, felt his need as strong and hard as her own. His lips, his hands, his whole body spoke of his desire, of the desperation of his hunger. He touched her, seemingly everywhere at once, until rational thought was lost and the stars seemed there for the picking.

She moved to take him inside her, arching with the pleasure, the sublime wonder of the joining. Together they moved, they pulsed, they danced to an ancient rhythm that took them into the heavens, soaring into the universe.

They clung as their world exploded and stars flew past them; then they clung even tighter as their breathing slowed and they floated back to earth. She was still lost in the wonder and the delight, but knew it when Kevin relaxed his hold to lie by her side. She cuddled back into his arms, laying her head against his chest.

"Nice," she said softly.

"You can say that again," he agreed, laughter on his lips.

She ran her fingers lightly down his side, still feeling the need to explore. A quiver ran through him as her caress went slower and lower. "Speaking of again . . ."

Kevin looked down at the darkened yard. One back corner caught the reflection of the streetlight, but the rest was all shadows. It was just past three in the morning. He knew because he'd heard the chimes from Saint Monica's. He'd heard them at two o'clock too. And at one.

He sighed and closed his eyes, leaning his forehead against the windowpane. The glass was cool, as was the night air. Fall was here and winter just around the corner.

How could something that felt so wonderful, so right, suddenly feel so wrong?

It was four hours since he'd taken Sam home. Four hours for him to feel the guilt and remorse building in his gut. It wasn't that it hadn't been perfect. It had. It had been everything he had dreamed making love with her would be. But he should never have let it happen.

He was too old for her. She was on the verge of life. He'd already played his hand. All right, he was still considered young in some circles. But not that young. Not that dewy-eyed.

He turned from the window and his gaze settled on the bed. It was the bed that he and Debbie had bought when they'd moved to this house, but it was Sam's presence that he felt in the room. It was her scent that lingered to tease and torment him.

If he closed his eyes, he would see her lying there. See the beauty of her young, firm body and feel her life and energy. The life and energy that he could barely keep up with now, and that would soon leave him in the dust.

He shook himself and grabbed his robe from the hook in the closet. Either awake or asleep, if he was lying in this bed, he would do nothing but dream of Sam. And that would get him nowhere in resolving his dilemma. He would sleep in the guest room.

He hurried out into the hall, closing the door on his room but not on the memory of Sam's presence.

Chapter Eleven

"It's not painted on."

Something in Kevin's voice made Sam jerk her hand back. She sat staring at him, puzzled, her hand hanging in mid-air.

They were sitting on a sofa in his family room watching TV. She'd been stroking the hair at the side of his head when his remark had popped out, falling out of the blue and hitting her broadside.

"What are you taking about?" she asked.

"The gray," he replied, indicating the hair at his temple. "It's not painted on, so you can't rub it off. No matter how hard you try."

"Talk like that makes you sound like an old poop."

He shrugged. "Maybe I am."

"Oh, for heaven's sake." She bounced over to the other end of the sofa, away from him, and glared. "Why are you letting my brothers get to you? I thought you were the Cool Hand Luke of the banking world."

"It's not a matter of who's getting to whom," he said. "It's who's right."

Sam made a face. Duchess came over and Sam patted her absently. Was it really age that concerned Kevin? Or did it have to do with their making love the other night? Maybe he was feeling guilty, a sense of having betrayed his first wife? She hoped not.

"You're as old as you feel," she said.

"Ah, the wisdom of youth."

His tone sounded rather sarcastic. Was he trying to start an argument? Trying to drive her away?

"What do you mean by that?" she asked, fighting to keep the sharpness out of her tone.

Kevin shrugged. "You're always bouncy and perky," he replied. "Like a twenty-something kid."

"Twenty-seven doesn't mean I'm a kid."

"You're not really." The sigh was thick in his voice. "I didn't mean to imply that you're immature."

"How kind of you." She paused to still the nervousness in her stomach and calm the demons of sarcasm that wanted to explode off her own tongue. "Besides, I am twenty-something. How else am I supposed to act?"

"You're acting fine," he reassured. "You're true to yourself. You're not the problem."

"I didn't think there was a problem."

His eyes wavered and he looked off toward the window where the other cat was sitting on the sill. Was she being a Pollyanna—something her sisters had always accused her of? Maybe there was a problem coming between them. Maybe he'd been disappointed with her the other night.

Sam had thought the other night had been wonderful, although she might be the only one who thought that. Kevin's opinion might be entirely different.

Or there might not be anything wrong at all. Men were such moody creatures. It was hard to tell from one minute to the next whether they were going to be high or low.

"You weren't old the other night," Sam said.

He turned back to look at her and Sam felt her cheeks warm. She probably shouldn't have said anything. That night had been so precious to her that she didn't really want to discuss it, analyze it. For all she knew, Kevin might feel the same way. But his attitude certainly didn't indicate any joyous memories.

"You were a man. Not an old man. Just a plain wonderful man."

Kevin sighed and raised his arm so she could slip underneath it.

"This feels so good," she said. "So natural. It's like we were made for each other."

"That's just a figure of speech."

"That's not how it feels to me." Sam wiggled her body to show how well she fitted. "I mean, we fit so well together."

"It's just a random happenstance."

She drew back slightly and stared at him. "Did you learn to talk that way at school? Or have you always been this cynical?"

"Boy," he snorted. "You're turning rather mean."

"You're inciting me. It's all your fault."

"It usually is the guy's fault," he said.

"You bet it is."

They fell silent and Sam could feel his body relax, but she knew it was temporary. Something was bothering Kevin and he was burying it for now. But it would rear its ugly head again. She turned herself so that she could look at the gray hairs at his temple.

It wasn't that she hadn't noticed them before. They were just a part of him. Like his dark eyes and dark hair. That easy smile of his that slowly grew until it filled his face. His long, lean, muscular body.

Sam loved those gray hairs. Just like she loved every single cell in his body. She made a fist and rubbed at the gray with her knuckles.

"Ouch!" he exclaimed. "That hurts."

She squirmed out of his arms, pushed him against the back of the sofa, and straddled him. "You needed it," she said.

"Says who?"

"Cassie," Sam replied as she settled herself on his body. "She said if a guy gets mopey, give him some pain. She said it cheers them up all the time."

"Wow, she's good. Maybe she should sell her plumbing-supply place and open up shop as a counselor."

Sam lightly bounced on him. "You're nice and firm."

"I'm glad you like it."

"I do. I do." She lay down on him and smoothed his hair. "So why are you so mopey?"

He shrugged.

"Tell me or I'll tickle you."

"No, you won't."

"Oh," Sam cooed. "Do I detect a touch of fear in your voice?"

"Not if you're paying attention," he replied. "Although, like someone once told me, a lot of people hear only what they expect to hear."

There actually wasn't a hint of fear anyplace that she could see. Not in his eyes, not in his voice, not anywhere. His expression was cool, his body relaxed. He might not be afraid but she was still tempted to tickle him.

But she decided not to right now. She just wanted him to be happy. And she couldn't help him be happy if she didn't know what the problem was. She smoothed his hair back off his forehead.

"Why are you so grumpy? Is it because your fortieth birthday is coming?"

"Of course not," he told her.

That had to be it. Put the fact that he was getting a year older together with all the nonsense her brothers had spilled on him and you had the explanation for Kevin's attitude.

She straightened and settled into a comfortable sitting position on him.

"Poor baby."

"You're being cruel."

"Why? Just because I won't let you feel sorry for yourself?"

He didn't say anything.

"You didn't act old the other night."

"I wasn't forty yet."

Kevin obviously needed some cheering up. Like a party. The problem was that she didn't know many of the same people he did. And it was pretty short notice to work up a good party list.

Her own family was always ready for a party but it would be best to keep her brothers away from Kevin for a while. That left just her, but she was positive that Kevin needed more people around. Suddenly she had an idea. His kids.

"Yes?" His tone sounded suspicious.

Sam glared slightly as she looked down at him. "What?"

"Your face turned bright all of a sudden," he said. "I just wondered what kind of mischief you were plotting."

"I'm a young woman with a healthy appetite, sitting on top of a handsome and virile gentleman. There's only one kind of mischief I could be plotting."

She could feel his body respond but when she pulled back, it was easy to see that suspicion still lurked in his eyes. "Don't you trust me?" she asked.

"Sometimes."

"Sometimes?" she exclaimed. "I just told you that I have the hots for your body and you just coolly look down your nose at me."

"It's hard to look any other way at you when you're lying on my chest."

Sam punched him in the arm. "You know what I mean."

"I do," Kevin said. "But you have a very active mind. I would guess you could have more than one idea festering in there at a time."

The more she thought about it, the better the idea seemed. Kevin would be thrilled to see his kids. It would be a great birthday surprise for him. The four of them could have a real fun day.

And there wasn't a home football game next weekend, so the bed-and-breakfast wouldn't be crowded. Between Melanie's and Beth's help, Dad should do just fine. He'd been on her case to take a break, anyway.

"You know," Sam said, wiggling her body on his. "I think we'd better make love again."

His body was responding very well so she kissed him, but small flickers of suspicion still danced in his eyes.

"I mean, before next weekend."

The suspicion left his eyes, was replaced by a hard sparkle, like a diamond's.

"Since you're liable to completely fall apart by then."

His arms wrapped themselves around her.

"Kevin, behave."

"Oh, I will." He rolled her over and onto the floor, then promptly was on top of her. "I promise."

His kiss indicated exactly what he meant by behaving.

"Oh, hell." Kevin threw his pen on the desk and leaned back in his chair, rubbing his eyes with his hands and groaning. "Buy a ticket or get out of line."

Then, throwing himself out of his chair, he walked over to the windows at the back of his office and stared out at the parking lot on the west side of the building.

It was one of those beautiful autumn days when the gods tried to make up for the soak-your-shirt days of summer and the freeze-your-ears-off days of winter. And today they'd done it in spades. Temperature in the high seventies, bright and sunny, a light breeze from the southwest, and humidity below fifty percent.

It was the kind of day that made a man want to be outside. Walking in the woods admiring the variety of nature's leafy palette. Running ten miles alongside the river. Playing a lively game of touch football.

The fact of the matter was that he was being more than lively—especially for a man his age. Ever since he'd met Sam he'd had this insatiable need to be with her. To hold her tight. To love her with his whole heart and soul, with every molecule in his body. No, loving Sam wasn't a problem. Not at all. The problem was the guilt that was overwhelming him. He closed his eyes, stuck his fists over them, and swore to himself.

He hadn't meant to get involved with Sam. Certainly not like this. He just wanted to help her and her father get their business off the ground. Guide her. After all, that was his job.

Kevin opened his eyes and glowered at a pair of cardinals—a male in a bright red coat and a female wearing her coat of plain brown—gamboling about, pecking at the berries filling the branches of the bushes lining the parking lot. Dumb birds.

Actually, they weren't the dumb ones. At least they had an excuse. They were just following instinct. They didn't know any better. Kevin, on the other hand, knew that he didn't have any kind of excuse. Yes, he had instincts, but they weren't something a man used to justify his actions. A real man knew better than to give in to his baser desires.

No, this was a relationship that should never have gotten to this point. But now that it had, it was time to stop it. Right here and now.

Yes, Sam was lively, intelligent, and filled with the energy of youth. But what the hell was he bringing to the party? Not a single cotton-picking thing.

A light tap on his office door just about put him out of his skin. But before he could calm down enough to reply, the door opened. He breathed a sigh of relief when he saw it was his secretary.

"I'm sorry to bother you," Cindy said. "But there's a Robert Scott outside who insists on seeing you."

Robert Scott? Kevin searched his internal memory bank of customer names. Nothing. "What's this relative to?"

"He won't say," she replied. "But I think he's Samantha Scott's brother."

"Oh." *That* Robert Scott. "Bobby. Send him in."

"Are you sure?" his secretary asked. "You have a loan-approval committee meeting in forty minutes. I could tell him to make an appointment for some other day."

"I'm sure this won't take long." He didn't know what the hell Bobby wanted, but he would make sure it didn't go long.

"Mr. Scott," Cindy announced and stepped aside to let Bobby enter Kevin's office, shutting the door behind her.

"Bobby." Kevin stuck his hand out. "How are you?"

Bobby didn't bother taking his hand. "We need to talk."

The words came out short and terse. Kevin didn't know what the big man wanted, but he had a strong feeling that it concerned Sam. Kevin indicated one of the chairs in front of his desk, seating himself once Bobby sat down.

They stared at each other across the wide expanse of his desk, like two gamblers waiting for the cards to be dealt. This was the first time they'd seen each other in a suit and tie. Since it was on his own turf, Kevin wasn't really nervous but he was somewhat on edge, anxious for Bobby to make his move.

The silence dragged on as Kevin waited. Waited and studied Sam's brother. He knew Bobby was big, but putting his bulk in a business suit seemed to accentuate his size. The man would be able to do a lot of damage if he wanted to.

Kevin frowned, irritated with himself for that thought. Bobby was a civilized man, a nice guy. Besides, Kevin didn't know anybody who dressed up to punch somebody out.

Not that there was any reason for that. He was sure that Sam wouldn't have told her brothers about them being intimate. But how about her sisters?

Shaking his head slightly, Kevin leaned forward, putting his elbows on his desk. His mind was needlessly going down the dumb path. He and Sam were adults, and what they did was their business.

"What can I do for you?" Kevin asked. He didn't have all day.

"Stop seeing my sister."

Her brother's words weren't really a surprise. In fact, Kevin had been expecting them. But expecting something was one thing. Seeing the words flung out in your face was another matter. For one of the few such times in his life, Kevin was at a loss for words.

Bobby leaned forward. "We've talked this over and—"

"I presume you mean you and Sam talked," Kevin said quietly. So quietly that he wondered whether Bobby had heard him.

But the pink flooding into the big man's cheeks indicated that he had heard. It also demonstrated that Sam's brother had more than a shred of decency in him. But not necessarily too much more.

"Look." Bobby's voice took on the gruff tone of a man who knew that he'd backed himself into a corner. "Sam is our baby sister and—"

"And she always will be."

Bobby's lips went into a hard, straight line, telling Kevin that he was in no mood for a reasonable discussion. That was fine and dandy with Kevin. Conciliatory thoughts had fled, once he saw that her brothers were going behind her back.

"Look, I know you guys feel a need to watch out for her. But Sam can take care of herself."

"In most cases, I'd say that was true," Bobby replied. "But she's never met anyone like you. You're sophisticated. You're smooth. You're cool."

The words were positive but Kevin knew Bobby wasn't singing his praises.

"I mean, you're older than her." Bobby's lips twitched in a grimace. "Hell, you're older than all of us."

"Is that against the law?"

They glared at each other, hard and uncompromisingly. Kevin said nothing. Absolutely nothing. Because deep down, Kevin had to admit that in a lot of ways he agreed with Bobby. And he would have come out and said so if he hadn't remembered how Sam had often told him about her brothers and how they babied her. How they seemed to find it difficult to understand that she had more than one brain cell. And that bugged him now more than the fact that he was thirteen years older than her.

"I know you mean her no harm," Bobby said. "And the difference between your ages might not seem like such a big deal right now. But in twenty-five years you'll be retiring and Sam will just be getting her second wind."

Bobby's words brought back memories of Debbie and how young she'd been when she'd died. Kevin was tempted to ask Bobby where he got his twenty-five-year guarantee. Kevin would have paid anything for one.

"I know how old I am," Kevin said quietly. "But don't you think, since Sam's an adult, who she goes out with is up to her and her alone?"

They stared stubbornly at each other and Bobby broke first. He looked off toward the painting on the wall to his left. Muscles rippled in his temples, indicating that Bobby was probably grinding his teeth in frustration. Well, that was tough. Kevin wasn't exactly enjoying this little conversation, either.

Yes, he enjoyed Sam's company. The way she grabbed at life as she raced along, like one of those people who won a keep-all-you-can-pick-up-in-five-minutes contest. It was enough to take at least ten years off his age, but Kevin was sure that it wasn't a one-way street. He was sure that Sam enjoyed his company as much as he enjoyed hers.

"Yes, Sam's an adult." Bobby shifted in his chair. "But she doesn't always show a lot of common sense."

So how many people did? Kevin almost laughed out loud. If Bobby had come in low-key and gentle, Kevin probably would have agreed with him. He most likely would have broken off with Sam. But the man coming at him the way he had, made Kevin dig his heels in; made him feel like maintaining a relationship with Sam just to spite her brothers.

"I think you ought to cut things off," Bobby said. "And quick. Before you guys get in over your heads."

Kevin almost laughed again. But he didn't, for fear he would cry. *Get out before they fell in over their heads.* What would Bobby say if Kevin told him how far things had already gone? But that wasn't something open for discussion. Certainly not when Sam wasn't here.

He was more confused now than before.

A light tap sounded before Cindy opened the door. "You have your meeting in five minutes," she said.

Kevin rose. Bobby was already standing.

"You know what's right, Mr. Delaney. So just do it." He turned to leave, then paused and looked back. "Or else we'll talk again. And next time, I won't come alone."

Kevin and Cindy stared at Bobby's broad back as he stormed through the lobby and out the glass doors. Kevin didn't care a fig about the man's threats. Bobby could bring his brothers and all his cousins, for all Kevin cared. The room could be filled to bursting with Scotts all telling him to break it off with Sam and it wouldn't force his hand.

No, he knew he had to bring all this to a head with Sam—but because it was the only honorable thing to do. Not because her brothers were threatening him.

"What was that all about?" Cindy asked.

Kevin shook his head. "He wants me to play golf with them."

"Golf?"

"Yeah, but I'm not going to do it." He picked up his folder for the meeting. "You know how I hate that damn game."

"So." Sam put a forkful of trout in her mouth and chewed for a moment. But only a moment. She was too full of energy to slow down.

Kevin just watched her. He was at one of South Bend's nicest restaurants, having a delicious dinner with a beautiful woman, but all he could think about was Bobby's visit today. And how right Bobby was.

"There I was up to my elbows in muffin batter," Sam was saying, waving her fork like a baton. "And the kitchen looked like a hurricane had passed through."

But how could he give her up? She brought such life and joy to his life. Was he strong enough to deprive himself of all that?

She swallowed her food and made a face. "I had made one batch, but they had stuck to the pan and I couldn't get them out."

"So what happened?" Kevin asked, forcing his gloom away for the moment. "You go to the store and buy muffins for your guests?"

"No." She looked sternly at him. "You weren't listening, were you?"

"I was listening," he replied. "You're just a little hard to keep up with at times."

"You'd better shape up." She wagged a finger at him. "There's going to be a test."

He put his hand over her free hand, needing to touch her; to feel her closeness. "And if I fail?"

"I don't think we should talk about it. Especially not while we're eating."

Another forkful of fish went into her mouth. Kevin wondered if she chewed any of her food. Obviously she'd never been a student of the chew-your-food-twenty-seven-times school.

"It would spoil your dinner." She snatched her hand from his and reached for a roll. "Anyway, like I told you—a miracle happened."

"Oh?" He was having trouble following her story. Mainly because he was having trouble concentrating on anything but her smile and the glow in her eyes. He was like a man who knew he was going to die of thirst; he wanted to drink in all the water he could while it was still around.

Sam buttered her roll, then went on with her story. "Aunt Hattie came in."

"She came to your rescue."

"Very good." She winked at him. "Now you're firing on all cylinders."

He smiled as he leaned back to watch her face, to bask in the pure joy that radiated from it. Sam had been excited ever since he'd picked her up this evening. And as their dinner progressed, she'd kept climbing higher and higher. The little alcove around their table seemed to sparkle and vibrate with her enthusiasm while the rest of the restaurant remained dark and gloomy.

"She going to take over the breakfast part of the bed-and-breakfast?" he asked.

"Yep. She wanted to do it just to help us out, but we were adamant about paying her. And her muffins are just great."

"That takes a load off your shoulders."

She shrugged. "It wasn't a lot of work, but I couldn't find a recipe I really liked. And the store-bought ones seemed so ordinary."

"Can't have ordinary muffins, can we?"

"But there's more," she said, quickly dissolving into a grin. "She's been talking about getting a job ever since Cassie and Jack got engaged. So Dad's going to ask her if she'd like to do more than just the breakfasts at the inn. You know, help out in other ways, too."

"That should work out well," he said.

"It'd be great," Sam said, as she polished off the last piece of fish on her plate. "The teenagers we hired are really for weekends, so it would be nice to have someone available at other times. And her hours can be flexible so she'll still be able to help out with the twins and the baby, once it comes."

Then, as she finished chewing, Sam neatly stacked her dishes to one side. She claimed it was a habit she'd picked up as a kid and, since she was still a kid at heart, couldn't break it.

"I need to go to the ladies' room." She put her napkin on the table and stood. "So don't do anything about dessert until I get back. I hear the sweets are just fabulous here."

"And delicious, too," he replied.

She punched him several times on the arm before hurrying off to the rest room, leaving Kevin sitting in a thick cloud of joy. Unfortunately, it wasn't enough to smother the doubt that wanted to take over his soul.

He really didn't know what to do. When he was alone, there was no problem. He would fill himself full of altruisms and define an honorable course of action: which was to tell Sam that he enjoyed her company but he just wasn't right for her.

But that sounded so pompous that he was sure Sam would just laugh in his face. And then they would both be laughing. And before he could blink twice, they would be hugging each other. Then they would kiss. And kiss some more.

Since that wouldn't work, what could he do? The problem was, it felt so good to be with her. Even talking to Sam on the phone was like soaking himself in some magical hot spring. He came away rejuvenated and refreshed. A completely different man.

And it wasn't just good for him. Sam enjoyed being with him also. He was sure of that. They enjoyed doing things together.

If her brothers had talked to Sam they would have been able to see that. But would it have made any difference to their opinion? Maybe, but more important, *should* it make any difference? After all, no matter how a person sliced it, he was still thirteen years older than her.

"Hey, big boy."

Strong but gentle arms grabbed him from behind and wrapped themselves around his head and neck. He could feel the softness of her breasts on the top of his head.

"You didn't have dessert without me, did you?"

"No, ma'am. I didn't."

"Good boy." She patted him on the head before going around the table and sitting down. "You will be rewarded," she said, signaling for the waitress.

He'd thought of discussing things with Sam tonight, but now he wasn't so sure it was the right time. Hell, maybe he should just forget about having any discussion with her. After all, relationships had a tendency to take on a life of their own. They usually went where they were going, no matter what the people involved did.

And as much as he hated to admit it, this relationship of theirs wasn't a permanent thing. It couldn't be. They would have their fling and then they would get on with their lives. She would find somebody younger. Somebody her own age. There was no use being dramatic about it. Just go with the flow and accept what comes.

"Don't plan anything for Sunday," she said.

Lost in his own thoughts, Kevin was finding it hard to respond. "Next Sunday?"

"Your birthday. Remember?"

"Oh." He shrugged. "I never do anything on my birthday."

"Good."

Suddenly her smile seemed a tad too bright. "Why? What are you planning?"

"It's a surprise."

"Some people don't like surprises," he said.

"Only old poops don't like surprises."

He was about to point out that he was as near to an old poop as she'd ever dated, but the waitress had arrived with the dessert tray and Sam's attention was seized. It appeared that, like it or not, he would have to have a talk with her about the wisdom of ignoring birthdays.

He watched as Sam's face lit up with the joy of choosing a dessert. Then again, maybe not. She would probably just take him out to dinner or something. No big deal. Certainly, nothing that would turn into a tradition or involve anyone else.

Chapter Twelve

"I don't care if it is my birthday," Kevin said, waving his hand at the muffins, fruit salad and juices on the table. "The two of us will never eat all this food."

"We don't have to," Sam replied.

"I should be slowing down on my eating as I get older," he went on. "And eat healthier—"

He stopped in midsentence, looking blank as his eyes seemed to search his kitchen for Sam's mysterious extra eaters. It took all her willpower and then some to restrain her impulse to laugh. She forced herself to settle for a small smile. The poor guy. He didn't have a clue. It was great.

His gaze stopped when it reached the counter, and the bacon and eggs ready to cook. "You didn't have to go through all this. If you wanted to have brunch, we could have gone to the Landing or Tippecanoe. They have great Sunday brunches."

"I wanted it here," she said, brushing his lips with hers as she went over to the cabinet to find a frying pan.

"But—"

There was a sound at the back door and they both turned in time to see it open. Stacy and Jon—they looked just like their pictures—rushed in.

"Surprise!" they shouted, grins covering their faces. "Happy birthday!"

There was a moment of silence as Kevin stood staring dumbly, like someone who'd wandered into the middle of the wrong century. Sam's own life passed before her eyes in slow motion.

He had admitted that he and his children were only now starting to get comfortable with each other again. Would this little surprise of hers be too much for a possibly still-fragile relationship? It couldn't be. It wouldn't be.

"Daddy!" Stacy cried and flew into Kevin's arms. A lump filled Sam's throat as she fought tears.

His son settled for a more macho, "Hey, Dad," as he walked forward to shake his father's hand.

"What are you guys doing here?" Kevin demanded as he put his children out at arm's length, a hand on each of their shoulders.

"Just passing through, man," Jon said.

Sam shook her head. The kid was certainly his father's son. The physical resemblance wasn't especially strong, but their personalities were out of the same mold.

"We're here for your birthday, Daddy." Stacy reached over and pulled Sam into the group. "Your girlfriend invited us."

Sam's stomach immediately went into a knot. She and Kevin had been going together a few weeks now, but they hadn't really formalized anything. No one had ever called them a couple before. She wondered, and worried, how Kevin would react to his daughter's words.

"Aha!" Kevin exclaimed. "That's what all this sneaking around was for."

"I didn't sneak around," Sam insisted. "I just told you not to make any plans for today."

"That doesn't sound like sneaking around to me," Jon agreed. "Sounds more like she gave you an order."

"And he obeyed," Sam said, causing the three of them to break into laughter while Kevin gazed at them with a rueful expression.

"Why are you guys picking on me?"

Kevin's tone was gruff but Sam could see the sparkle in his eyes and the softness in his smile. He was happy. And his kids were happy. This was absolutely great. It couldn't get any better.

"Why don't you guys go in the living room?" Sam suggested, trying to shoo them out of the kitchen. "Sit around and visit. I'll have brunch ready in about ten minutes."

"I can't do that," Stacy protested. "I promised you I'd help."

"Hey," Jon said. "I'm not going to sit alone with Dad. He'll just grill me about my classes and how I'm doing in them."

Everyone laughed except Kevin, who put some stern lines across his face. "And exactly how are you doing with your classes?" he asked.

"See?" Jon looked at Sam. "Now look what you did."

"I didn't do anything." Sam grinned up at the kid who stood taller than she'd ever dreamed of being. "Maybe the real problem is that you haven't, either."

"Oh, dirty pool." Jon looked at his sister. "Come on, let me stay and help."

"No," Stacy said. "Get out. Both of you. Go do some of that male-bonding junk people are always talking about."

Stacy was definitely an older sister and Sam suddenly felt sorry for Jon. "You can all stay here," she said. "Your father can relax and the two of you can help me."

"I want to help, too," Kevin said. "And since it's my birthday, I can do what I want, right?"

"That's silly," Stacy replied. "Take it easy."

"Jon and I can set the table and do that male-bonding stuff right here. Just like you said we're supposed to."

"I'm doing fine with my classes," Jon said. "Honest, Dad."

"Sam!" Stacy wailed.

For a moment Stacy sounded like one of Sam's sisters, pleading a case with their mother. Sam was less than ten years older than the girl but she definitely felt of a different generation.

"It's his birthday," Sam reminded. "He can do what he wants. Even if it is something dumb like setting the table."

Jon smiled while his sister groaned.

"Come on." Stacy punched her brother on the shoulder. "Let's go get the presents and the cake."

Once his kids had stepped out, Kevin was over next to Sam, taking her in his arms. It was like coming home. Her heart was happy, and her smile was bright.

"Thank you." He bent down and kissed her, his lips tickling her soul into wanting nothing more than to stay in his arms forever. "Thank you very much."

The bickering voices on the porch told her that Kevin's children were returning. She slowly eased out of his arms, missing him before he was even an arm's length away.

"That's enough of that," she scolded. "I don't have time for this right now."

"Boy," he said. "You're pretty darn bossy for a youngest child."

"I've spent a lifetime suppressing my need to control," she replied. "It had to come out sometime."

Slipping around behind her, Kevin had his arms around her again. He bent down and nuzzled her ear. "I can't wait to see what else I can uncover."

Desires flared in her heart, trying to drown out all sense of reason. She wanted to turn in his embrace, to find those lips that so haunted her dreams and lurked just below the surface of her thoughts. She wanted to play that dangerous game with the fire of their passion, flicking in ever closer and trying not to get burned. But his kids were on the porch and about to burst into the kitchen.

"Kevin." Sam put an elbow in his ribs, getting a satisfying grunt in response. "Later. Your kids are here."

"So what do you want to do now?" Stacy asked as they cleaned up the dishes after brunch.

"I don't know." Kevin shrugged and went back to loading the dishwasher. The meal had been just fine—casual and easy. Everyone was sitting around, getting to know each other. It had been a great birthday. "We could relax and chat."

"You mean sit around and talk?" Stacy wailed.

"You're letting this 4-0 thing take the air out of your tires, dear old Dad."

Kevin looked hard at his son, not needing any reminders of his age today. "Maybe you'd like to do a little run down by the river," he said. "How about six or seven miles?"

"No," Sam and Stacy shouted in unison. "No way."

"We just ate," Jon protested and grabbed the frying pan from his sister's hand and began to dry it. "Besides, I have a meet tomorrow."

"We can play a game of Monopoly," Sam suggested.

His kids hooted at her.

"All right," she said with a laugh. "It was just an idea. Someone else can make a suggestion." She accepted their teasing so good-naturedly that it took Kevin's breath away and sent fingers of warm hunger along his spine.

"It's a nice day." Stacy let the dishwater out of the sink. "We should do something outside."

"I agree," Kevin said. It was too beautiful a day to stay inside, and he was feeling too good to be cooped up.

"We can play Monopoly outside," Sam said.

This time the groans were more subdued.

"Let's go in-line skating," Stacy suggested.

"Yeah," her brother agreed. "At the university. There's a lot of neat places there."

"How about it, Sam?" Stacy asked. "You game?"

"Sure, I enjoy in-line skating." Sam looked for a long moment into Kevin's eyes as if trying to read his thoughts. "Although I think the birthday boy should choose. After all, it is his day."

"Dad?" Jon prompted.

Kevin shrugged. It wasn't what he would have chosen—or even thought of—but if it was what they all wanted to do, it was fine with him. He felt young with Sam's smile on him. Young and able to keep up with anybody. This was his chance to prove to himself that all his worrying was nonsense.

"Sure. Why not?" he said.

"Have you ever been in-line skating?" Sam asked him.

Traces of annoyance danced in his stomach. "Yes," he replied. "I've been roller-skating."

"In-line skating is—"

"I know." She was going to tell him it was different; the wheels were in line rather than at the corners of a rectangle. "I've also ice-skated."

It was a long, long time ago, but nobody knew that. And nobody had to know that. A reasonable athlete could do any of these things. Besides, it wasn't like they were going to play hockey or anything like that. They were just going to skate around on some sidewalks. Big deal.

They finished cleaning up the kitchen and then Sam drove them to a small sporting goods store on the eastern edge of town, not too far from the university. They rented the skates and the necessary protective gear. The clerk seemed to know her well, calling her by name and asking about all her siblings. It was obvious that she'd been there before. Probably with her young friends.

The skies were clear and sunny as they drove on to the university, but Kevin could feel the dark clouds crowding in. What the hell was he doing? Who was he trying to kid?

This was going to be fun. He could feel it in his bones— the ones he was going to break.

Sam parked and they all strapped on their skates, knee and elbow pads. While the kids and Sam tried a few practice runs over the paved parking lot, Kevin tried to stay standing. His ankles wanted to wobble and collapse. It felt a lot different than roller-skating.

Or maybe his memory was going, and he couldn't remember what roller-skating was like. This was a really bad idea.

"Sure I couldn't have rented a body cast right off the bat?" he asked. They all laughed. What a card old Dad was. A joke a minute.

"Come on, Dad," Jon said, obviously anxious to do some real skating. "Race you to the end of the quadrangle."

Right—only if they could find a quadrangle with a fence to cling to the whole length.

"He doesn't want to race." Sam took Kevin's hand. "He wants to stay with me."

"Aww," his kids sang out in a chorus, with stupid grins on their faces.

They thought it was cute. He thought it was pitiful. Sam obviously saw him as a miserable old man, unable to do the simplest athletic thing. And the awful truth was that he couldn't. He just knew he was going to fall. He could feel his ankles ready to sprain, his wrists ready to break.

He should get back in the car. He should say an old football injury was acting up, except that he'd never played football and the kids knew it. He should say he'd changed his mind and wanted to play Monopoly, after all.

"Come on," his son said. "Are we going to stand around or skate?"

"What are you waiting for?" Kevin said lightly. "You want me to hold your hand?"

"Ha, ha," Jon sneered as he and Stacy took off, moving with the smooth natural grace of the young and athletic.

"Come on," Sam murmured to him. "Let's go."

Something in her voice hit him hard, like he'd been slugged in the solar plexus. His breath was gone for the moment and his head spun. She had read every doubt and worry that had flitted through his mind. She was dividing the group mentally into the young and the old; chronologically she knew she belonged with the young, but emotionally she was going to stay with the old.

He hated the idea of it and pulled his hand out of hers. "I think it would be best if I didn't hold your hand, either."

She gave him a questioning look and he tried to make light of it, tried to joke away his depression. "You have to learn to stand on your own sometime."

She still didn't say anything.

"Come on, come on," he said, forcing his voice to sound enthusiastic. "Let's get going. We came to skate, didn't we?"

Sam turned and followed after his kids, slowly and uncertainly. And they proceeded in this manner—his kids way up ahead, Kevin bringing up the rear, and Sam floating back and forth in between—down the length of the quadrangle. But it was all right. He wobbled a few times, but he didn't fall. He felt brave enough to even pick up his speed a hair when they turned onto the main quadrangle.

Other college-age kids were around, some biking and some in-line skating, too. A few were on the grass studying or playing Frisbee. He might be the oldest one around, but he wasn't old. Not yet.

He took a deep breath and let the beauty of the day relax him as he skated in and out of patches of shade. From the other side of the campus, steeple bells were chiming and from up ahead, he could hear Stacy's laughter. It was going well.

Jon and Stacy went around the side of a building and onto a parking lot. They were heading for the wide sidewalk that ran around the lake—except that they had to go down a steep slope first to get there.

The kids went down it as if they were flying. Sam went down just as smoothly. Kevin just stared at like it was a ski jump looming ahead, refusing to let his feet slow. He could do it. He could do it. He could—

Some bicyclers came around the corner of the building and sped by him. They didn't touch him; they didn't even brush close to him. But they startled him and he felt his sense of balance evaporate. His feet were skidding one way and his body another. His arms were waving like he was a windmill.

The slope loomed ahead and he knew he would never make it down alive. He turned and with awkward, crablike steps wobbled onto the grass and into a nearby tree.

"You okay?" Sam was asking.

"What happened?" Stacy wanted to know.

"Nice move, Dad," Jon said.

"Nothing happened," he said, trying hard not to show his impatience. "I just wanted to take a closer look at this tree."

"Right," Jon said with a snicker.

"You sure you're okay?" Sam pressed.

"I'm fine. I'm fine." He pushed away from the tree. "Let's get going, shall we?"

The kids hurried back over to the lake, but Sam lagged behind as if he needed a keeper. He got back on the side-walk—down below the slope—and made his way over to the lake.

"We could stop up there and wait for the kids," Sam suggested, nodding ahead toward a kiosk at a bus stop.

Sure, Kevin thought bitterly. There was even a roof over it to keep his old gray head out of the sun.

"I'm fine. This is fun," he insisted.

"Are you sure?" she asked.

"Hey, this is just my first time," he protested. "You can't expect me to be up to their speed."

They looked up ahead at the kids who were doing fancier stuff—skating backward, along with some dips and spins. Stacy did a jump that would put Kevin in traction for months if he even thought about doing it.

"Cool, Stacy!" Sam called out. "How'd you do that?"

Stacy waited for them to catch up, then she went through the jump again for Sam as Jon tried to convince Sam to try some of his moves. Kevin purposely let himself fall behind again.

The three of them were really getting along. But then, why shouldn't they? They were all young, athletic, full of life. In other words, they were contemporaries.

He was the oddball. There was no denying reality.

"You can't light all the candles in here," Kevin protested. "You'll burn the house down."

"Have no fear." Sam was laughing as she reached into the pocket of the sweater vest she wore. "I have everything under control."

They were back at the house after a few hours of the torture of in-line skating. Of the agony of staring reality in the face. He had to be a man and end this thing with Sam. But first he had to get through this next hour of having the birthday cake with the kids. Once they went back to school, he would find the words to say goodbye to Sam. He tried to maintain a happy face, but it was getting harder and harder.

Sam pulled out four large candles. "See? Only four. No need for the fire department to be on standby." She stuck them into the top of the cake.

"I take it those are decadent candles," he said.

Three pairs of eyes stared at him. Boy, sometimes it seemed that the younger the person, the more dense their brain.

"You know," he said. "I'm forty. Four decades."

"We knew what you meant," Stacy said.

"Yeah," Jon added. "We just can't believe you'd say something like that."

"Aw, come on, guys," Sam interjected on his behalf. "It was kind of cute."

Stacy groaned. "Don't say that," she told Sam.

"Yeah," his son said. "If you keep on praising and encouraging him, he'll never change."

"I hope he never does." Then, smiling, Sam lit the four candles and pushed the cake toward Kevin. "There you go, hon."

"Happy birthday to you," the three of them sang.

Hon? That was the first time she'd called him that. At least in public. And, as he looked deep into those doe eyes, a galaxy of emotions danced in him: passion, desire, love.

Love.

"Happy birthday to you."

He loved her. He wanted to spend the rest of his life at her side. He wanted to see her the first thing when he awoke and the last thing before he slept. He wanted to give her the world. He wanted her to be happy.

"Happy birthday, dear—"

"Kevin."

"Dad."

There was a jumble of giggles as they said different words.

He looked at the laughing faces around the table and felt a pain stab at his heart. It matched the twinge in his wrist from when he'd skated into the tree and the ache in his knee from trying to avoid the bicyclers. He was so wrong for her. She deserved someone who could keep up with her. A true partner. One who would be a match for her forever.

"Happy birthday to you."

The words died away and Kevin found it hard to keep his smile in place.

"Now you have to blow out the candles," Sam said.

"I'm too old for these birthday-boy games."

"You're as old as you feel," Jon muttered.

"I told you," Stacy said, looking at Sam. "I told you he wouldn't do it."

"He has to," Sam insisted. "Otherwise he'll have a year of bad luck."

Kevin wanted to put his foot down, but he was afraid that would just generate a derisive laugh from Sam. And an announcement that he was acting like an old poop.

"Come on, Dad. They're going to start dripping wax all over the cake."

"You want me to blow them out for you?" Jon asked.

Kevin took a deep breath and blew out the candles—all four of them in one fell swoop.

"Very good, Dad."

Kevin picked up the knife and sliced the cake, passing out pieces to everyone. It seemed they all ate it on the run. One second everyone was laughing about the candles and the melted wax, and the next, the kids were taking their empty plates to the dishwasher and talking about the drive back to school.

"Do you really have to go back so early?" he asked.

"Sorry, Daddy," Stacy replied. "I have to finish a sociology paper and study for a contemporary lit test."

"I have a cross-country meet tomorrow afternoon," Jon said.

Nodding, Kevin struggled to hold the smile on his face. His kids had lives of their own, which was the way it should be. Which was the way he wanted. Still, there were times....

His eyes met Sam's across the table and her gaze said, I'll be here. But while his heart wanted to sing, he knew it couldn't. Once the kids had left, it would be time to set his treasure free.

* * *

"Well, that was fun," Sam said.

Kevin didn't reply. Instead he gave one last wave and stared after the car as his kids rounded the corner, turning to go south across the river.

She tried again to get a response from him. "Maybe we can get together with them again sometime," she murmured.

"Yeah." He continued staring at the bridge, even though his kids were long gone. "Maybe."

His words were positive but his tone certainly wasn't. The black cloud he'd been carrying ever since they'd gotten back from skating seemed to have grown darker.

She put an arm through his, wanting to pull him back from whatever shadow he was living in. "How about another piece of cake?" she asked. "I can make some iced tea to go with it."

"No, thank you."

Her arm slipped out from his. Kevin hadn't been rude, but he definitely didn't want any cake. Actually, it felt like there were a lot of things he didn't want, starting with her. Maybe he just needed some time alone.

"I'd better get going," she said. "Dad might need some help. We've got a fiftieth wedding-anniversary party scheduled for tomorrow afternoon."

"Could you stay a few minutes?" Kevin asked. "I think we need to talk."

Something in his voice made her heart flutter with fear, but she kept her voice steady. "Sure."

Silently, she followed him into his house. She hated silence more than anything, especially this heavy kind that hung around, waiting for misunderstandings to happen.

"I'd been hoping to bake your cake myself," she said, trying to break the mood somehow. "But I didn't know what kind you liked."

"It was fine."

"Stacy said you liked chocolate, but then who doesn't?"

He didn't answer and Sam bit her lip to keep from chattering on. She could do that; she could fill up any silence with words as if they were a weapon to fight the darkest demons. But they were only weapons to fight back her own fears, and they were weak weapons at that.

Kevin turned into the living room and sat down in a straight-backed wing chair—the most uncomfortable chair in the room. Sam's heart skipped a few beats. Bad news was coming.

"Maybe I can bake you a cake some other time," she said quickly. "After all, there's no rule that says a person can only eat cake on their birthday."

"Sam, would you sit down? Please."

She swallowed hard and stood there clenching and unclenching her fists. She was talking too much. She knew it.

She sat down on the edge of the recliner across from Kevin. It was a chair that was made for relaxing, but sitting on the edge made her as uncomfortable as Kevin. Made them even.

"I don't think that in-line skating was such a good idea," she said. "I'm going to feel it for a week."

"Actually, I think it was a good idea." A sad smile flickered on his lips. "A very good idea."

"It was? Then why are you so down? You said the cake was fine. Was it my scrambled eggs? Or the fruit salad?"

"Sam." Kevin held both hands up. "Everything was fine. The food was great, the skating was fun. The whole darn day was so special that I'll never forget it."

Then what are you brooding about? But the words wouldn't come out and she just sat there, her stomach jumping while the outside of her did nothing.

"And I'll never forget you."

He would never forget her! Why should he? Then she looked at Kevin—really looked at him. She saw the slump of his shoulders, the sadness in his eyes. And she understood.

But not really. And that lit a fire under her fears and turned them into anger.

"What are you talking about?" she cried. "What is all this?"

"Sam, don't make it harder than it already is."

She was on her feet, glaring at him. "This is just all some stupid birthday thing, isn't it?" she demanded. "Now that you've crossed that great threshold of forty years, you've become a martyr."

"Maybe I've just taken a good look at things."

"Come off it, Kevin," she snapped. "You've been dragging around for the last week. You've been looking for a reason to be more depressed."

"I have not. I gave it my best shot, but it's just not working out."

That sent an icy sliver right into her heart. "What do you mean, it's not working out?"

"Exactly what I said." He took a deep breath and leaned forward slightly. "Look, Sam. We've both had a good time but it was never meant to be."

"Why not?" she demanded. She had to talk him out of this insanity. He was just feeling glum about his birthday; she knew it. "What went wrong?"

"Nothing," he said, clearly exasperated. "It's just that we're too different. It was a short-time thing. A summer romance."

"We had fun." How could he forget all the laughing? The talking? The loving?

"Had," he repeated. "Past tense."

She just shook her head. "I should have seen this coming. I knew you were upset over your birthday, but I didn't realize how much."

"You make it sound like a case of the flu. Something that could have been avoided if I'd just had my shots. It's not that way at all."

She had to make him slow down. "Now is not the time to start making decisions," she said.

"Now is the perfect time.

"Kevin, in a week or two—"

"I'll feel the same." He got to his feet and suddenly she saw something beyond his words, beyond her fear. She saw a flatness in his eyes, no feeling at all. "It's over."

"This is crazy," she said, grasping at whatever straws she could find. "Age doesn't matter."

"It does to me."

"I'm not giving up on us."

Fear was strangling her heart, though. She had found love and she was going to lose it. Where were those stupid spirits who were supposed to come help her fight? It was probably their bowling night so they weren't paying attention.

"There isn't an 'us' anymore," he said, his voice quiet. Resigned.

"This isn't the end. I'm going to find a way to make you see how silly all this is."

"Give it up, Sam," he told her. "Unless you can find a way to make me ten years younger or you ten years older, it's over."

She wanted to stamp her feet and tell him he was being idiotic. She wanted to laugh at the ridiculousness of it all and cry at the fear that she would never be able to get him to see it that way. She wanted to go over there and shake some sense into him. Or kiss some sense into him.

But the distance was greater than just the few feet that separated them. That look in his eyes put them miles and miles apart. She needed a map if she was going to find her way back into his heart. She needed to think this out.

"I guess I'd better be going," she said. "See you around."

She stomped to the door. A million different voices were shouting inside her, each with their own different plan. Kevin took a step after her, but she didn't slow a bit.

"I'll never forget you, Sam," he said.

"You're not going to get the chance," she informed him before she let the screen door close behind her with a bang.

Even as it did, it let loose a demon of fear in her. What if she couldn't find a way to convince him?

Chapter Thirteen

Sam spread the calendar out next to the reservation book and began to compare the two. She had too much free time, and needed to fill it, even if it was just on paper.

"You staying in on your day off?" Her dad was in the office doorway, a frown of concern on his face.

She chose not to look at him for too long, having found she tended to get a bit weepy at the slightest hint of sympathy. She had called Kevin twice in the last few days, and each time it was exactly the same—he said was it was over. He never listened to her arguments. He was like a broken record: It's over. It's over. It's over.

Sam took a deep breath before smiling over in her father's direction. "I was just checking the schedule for next weekend," she said briskly. "I thought I'd switch days off with Amy so I can be here all day Saturday."

"Hattie'll be here," her dad said. He came farther into the room and sat on the edge of the worktable.

Sam bit back a sigh. She had hoped this would be a short visit. She could only manage brief spurts of cheeriness. "I thought she was just working part-time."

He shrugged. "Cassie and Jack are back from their honeymoon and she wants to give them some space."

"I see." She stared down at the reservation book as if it held some secret formula for cracking Kevin's defenses. The words might as well have been written in some ancient rune, though, for she couldn't make sense of them. But her heart felt just as terrified.

"Well, maybe I should take a look at the attic, then. You know, we were talking about changing it into a three-room suite."

"Where's your banker friend?"

She glanced at him only briefly before letting her eyes focus on the rain running down the window. The world outside was all blurry and distant, unable to touch her.

"Oh, at the bank, I imagine," she said and went back to the reservation book. "We've both been kind of busy lately."

"I see."

But her father didn't budge. Maybe her attitude hadn't been quite as carefree as she'd thought it was. She picked up a pencil, but then tossed it across the desk in disgust.

"He's decided he's too old for me," she said. "He broke it off."

"I take it you don't agree with him."

"No." Her voice sounded defensive, even to her, as if she was daring her father to take Kevin's side. "I think we fit very well together."

"So, what are you going to do about it?"

"I don't know." Sam sighed. "He's being a stubborn idiot. He won't listen to reason."

Her father sat for a long moment, letting the silence build until Sam thought she wouldn't be able to breathe. It was four days since Kevin had told her it was over. Four eon-long days for her to try to figure out a plan to refute his arguments. But all she did was relive every single thing he'd ever said to her. Every single look. Every single kiss. And begin to wonder if there was a way out of this maze he'd led them into.

"Why don't you take a few days off and get away?" her father finally said. "You've got friends all over. Go visit some. Things might seem clearer from a distance."

She glared at him. "You think he's too old for me, too."

He just shook his head. "I think love's a rare gift and when the gods give it to you, you should run with it before they change their minds and take it back."

"Kevin thinks he's being noble."

"A man can dig his heels in mighty deep when he think he's being noble," her father replied. "All the more reason for you to get away. Give all that 'nobility' time to get tiresome."

"I can't leave," she protested. "We've just opened the inn."

"You can and you should," he said, then reached over and took her hand. "Your heart's not in this business, honey. You've given it your time and your head, but your heart's not in it and never has been."

"Dad, that's not—"

"It is true," he said. "And I love you to pieces for helping me get it started. But you're too young to be cooped up here. Hattie and I get along just fine. It suits us to be tied down to the place."

"I like working here."

"You like any place where you can make people happy, but right now you're hurting and you need to take care of that." He paused, frowning. "What was that phrase Fiona said your other dad used to say? 'Heal the heart.' That's what you've got to do. Heal your heart. Stop it from hurting like it is right now and maybe you can find an answer to Kevin's argument."

Sam just stared. "My other father had a medical problem. He meant he had to go to the hospital."

"Did he?" her father said with a slight smile as he got to his feet. "I don't know. Doctors fix stuff. Healing comes from rest and time and mostly love." He patted her shoulder. "You think about getting away. It'd do you a world of good."

She watched her father leave, then slowly closed the reservation book and wandered into the living room. Toby was lying in the window seat, his back to the pouring rain. She sat down by him, stroking him gently as she watched the rivers of water wend their way down the glass.

"It's not me that needs to be healed," she told Toby softly. "It's that hardheaded fool over at the bank. Sometime between now and the next time he drops by to check our accounts, I have to figure out how to convince him that age doesn't mean a thing."

A knock sounded at the outside door and Sam got a sudden vision of a deliveryman out there, loaded down with a big box of answers. She gave Toby a last pat and got to her feet. There was no such thing as an answer man, of course, but the idea was nice. She would like it if there was someplace she could go with her woes, and be presented with a three-part plan of how to bring an obstinate fool to his senses.

She pulled open the door. A young man in a business suit stood there, briefcase in hand and a bright smile on his face.

"Samantha Scott?" he asked, his voice trying to come out businesslike but sounding more eager than anything. "I'm Gary McClain. From Michiana Savings and Loan."

Sam just frowned at him. "Yes?"

He seemed only slightly daunted by her cool welcome. "I just wanted to drop by and meet you. I've been assigned to go over your accounts with you occasionally. Give you advice. Maybe suggest some sources you could go to for help."

Her frown grew deeper. "I don't understand. I thought Mr. Delaney was doing that."

"Oh, no," Gary said, his tone suddenly serious and his voice hushed. "Mr. Delaney's a vice president. He's far too busy to do this type of thing."

Too busy, suddenly, or too chicken? "I see," Sam said carefully, a slow anger festering deep in her soul. He wasn't coming over again. He was avoiding her completely.

But Gary wasn't too good at reading minds. "He's a very important man at the bank," he went on. "It's up to us younger guys to handle this sort of thing."

Sam's eyes narrowed and she took a good long look at Gary McClain. Younger guy. He was certainly that. Probably in his late twenties, although he looked even younger. A suspicion fed her anger, stoking it until it was ready to explode. He was no better than her brothers!

"And did he assign you personally to this account?" she asked, hoping the question sounded casual.

"Yes, he did," Gary admitted with a smile. "He told me that you were a special customer and that I should drop by often to offer my help."

"How kind of him," Sam snapped.

Gary frowned. Apparently her tone was finally penetrating his thick veneer of cheeriness. "Is there a problem?" he asked. "Is this a bad time to come?"

"Not at all," Sam said, holding the door open for him. "Let me get my father for you. I was just on my way out."

Kevin signed the document and reluctantly put it on top of the pile. Reluctantly, because it was last chore he had to do. He pushed himself slowly back from his desk and took a deep breath.

It was no big deal. There were lots of things he could to do to fill his time. Learn that new accounting program. Catch up on his reading. Write that article for *Today's Banking* that he'd been mulling over for a few months.

He could avoid thinking of Sam. He had done all right for the past several days. Sure, he hadn't been totally successful. And he hadn't been successful at all, once he went home. But it would get better. It had to. He was right in breaking off with her.

There was a knock at the door and Cindy stepped in. "Miss Scott would like to see you," she said. "I told her you were busy but she was most insistent."

Kevin frowned. "Gary's handling her account now," he said. "Why don't you tell her—"

Sam burst into the room. "Good old Gary's not here," she retorted. "He's at the inn, going over the books."

Kevin tried to keep his heart from leaping at the sight of her. She looked so wonderful, even with angry fire shooting from her eyes. It was all he could do to keep from rushing over to pull her into his arms. But he was strong.

"Sam," he said evenly and nodded for Cindy to go. "What can I do for you?"

"Stop being a jerk."

He winced slightly at her words, and then again when he realized that Cindy wasn't quite out the door yet. He stood, waiting in silence until he heard the click of the latch; then he waved Sam into a chair.

"Sam, please," he said softly when she just stayed there glaring at him. It hurt to see her so upset. And only made him more convinced that he had been right to break it off.

She finally gave him a dark look but stomped across the room to take a chair. He sank into his.

"Gary's really a fine businessman," he said. "I'm sure that he'll be able to offer you lots of very good advice."

"And I'm sure it was just a coincidence that he's so young," she snapped.

"Surely, you wouldn't hold that against him," Kevin said.

"And I bet he's unmarried, too," she went on.

"Most of our young executives are," he noted.

"What a surprise."

He leaned forward, remembering, against his will, the first time she'd been here. There had been such a glow about her, such a warmth in her eyes that it had drawn him. He had been unable to resist moving closer to her.

She looked far different today. The glow was from anger. The warmth in her eyes was from hurt. But he was drawn just as strongly. Maybe more so. He ached to take her in his arms, to kiss away that anger and soothe away that hurt. More than anything, he wanted to feel that wondrous rush of fire that would sweep over him at her slightest touch; that rush that suddenly made him feel alive again.

"I know what you're doing," she told him.

"Oh?"

"You figure if you push some young guy at me, I'll change my mind about you."

"I wasn't thinking that." The idea of her with another man actually hurt, like a knife being slowly twisted in his belly. "I just thought it would be easier for us both if I wasn't coming over to see you."

"It would be easier for us both if you'd just forget about all this age nonsense."

He looked away from her, unable to keep his mind in order when her lips tempted him; when his eyes just wanted to dance over the soft curves of her slacks. He took a deep breath.

"This really isn't accomplishing anything," he told her slowly. "My mind is made up. I'm not going to change it."

"My mind is made up, too," she said. She was on her feet and coming around to the side of his desk; coming into his line of vision once more. "And I'm not going to change it."

She was too close to him; his will wasn't that strong. He leaned back in his chair, but she was still too close. He just had be tough a little longer, he told himself. Just a few more minutes.

"Sam, I'm sorry that you're hurting," he said. "But you'll meet someone else—"

"Don't give me that nonsense about someone else," she retorted. "You care about me and I care about you. We don't need someone else."

He frowned at her and wondered how good he was at bluffing. "I'm fond of you, certainly," he said. "As I'm fond of a lot of people, but—"

"We shared more than a fondness for one another," she insisted.

"It was just for fun," he countered. "Didn't we say that a number of times?"

"It changed. We changed."

He just shook his head slowly. For her sake, he had to make her believe it was over. She had her whole life ahead of her. He had to let her start living it again. "*I* didn't."

She stepped back, then. Her eyes were flashing with emotion, but it still looked more like anger than pain. "You'll admit the truth one of these days," she said. "You'll have no choice."

"I won't?"

"No." Her eyes softened, and her voice held a touch of laughter. "You see, I have Romeo and Juliet on my side," she said. "You know, the swans."

He felt a chill race down his spine, remembering her brothers' words at Cassie's wedding. Something about when Sam told him the story, he would be a goner. But that was crazy. A story was a story.

"What are the swans going to do?" he asked, trying to sound amused. "Beat me into loving you with their wings?"

"Laugh all you want, but years ago Fiona, Cassie and I saved Juliet's life and we were promised that the spirits would come fight for our love in return."

His heart worried that he would have no chance, but he was determined not to show it. "What kind of spirits?" he asked.

"Fiona found Alex and Cassie got Jack. All because of the swans."

"So if I should see a big swan heading toward me, I should look out."

She just smiled and turned to the door. "You won't see it coming," she said. "But in my family, love always wins."

She was gone then, but her smug little smile hung in the air along with her words. It didn't matter what happened in her family. This was going to be the exception. He was not going to budge, come big swans or not.

Sam stared at the swans, her left hand on her hip and the bag of bread held closed by her right hand. "Look, you guys, you owe me," she told them. "All right, so I didn't do that much in the big rescue—I did all I could. I was just a little kid, remember."

The swans just glided about in the water, as if content to wait forever. As if they were more interested in the changing colors of the leaves and the chill in the air that said winter was coming. Sam sighed and tossed a few bread crusts out onto the water. They pretended not to notice it.

"Even if I wasn't the one who actually rescued you, I've been feeding you for years," she told them. "So when are you going to sic the spirits on Kevin? It's been two weeks already."

The swans went over to daintily nibble at the bread.

"Gary's been over twice and Kevin won't even take my calls. Don't you think this has gone on long enough? What are you guys waiting for?"

"Auntie Sam!"

Sam turned and saw Jennifer running down the slope toward her, golden and reddish leaves flying at her feet. Alex was following more slowly.

Sam caught the girl in a big hug. "Hi, Jen. How's it going?"

"Can I feed the swans?" she asked, reaching for the bag of bread.

"Sure. They're mad at me, anyway."

"How come?"

Sam shrugged. "I don't know. They're not telling."

"I'm going to be a princess for Halloween."

"I bet you'll be the best princess in town," Sam told her.

"Hi, Sam," Alex said, giving her a hug. "How're you doing?"

"Okay." She didn't have the strength to pretend for the family.

"The swans are mad at her," Jennifer told Alex.

"Oh?" He looked at Sam. "You give them stale bread again?"

She just shook her head. "They're supposed to be working their magic about now," she replied. "They did it for Fiona and for Cassie. Why aren't they helping me?"

"Maybe they're working behind the scenes," Alex said.

"Yes. Or maybe there *is* no magic." Sam sank onto the bench. She was getting so discouraged. Everything she'd tried had failed. There didn't seem to be any way to wear Kevin down.

She turned toward Alex and tried for a smile. "So where's little Michael?"

Alex sat next to her, his eyes on Jennifer who was engrossed in feeding the swans. "He's having one of his clingy days," Alex explained. "Fiona thought it might be better for Jen to get out. She starts to feel guilty if she doesn't share her brother's moods."

"It's been a rough time for them both," Sam said. "For all of you."

"Yes." Alex leaned forward, resting his arms on his knees. "I love having them with us, but I wish they hadn't had to go through all they did to get here."

"I know what you mean. But you know, sometimes I think things happen for a reason," Sam said. "I mean, it's terrible for the kids to have lost their mom and have their dad so ill, but because you and Fiona found each other, you were able to offer the kids a home. Sometimes I think there's a great big plan behind everything."

Alex looked at her for a long, silent moment, then reached into his jacket pocket. "Funny you should be thinking along those lines," he said. "Maybe you can make sense of this."

Sam took the paper that Alex offered her and unfolded it.

"It's a copy of the report of your parents' accident," Alex said. "I requested it ages ago, but it just came the other day. Fiona's so occupied with the kids, she hardly looked at it. Cassie's just barely back from her honeymoon and I didn't want to bother her with it. And with you being upset over Kevin, I wasn't going to show it to you now, either, but then I thought you might like a distraction."

Sam just frowned at him, then looked down at the report. "Is there something here you didn't expect?" she asked.

"Well, it's pretty much as the newspaper articles reported it," he said. "So maybe I just interpreted it wrong."

He pointed to a small diagram of the accident scene at the corner of the page. "Look at this and tell me what you think."

She had never been good at guessing games and wished he would just come out and say what he was thinking. But she did as he wished and looked at the diagram. It showed the highway, the exit and the path of her parents' car as well as the one that had hit them, forcing them off the road and into a bridge abutment.

"What am I supposed to be seeing?" she asked.

"They were past the exit when the accident happened," he said. "They should have taken that first exit if they were going to the Mayo Clinic."

Sam looked up at him, not knowing what to make of any of it. "Maybe they missed it."

"Maybe. Or maybe they weren't going there."

Sam looked down at the paper. "But you said he was ill."

"Yeah. I got that verified. And I don't believe for a second that they were leaving you guys."

"So what does this mean?" Sam stared at it for a long moment.

"You got any more bread?" Jennifer asked, interrupting Sam's thoughts. "The swans said they're still hungry."

Sam got to her feet. "I think the swans have had enough," she said. "But I'll bet Grandpa's got some cookies that you could have."

"Okay."

Jennifer ran ahead of Alex and Sam and was in the house before they were even climbing the back steps. Sam didn't know what to make of the accident report. It threw all their suppositions into disarray, so she ought to be upset. But after all that she'd gone through with Kevin, she just wanted some answers.

Her dad was in the kitchen with Jennifer, so while Alex stopped to chat, Sam hurried into the office. A slow idea was forming in her head and she needed to check something out. She found the atlas on the bookshelves and opened it to Minnesota. If she followed the highway that her parents were on, it would take her to . . .

South Dakota. Her father's home.

Sam wandered over to the windows and stared out at the lake. He had been going to "heal his heart." What if he hadn't been going to a doctor for healing but had been going home to make peace with his family? He'd never made it. Would his family ever have known what had happened to him? Or that he'd wanted to make peace with them?

Suddenly Sam noticed that the swans were still there, near the feeding shore. Why? They always left when the bread ran out. Always. Was something wrong?

She slipped out the kitchen door and hurried down to the lake. The swans were gliding in their usual circles so there was no need to call for Cassie and her scissors; but they were watching her.

"I need to go there, don't I?" she asked them. "Instead of being so selfish and thinking only about me and Kevin, I've got to find my dad's family and ask them to forgive him."

They stopped their gliding to stare at her.

"But how am I going to do that?" she asked them. "I still haven't gotten an answer to my inquiry about them."

There was no movement, no sound. All the world was standing still. Waiting.

Sam took a deep breath. "Okay," she told them. "I need the magic to find my dad's relatives. Wake up the spirits and tell them my dad's love for his family is the love I need their help with."

They left then, gliding away as silently as ever. But they took with them a piece of her heart. It was over between her and Kevin. She had just given away her last hope of making it work.

She turned and slowly climbed the slope to the house.

Sam walked slowly into the community center on the west side of Sioux Falls, South Dakota. Like the whole neighborhood, it had seen better days, but the brightly colored drawings all over the walls said there was still life and love in the place. She looked around her. After five days of searching through tribal council lists, and phone books, of asking questions and reaching innumerable dead ends, she was almost at the end of her quest. And she was suddenly nervous.

"May I help you?" a young woman had stopped in the middle of the lobby to ask her.

"I'm looking for a Mr. and Mrs. Stonebreaker," Sam said. "I was told they were here on Friday afternoons."

"Oh, you mean Joe and Martha? Sure, they're down in the library. It's story time."

The young woman led Sam down a hallway and opened a door at the end, waving Sam to go inside. It looked like a school library—a small collection of battered books on shelves around the edges of the room. In the center, though, on the floor, sat twenty-or-so children ranging in age from about three to thirteen or fourteen. Behind them, on a mixed collection of chairs, sat a dozen adults, some young, some older.

And across the room, at the center of everyone's attention, was an old man—wearing—unbelievably—a swan mask!

Sam slid into an empty chair at the back of the circle. The old man—must have been her grandfather—was telling a story, the story of the Ugly Duckling. Or a version of it.

"And when the last egg hatched, out came this big old bird," he was saying. "He was not at all like the other ducklings, so soft and yellow and small. He was bigger, with gray fuzz all over him. The other mother ducks came over to see the babies. 'Oh, he is so big,' one said. 'He looks so different,' another said. 'He is beautiful,' said his mother."

The old man's voice was soft but carried a whole range of emotions—haughtiness, love, pain. With simple words and a few gestures, he was painting a vivid picture of the ducks.

"But the little ducklings all loved him. He could swim fast and chase the older ducklings away. Little by little, though, some of the young ones learned to be afraid of him. 'He's too big,' the old turkey said. 'He's too different,' the old hen said. And little by little, the big duckling began to believe he was different. That he wasn't as good as the others. He began to stay away from the others, to swim by himself, and he shunned even the little ducklings who still wanted to be his friends."

The children at the man's feet sat enraptured. No one moved. No one spoke.

"Then one day, there was a terrible storm," her grandfather went on. "Lightning flashed and thunder crashed and the rain came down for days and days and days. And when it was all over, the ducks discovered that other birds had taken refuge in the pond. Big, beautiful white birds. When they saw the big duckling, they called to him. They said he was one of them and he shouldn't be there with the ducks. That he should come with them to the place where swans lived. But his duckling friends begged him to stay. The big duckling didn't know what to do. He was afraid to go with the swans and afraid to stay with the ducklings.''

"So what did he do?" a little voice piped up.

The old man sat down, taking off his swan mask. "I don't know," he said slowly. "What should he do? Do you think the ducks and the swans could live together in peace?"

Sam blinked back sudden tears as she got to her feet. This man had turned the Ugly Duckling into a discussion on prejudice and fear.

She watched as he led the discussion down many roads until they decided the big duckling should invite the swans to stay at the pond, too, so they could all live together.

After a few minutes, the children were rushing over to examine the man's mask while the adults were exchanging greetings. Sam just stayed at the back, watching.

"Hello," an old woman said. "You're new here, aren't you? I don't think I've seen you here before."

"Yes. I'm here to see Mr. and Mrs. Stonebreaker." Sam took a deep breath. There was something familiar about the woman's eyes. Like they were mirrors of her own. "You wouldn't be her, would you?"

"Yes, I am. How can I help you?"

Sam looked over at her grandfather. The kids were starting to leave.

"Maybe you'd like to wait a few minutes," Mrs. Stonebreaker said. "And tell us both at once."

Sam nodded and tried to gather her thoughts. How did you tell someone that they were your grandparents? Then suddenly the old man was over there with them, and the others were all filing out of the room.

"This young lady wants to see us, Joe," the woman said.

"I'm Samantha Scott," Sam said. "From South Bend, Indiana."

"My, goodness," her grandmother said. "What would someone from so far away want to see us about?"

"Maybe we could sit down," Sam suggested and led them toward some chairs. Once they were all seated, she hesitated.

"I'm not sure where to begin," she said slowly. "But I think that my father was your son."

She cursed herself for letting it come out so bluntly. The two old people just stared at her. The sound of kids' laughter came from the hallway, but might have been from miles away. From another world, even.

"Joe Junior?" Mrs. Stonebreaker finally asked. "You mean, Joe Junior?"

Sam nodded, then bit back a sudden rush of fear. What if she'd been wrong about everything? What if they'd thrown her father out, all those years back? Maybe he hadn't left of his own choice. Maybe they didn't want to hear about him.

"Joe Junior?" Mr. Stonebreaker repeated, shaking his head slowly. "We haven't heard from him in more than twenty years."

"Thirty years," his wife corrected and clasped her hands tightly together. "He was so unhappy here. So sure that if he could just escape, life would be great."

"But you take yourself with you," the old man said.

"I think he regretted his silence, though," Sam said softly. "He was on his way back here twenty years ago when he and Mom were killed in an automobile accident. He told his friends that he had to heal his heart."

"Joe died?" the old woman asked.

Mr. Stonebreaker's hand came over to cover his wife's. "We'd thought for a while now he must've died. You lose your anger when you get older. He'd have come back by now."

"He was trying to," Sam said. "He wanted to say he was sorry for all the years of silence."

Mrs. Stonebreaker just nodded, her eyes teary. She looked at her husband, and for a long time they seemed to share their sorrow and their memories. Although no words were spoken, Sam knew they were communicating. That's what love lets you do—open your thoughts to another person, she mused.

Would she ever have that kind of love?

Chapter Fourteen

Kevin hurried through the parking lot. He'd spent his morning in a civic planning meeting at city hall and had grabbed a sandwich at the Amish lunch shop. He would eat it at his desk while he went over loan applications. He'd learned over the last few weeks that the key was keeping busy. Real busy.

He stopped with a frown when he entered the bank. The place was festooned with Halloween decorations—corn stalks, pumpkins and people in costume. Tellers were all dressed up as pirates and witches and football players. He just cringed and hurried back into the office area.

He wasn't into all this dress-up, even if it was a commendable effort by the downtown merchants to provide safe areas for the kids to celebrate Halloween. Further proof that he was "an old poop," as Sam would say.

He walked past an angelic Cindy—complete with halo—and snapped, "Good afternoon."

"Well, aren't we cheery today?" she said with a bright smile. "And in your 'grumpy banker' costume, too."

He glared at her. "Costumes weren't mandatory." He went into his office.

She followed him. "You know, you were a lot more cheerful when you were dating Sam."

He increased the intensity of his glare. "Thank you for that little tidbit."

She just smiled even brighter. "We think you should get back together with her."

"We?"

"Oh, you know. The staff here."

He clenched his teeth. Great, now his disposition as well as his love life was the topic of discussion at the bank. "I was too old for her," he said.

"Well, you're sure hell-bent to prove it, aren't you?" she returned. "Funny, when you were with her, you seemed a lot younger."

"Maybe it was before my birthday," he said.

She just raised her eyebrows, then pointed to his desk. "Your messages are there with your mail, and that package came for you." She took a few steps toward the door. "Oh, and don't get tied up around two. The kindergarten classes from Perley School are having their costume parade this way and Mr. Cartwright's got a storyteller coming to entertain them. He wants us all to pass out candy to them. Yours is in that bag." She pointed to a sack of chocolate bars.

"Great," Kevin muttered and sank into his chair as Cindy left. He should have scheduled meetings for this afternoon, too.

He picked up the package and ripped the tape that closed it. Probably some free sample or some other useless—

He stared into the box. Two small wooden swans lay in it. He dropped the box on his desk like he'd been stung.

Damn. Things should be getting better by now, not worse.

He took deep breath and picked up the box, holding it carefully as if it might contaminate him. They were from Sam, of course. Why couldn't she just let things be?

He put the box, with the swans still in it, into his file cabinet. Then he went back to his desk and pulled over his mail. There was a lot of it. With luck, he would be busy for a few hours.

He got through part of the stack before his attention started to wane. He wondered how Sam was doing. Had she started to date someone else? The thought hurt. No, she wouldn't have sent him the swans if she was involved with someone else. That knowledge brought relief.

Damn. This wasn't going the way he wanted.

He pulled a letter out of an envelope, but his eyes couldn't seem to focus on the paper. He kept seeing Sam here in his office as she'd been that first day, so soft and eager. Or how she'd been a few weeks ago when she'd been spitting fire at him. He kept feeling the presence of her swans. He kept hearing her laughter.

There was a knock at his door and William Cartwright looked in. "It's past two," he said. "Where's your candy for the kids?"

Kevin sighed as if he'd been in the middle of delicate negotiations, and got to his feet. He needed this like he needed a root canal. He grabbed the candy and went into the bank's lobby. It was crowded with little kids in costume, but it was quieter than he'd expected. Maybe because they were all settling down on the floor around some woman dressed up like a—

Like a swan.

He took a deep breath and tried to settle his racing heart. Tried to slow the shaking of his hands. It was Sam wearing a swan mask. He closed his eyes and let her voice flow over her. God, how he loved her.

"There once was this mother duck," she was saying. "And all of her babies had hatched except one. She had one big egg left in her nest."

Everything came rushing back. All the little smiles, the touches, the way they loved. John Wayne and Scarlett O'Hara. His birthday. Her throwing him out of her house.

"...came over to see the babies," Sam was saying. "'Oh, he is so big,' one mother said. 'He looks so different,' another said. 'He is beautiful,' said his mother."

He remembered the way her eyes would light up when she spoke. The way her whole body would shimmer with excitement. The way her laughter could fill even the gloomiest day with sunshine.

"Little by little, the big duckling began to believe he was different. That he wasn't as good as the others. He began to stay away from the other ducklings. He swam by himself, and avoided even the little ducklings who still wanted to be his friends."

She tried so hard to make everyone happy. Her father. Her sisters. Himself. When was she going to worry about making herself happy? When was someone going to put her happiness first? That was all he wanted for her—to be happy.

"Other birds were now in the pond. Big, beautiful white swans. When they saw the big duckling, they called to him. They said he was a swan and shouldn't be there with the ducks. They wanted him to come with them to the place where they lived."

He opened his eyes and let them rest on her. She had to know he was there, but her gaze was focussed only on the kids. Her voice was so full of the story, so full of excitement. He wanted to be there with them, to sit mesmerized by her voice, to admit to being her captive.

"But the big duckling didn't know what to do. He was so used to being alone that he was afraid. He was afraid to go with the swans and afraid to stay with the ducklings."

"He shouldn't be afraid," one of the kids called out.

Sam's eyes suddenly met Kevin's, locked with his as if speaking straight to his soul. "No, he shouldn't be," she agreed.

"My mommy says we're all different," another kid said.

Sam's gaze hadn't budged. "Yes, we are," she said. "That's what makes us special."

"If the ducks want to be his friends, he should let them."

He could feel her smile from across the room. "He certainly should," she said.

Then she sneezed and it broke the spell—ended the trance he'd been in. But then she sneezed again. And again. The swan mask wobbled.

The kids all stared at her. Kevin frowned.

"Sorry," she said amid a sniff. "My antihistamine must be wearing off." She sneezed again.

Kevin pushed through the small crowd of adults, hopped over the low railing that separated the office area from the lobby and wove through the kids. He pulled the swan mask off Sam.

She sneezed again. "I'm allergic to swan feathers." Another sneeze.

"Then why are you wearing the stupid thing?" he asked, sounding a bit annoyed.

"The story wouldn't have worked quite so well without it."

"Maybe there are things more important than the story," he argued.

"It was only for a few minutes," she said and punctuated it with a sneeze.

"That obviously was a few minutes too long," he snapped.

"I took an allergy pill."

"Maybe you should have taken a break."

She glared at him. "Who died and made you John Wayne?"

"At least he had some common sense."

"I see," she snapped right back. "And Scarlett didn't."

"No, she didn't," he told her. "She just charged around, doing whatever she wanted, regardless of what anybody thought or wanted. Obviously, she's your role model."

"Better that than some stuffed shirt who has no feelings," Sam barked.

"I have feelings," he cried.

"Oh, yeah," she agreed. "Big bossy ones. Tell everybody what to do. Don't go barefoot. Don't wear a swan mask. Don't fall in love."

With that, she burst into tears. Kevin just stared at her for a long, frozen moment. And stared around in horror at everyone staring at them both. What in the world had come over him?

But then the pain in his own heart suddenly woke him up and he pulled her into his arms.

"Why is the swan lady crying?" one of the kids asked.

"Is that banker man being mean to her?"

"Is he a bad guy?"

"Sam," Kevin whispered into her glorious hair. "Sam, stop crying."

"No."

"Sam." Panic was growing in his heart, as the sea of frowning little faces around him grew more frowning. "Come on, you can stop if you want to."

"Is the bad man hurting her?" a little kid asked loudly.

Sam quivered in his arms, but she didn't move. "Sam," he hissed. "They're going to attack me."

"Tell me you love me," she whispered back.

"Sam!"

"Say it."

He looked up and saw not only the frowning faces of the children, but those of the adults, too. And then he felt the soft, warm presence of Sam in his arms and he gave up all pretense. It was hopeless, as it had been hopeless right from the beginning.

"I love you," he whispered.

"Say you've been a fool," she demanded under her breath. "Say that age doesn't matter."

"You aren't crying at all, are you?" he muttered.

She let out a wail that could have been rented as a siren by the fire department. The kids all gasped.

"All right, all right. I've been a fool. Age doesn't matter," he whispered and then sighed. "Any more demands?"

She pulled away from him with a slight smile. "No, I think that'll do."

He wanted to be annoyed with her. He wanted to scold and be huffy and retreat to his office to build his defenses all over again. But when he looked into her eyes, he forgot all that. All he knew was how beautiful she was—and how much a part of his life.

He couldn't imagine even breathing without her at his side. He couldn't imagine wanting to.

He slowly reached out and she came into his arms again, but this time to plant a quick, fervent kiss on his lips. It was a reminder of yesterday and a promise for tomorrow. It was a pledge of all the happiness that they would find together.

"Are you okay, swan lady?" one of the kids asked Sam.

She smiled down at the little girl. "Yep, I'm fine."

"What's the end of the story?" another kid called out.

Kevin just let his arms slide around her once more, resting again under the spell of her magic. "They lived happily ever after," he said.

Epilogue

"No, just sit," Sam told her grandmother. "I'll get the rest of the stuffing."

"And don't let Kevin go in the kitchen with her," Cassie called out. "We won't see them again for hours."

"Hey, I think you're picking on me," Kevin protested.

"Get used to it, Dad," Stacy told him. "It's good for you."

Sam just laughed and hurried into the bed-and-breakfast's kitchen. It was the best Thanksgiving ever. Her grandparents had come in from South Dakota and Kevin's kids were up from school. Fiona, Alex and the two children were here, along with a glow on Fiona's face that said next spring they were going to have three kids in their house. Cassie and Jack had brought the twins and an ultrasound photo that they claimed showed Cassie would be having twin boys. And Sam had her own little secret that she hadn't even told Kevin about yet.

She glanced out the window and saw Romeo and Juliet out on the lake. Sam thought they knew how happy she was. She heard the kitchen door swing open behind her, then felt Kevin's arms slip around her.

"I thought they weren't going to let you in here," she said with a laugh.

He held up an empty dish in one hand. "We're out of cranberry sauce."

She just shook her head. "And how much of it went on your plate to give you this excuse?"

"Hey, what can I say? I love cranberry sauce."

She laid her head against his chest and closed her eyes, so perfectly content that this moment could go on forever.

"Your dad and Aunt Hattie were holding hands under the table," Kevin told her.

"I know. I saw them." She felt his fingers touching the wedding ring on her left hand and opened her eyes.

"You're not getting moody again, are you?" she asked.

"My moods will all be bright from now on," he promised.

"Oh, sure," she replied. "Can I get that in writing? I want to use it the first time you complain about a two o'clock feeding."

He pulled back enough to look down into her eyes. "You're pregnant?" he asked, his voice so full of hope and fear and awe that it tore at her heart.

"That's what the test I took this morning said," she told him gently. "Is it all right? I know you've already got Stacy and Jon, but—"

"All right?" he cried and pulled her back into his embrace. "All right? Of course, it's all right. It's wonderful."

"We just never really talked about it," she began, but then his lips were on hers and she lost all coherent thought.

The kiss was a celebration of everything they had. Everything they would have. It was his love meeting hers. It was definitely all right.

"Hey, you two," Cassie said as she opened the kitchen door.

They split apart, but only by inches.

"I should have known," Cassie said with a laugh. "Never send newlyweds into the kitchen together. Not if you want them back out the same day."

Sam shoved a dish of cranberry sauce into Kevin's hands and grabbed up the extra bowl of stuffing. "See what you've gotten yourself into," Sam told Kevin as they went back into the dining room. "One big happy family."

* * * * *

MILLION DOLLAR SWEEPSTAKES

SWP-M96

As seen on TV!

Free Gift Offer

With a Free Gift proof-of-purchase from any Silhouette® book, you can receive a beautiful cubic zirconia pendant.

This gorgeous marquise-shaped stone is a genuine cubic zirconia—accented by an 18" gold tone necklace.

(Approximate retail value $19.95)

Send for yours today...

compliments of ♥ *Silhouette*®

To receive your free gift, a cubic zirconia pendant, send us one original proof-of-purchase, photocopies not accepted, from the back of any Silhouette Romance™, Silhouette Desire®, Silhouette Special Edition®, Silhouette Intimate Moments® or Silhouette Yours Truly™ title available in August, September, October, November and December at your favorite retail outlet, together with the Free Gift Certificate, plus a check or money order for $1.65 U.S./$2.15 CAN. (do not send cash) to cover postage and handling, payable to Silhouette Free Gift Offer. We will send you the specified gift. Allow 6 to 8 weeks for delivery. Offer good until December 31, 1996 or while quantities last. Offer valid in the U.S. and Canada only.

Free Gift Certificate

Name: _____

Address: _____

City: _____ State/Province: _____ Zip/Postal Code: _____

Mail this certificate, one proof-of-purchase and a check or money order for postage and handling to: SILHOUETTE FREE GIFT OFFER 1996. In the U.S.: 3010 Walden Avenue, P.O. Box 9077, Buffalo NY 14269-9077. In Canada: P.O. Box 613, Fort Erie, Ontario L2Z 5X3.

FREE GIFT OFFER
ONE PROOF-OF-PURCHASE

084-KMD

To collect your fabulous FREE GIFT, a cubic zirconia pendant, you must include this original proof-of-purchase for each gift with the properly completed Free Gift Certificate.

084-KMD-R

Add a double dash of romance to your
festivities this holiday season
with two great stories in

Christmas Celebration

Featuring full-length stories by bestselling authors

Kasey Michaels
Anne McAllister

These heartwarming stories of love triumphing
against the odds are sure to add some extra
Christmas cheer to your holiday season. And this
distinctive collection features **two full-length novels,**
making it the perfect gift at great value—for
yourself or a friend!

Available this December at your favorite retail outlet.

Silhouette®

...where passion lives.

The collection of the year!
NEW YORK TIMES BESTSELLING AUTHORS

Linda Lael Miller
Wild About Harry

Janet Dailey
Sweet Promise

Elizabeth Lowell
Reckless Love

Penny Jordan
Love's Choices

and featuring
Nora Roberts
The Calhoun Women

This special trade-size edition features four of the wildly
popular titles in the Calhoun miniseries together in
one volume—a true collector's item!

Pick up these great authors and a chance to win
a weekend for two in New York City at the
Marriott Marquis Hotel on Broadway! We'll pay
for your flight, your hotel—even a Broadway show!

Available in December at your favorite retail outlet.

NEW YORK
Marriott.
MARQUIS

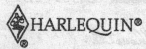